FIRST TANGO
IN PARIS

By the Author

The Storm

First Tango in Paris

FIRST TANGO IN PARIS

by

Shelley Thrasher

2014

FIRST TANGO IN PARIS

ISBN 13: 978-1-62639-073-7

This Trade Paperback Original Is Published By
Bold Strokes Books, Inc.
P.O. Box 249
Valley Falls, NY 12185

First Edition: July 2014

Credits

Editor: Ruth Sternglantz
Production Design: Susan Ramundo
Cover Design By Sheri (graphicartist2020@hotmail.com)

Acknowledgments

Thanks, Cheryl C. and Jean R, for your early encouragement and contributions.

Radclyffe, Lee, Vic, Jo, Pam and Cheryl, and Sheri—I appreciate your help with my writing, website, and cover.

Justine and Ashley, you're the best betas ever.

Ruth, your suggestions have made all the difference.

And, Connie, many thanks for running errands while I sit home in front of the computer, for listening to me, and for suggesting interesting plot points.

Dedication

To Connie, for indulging my love of travel abroad and for giving me the space and encouragement to write about it.

Chapter One

New Orleans
February 14, 1972

Brigitte Green lounged quietly on Rosa Rios's overstuffed burgundy love seat—one leg tucked under her and both arms wrapped around her other leg—and gazed at Rosa. She'd gained more than a few pounds lately, and the silver streak in the bangs of her shoulder-length black hair definitely hadn't been there years ago, when Brigitte first knew her. But she still found Rosa alluring.

"Have you thought about finding someone special in your life, little one?" Rosa asked from her armchair near the gas space heater across the room. Strange. Rosa seldom sat still. Instead, she hustled around the apartment, large brown eyes snapping up every detail, constantly offering Brigitte a piece of freshly baked chocolate cake or a glass of merlot. Now she offered only advice. "You're thirty-five. Time for you to quit working."

Brigitte had loved Rosa since she was five and had lived with her since she was eighteen, after her grandmother died. Rosa was aunt, older sister, and mother to her.

"I'm mostly content with things the way they are," Brigitte said.

Rosa frowned. "Stop kidding yourself."

"Well. Maybe you're halfway right. As always." She glanced down at her carefully manicured toenails. She needed to repair the chipped paint on her big toe.

"Of course I am." Rosa shifted her weight and settled into her favorite chair even more thoroughly. "And you should listen to me."

"Come to think of it, maybe I should get out of New Orleans." She snapped her fingers. "I know—I'll quit working, go to Paris, and find the love of my life." Brigitte picked up the cup of steaming hot chocolate Rosa had brought her and entertained the fantasy.

"That's exactly what you should do." Rosa wasn't smiling. Her brown eyes bored into Brigitte.

She laughed. "Yeah. Like I'd ever leave you." She sipped her chocolate.

Rosa held out her chubby hands to the gas heater, warming them. "No. I mean it." She pointed at the book that lay beside Brigitte on the couch. "After all, you've done a great job learning to read and speak French. You should get along fine in Paris." She finally grinned. "Listen to me. We Latin people know a lot more about love than you Americans do."

Brigitte's heart began to tap-dance. "Hey, why don't we go to Paris together? I can just see us now." Her heart was pounding a three-against-two jazz rhythm by this time. Maybe Rosa was on to something.

"Yeah. Two over-the-hill call girls riding to the top of the Eiffel Tower and sitting in a sidewalk café drinking wine." Rosa shook her head dismissively.

"Ooh-lah-lah." Brigitte was getting into the idea now. "I could teach you enough French to get by on."

Rosa chuckled. "If I left New Orleans I'd head straight for Buenos Aires. After all, I was born there."

"And what would you do there? It's probably changed completely." Brigitte warmed her hands on her cup and took another drink.

Rosa straightened a bit in her chair. "Ahh. I could tango to my heart's content. Boom, boom, boom, boom—boom-boom-boom-boom-boom…" She hummed "La Cumparsita," the world's most popular tango tune.

Brigitte grinned but then put down her cup and tightened her grip on her legs. Just the thought of losing Rosa panicked her. She'd never find anyone who cared for her as completely as Rosa did. No one else would understand what she'd done all these years—who and what she was—and love her in spite of it. Like Rosa, she was used goods, no longer eligible for the real love she might have found when she was still young and fresh, before she'd joined Rosa in New Orleans half a lifetime ago.

She let her dream of Paris fade. "I suppose I could go with you, though my Spanish is terrible."

Rosa warmed her hands at the heater again, then clasped them together in her lap. "Let's face it. I'm not going anywhere."

"Why not?"

"Because I'm too old to start a new life, little one." She looked forlorn for several seconds, but then she brightened and seemed like her usual cheery self again. "You really should go to Paris, though, and find somebody special to settle down with."

Brigitte picked at her chipped toenail. "Fifty-five's not that old, Rosa. Why the hell would you want to stay here? It's a dead end for women like us."

Rosa's smile disappeared, as if she'd just learned a client had the clap. "You know perfectly well why I'd stay. Because of Leo, of course."

"Humph. A married man's not my idea of somebody special." She flaked off part of the polish on her flawed nail. Did Rosa think Leo would miraculously leave his wife for her? He had the best of both worlds and would never change. Yet Rosa was a sucker for his lies.

"I've had my fill of men like him," Brigitte said, "and you should too. He's rotten to the core." She shrugged. "I guess we're both stuck here then, so let's make the best of it. Come on. Get up. I'm ready for my dance lesson."

Rosa nodded and rose, then stretched, uncharacteristically somber again. She bent and changed from her bedroom slippers to her tango shoes. Usually she couldn't wait to dance, and she'd told Brigitte why a lot of times. Back in Argentina, her parents had been happy when they tangoed. But that was about the only time they were. Apparently that one bright recollection of them from her childhood helped her forget all their drunken brawls. Tonight, however, she seemed preoccupied, almost depressed. What was wrong? Maybe it was the foul weather. She'd get over it. Rosa always bounced back.

But just as Brigitte started to ask what was bothering her, Rosa gently lowered the arm of her Garrard turntable onto a gleaming black record. The haunting sounds of violins and a piano filled the living room. Brigitte breathed them in as she would the rich aroma of strong coffee. Then the accordion-like bandoneon joined in. Blending the powerful fullness of an organ with the personal quality of a harmonica, it enticed her into a web of auditory magic. Like a high priestess, Rosa gestured toward the record player with her head, then toward the empty space in the middle of the room.

Brigitte uncurled herself from her usual spot on the comfy velvet love seat, then stretched her calves and made circles with each foot. The passionate music engulfed her as she continued to prepare. Finally, she bent and slipped her bare feet into the red leather shoes with their sturdy, medium-height heels that she always left here. Their well-worn straps fit snugly around her ankles, and special insoles cushioned her feet as she sauntered toward Rosa, who'd just turned the record over.

She stopped and stood still, letting her devotion to Rosa and to the drama of the music fill her senses. The violins wheedled, the piano beguiled, and the bandoneon enthralled. The music surged, the various melodies creating a rapid rhythm inside her. Yet she sensed a somber slowness in Rosa and forced her own inner cadence to ease off to match that of the woman she would follow anywhere. She noted Rosa's erect yet expectant posture, envisioned the ideal space that should exist between them as they danced, and then straightened her shoulders. Finally, she glided into Rosa's outstretched arms and felt, as always, at home.

How could she ever leave Rosa and seek a new life of her own?

"You do need to go to Paris, little one," Rosa remarked as they began to move together in harmony, their shoulders parallel and an appropriate distance between them. "And when you get there, remember how the tango has taught you to carry your own weight." She squeezed Brigitte's shoulder for emphasis. "During the dance, you and your partner must keep apart, yet depend on each other and stay connected. You and I have perfected that art." She smiled with what appeared to be satisfaction. "Now you're ready to find a woman you can devote yourself to, body and soul."

Brigitte executed a sharp head snap, avoiding Rosa's eyes. "You've always told me not to talk or even look at my partner while I'm dancing the tango. And never to smile."

"I've also taught you it's okay during practice, especially with someone you're not interested in romantically." She raised her voice a bit. "How many times do I have to repeat myself? Find a new life and somebody to love. You deserve it."

Listening to the tumultuous music, Brigitte walked in the special way Rosa had taught her. Then Rosa built a step of her own in the spaces between the pattern Brigitte had laid out. Finally, both of them decorated these interwoven steps with a layer of adornments they'd created and polished together. It always amazed Brigitte how they could kick so precisely around one another's legs without tripping each other and falling on their asses.

As they danced, the eerie sound of the bandoneon insinuated itself deep into Brigitte, and she glimpsed the burgundy love seat as she whirled into a new space. She sensed someone else's arms around her, and the fresh odor of spring rain tickled her nose, replaced the heavy, opiate scent of Rosa. The face of the woman Brigitte held was as blurred as the remnants of an image just erased from a blackboard, but she could see the taut skin of the stranger's neck. The woman felt lighter, moved more restlessly than Rosa did. Yet she lacked Rosa's certainty and decisiveness.

"Hey, do you want to lead?"

Rosa's words broke the momentary spell into which Brigitte had wandered. "No. I just lost focus for a second. Sorry. I'll be fine." She settled back into the practiced ease she always felt with Rosa, the dip into another reality not new to her. She'd always sensed and experienced things that others didn't seem to notice.

As the music wrapped around them and they completed another complicated sequence, then began their closing moves, Rosa asked, "So. What would your dream woman be like?"

Brigitte almost stopped. Was Rosa a mind reader? And why in the hell was she being so insistent? She gazed down at Rosa and grimaced as she tried to concentrate on the question. "My dream woman? Well, until now I've considered money and power enough. But maybe I could find someone loyal, someone who'd love me in spite of what I've been. Like you do."

Rosa scowled. "While you're looking, you might as well find someone rich. Leo has loads of money and power. That's why he appeals to me. To hell with true love and loyalty. They're fairy tales."

Was Rosa trying to convince herself, or did she actually believe what she was saying? Surely she wanted more out of life than Leo could give her, even if he ever did leave his wife for her. "I have more than enough money, thanks to your help. And I've had enough power over men to last a lifetime." For some reason, Brigitte didn't want their tango lesson to end. "You're the only person I've ever experienced love and loyalty with—"

"And I'm too old for you and definitely not interested in women." Rosa's dark eyes flashed like they did when she was reprimanding one of her girls. "You're like my daughter."

The music ended, and Rosa turned off the record player.

"I told you I'm content with things the way they are," Brigitte said as she slipped out of her tango shoes. "Think I'll go turn in early and read myself to sleep. I've started another great novel by Colette."

Rosa beamed, as if she were a teacher and Brigitte her star pupil. "Okay. Leo's coming over later, so I'm gonna rest awhile before I get dressed." Rosa's smile dimmed. "You know how he always wants me to look my best. Enjoy your book. I'm glad you're hooked on reading instead of pills, like too many women I've known."

"I don't need pills. My books take me interesting places." *And my crazy mind doesn't do a bad job either. Like that mystery woman I just danced with for a second.* That was the one thing she couldn't confide in Rosa about. She'd tell her she was nuts. "But thanks for being concerned." She shook her finger at Rosa in a mock-motherly way, trying to lighten the mood. "Now you and Leo be quiet. No fighting for a change."

Rosa poured herself a shot of whiskey and smiled mysteriously. "Don't you worry. I've got him right where I want him. I'll make him behave. Besides, it's Valentine's Day. I want tonight to be special."

A sudden blast of rain hit the windows, and a chill February wind rattled the panes. Shivering, and feeling even more protective of Rosa than usual, Brigitte walked over and hugged her. "I believe you, but don't expect too much from him. I don't like to see him disappoint you."

Rosa held Brigitte against her longer than usual, then squeezed her before she let go. "Thanks for that. I love you, little one. Sleep tight."

As Brigitte left to go downstairs to her apartment, she shivered again, like someone was walking over a grave.

❖

Crash, thud.

Brigitte moaned and tried to rouse herself from a deep sleep. She felt like she was drowning in the bayou, muddy water sucking her down while she struggled to the surface.

Damn Rosa. Had she dropped something? Thrown something at Leo? They'd been fighting more than usual lately.

The hinges on the door to Rosa's upstairs apartment creaked, and a few boards squeaked as someone crept down the stairs and quietly shut the front door. It had to be Leo. He was the only one who ever visited Rosa here in their old house in the French Quarter, and Rosa had said she was expecting him.

Brigitte cuddled her feather pillow a while longer, drifting into oblivion, then rocking back into the light. Dark, light…dark, light. She relaxed and embraced the darkness for a long, luxurious time.

She'd been sleeping so well for a change. What a relief. She hated insomnia. She'd been tempted to take sleeping pills, but she'd rather wear her brain out reading in French than drug it into oblivion. So far, so good. She'd even begun to dream in French. Tonight, she'd been having marvelous dreams about strolling down the Champs Élysées, eating elegant pastries, shopping for a new wardrobe in expensive Parisian boutiques. She couldn't wait to tell Rosa about them.

A clinking, clattering noise from upstairs roused Brigitte again, and she forced herself to sit up in bed. What time was it? One thirty-two, her clock radio said. She groaned and lay back down for a while. Oh well, she was halfway awake. Might as well go check in with Rosa, catch up on the latest in her on-again, off-again affair with Leo, see what they'd fought about this time.

She turned on the light and pulled on her fuzzy white chenille robe to ward off the cold air that invaded Rosa's old house. The robe wrapped around her like a fur coat, soft and comforting, though she couldn't completely shake the damp cold of winter that seeped in around the windowpanes. Yanking one hand through her hair, she noticed how red-rimmed her eyes appeared in the bathroom mirror—the only downside of reading too much—but Rosa wouldn't give a shit what she looked like. She'd better not. Brigitte slid her feet into her plush red mules and shuffled upstairs. She'd make it quick. She really just wanted to get back to sleep.

"Hey, Rosa. I know you're in there." She'd heard only one set of footsteps leaving earlier. Besides, Rosa never went out this late at night anymore. She said she was too old for that shit, and Brigitte agreed. Even at thirty-five she felt too old to party. Home, tangoing with Rosa, peace and quiet, a good book—that was her idea of a good time.

Standing outside Rosa's apartment, she knocked. No answer. She knocked again. "Come on. Hurry up. I'm freezing my ass off out here in this drafty hall. It's the least you can do after waking me up. Rosa!"

No answer. Probably didn't want to be bothered. But Brigitte was curious now, so she pushed the door open.

"Hey, anybody here?" The aroma of the spicy crawfish étouffée Rosa had fixed them earlier permeated the living room. She stopped and inhaled deeply, recalling how Rosa had stood at the stove earlier tonight and stirred the roux in her big black iron skillet, then added various other ingredients until she sprinkled thyme on the completed dish.

But under the reminders of the onions, garlic, and bell peppers in their evening meal, Brigitte detected a strange smell, almost like rust. She walked through Rosa's well-furnished living room with its expensive yet comfortable furniture and her top-of-the-line stereo equipment. Paintings Rosa had bought from artists in the French Quarter covered the walls. In Rosa's bedroom, Brigitte glanced at the huge, tastefully painted nude that hung over Rosa's neatly made bed. Where was Rosa? The cooking odor from the kitchen subsided as Brigitte neared the bathroom, and now the new, odd smell grew stronger.

She wanted to turn around right here and leave. She could return to her bed, her book, and her enticing dreams of being in Paris, then wake up late and come back again. In the morning Rosa would call out for her to come in. The aroma of brewing coffee would overpower last night's étouffée and this odd smell. But she pushed on through the closed door.

The odor overpowered her. Blood everywhere. The beautiful pink water in the tub deepened to rose as blood trickled from Rosa's forearms.

Brigitte stooped and clasped Rosa's shoulder, shook her gently. "Rosa, talk to me." Her heavy hair had pulled her head backward. Her brown eyes stared at nothing. Her chest didn't move. Her breasts floated on the blood-ribboned water.

Brigitte felt for a pulse. Stopped, like an unwound clock. She dropped the familiar hand that felt like a dead catfish now.

Dead! Rosa was dead. Oh, goddamn it. No. Rosa couldn't be dead. Not Rosa. No, no, no—Rosa was too alive. She'd never lie here so still and silent. She'd jump up any minute, grab on a robe, and rush into the kitchen. She'd fix coffee, send her down the street for some fresh beignets, put on some dance music, and they'd tango before breakfast. Rosa couldn't be dead.

Brigitte sank to her knees on the cold tile floor, clung to the side of the stark-white bathtub, and sobbed. "Rosa. Rosa. Why did you do it? Why?"

Finally, she rose and stood staring, the blood throwing her into a stupor. The knife lying beside the tub pointed at her like an exclamation mark. She saw everything happen again as if she'd been there.

They quarreled. Leo left in a huff. Rosa cursed him, then kicked off her heels, jerked off her panty hose, slung them after her shoes.

Gradually Rosa's breathing slowed. She took off her new dress, hung it carefully on a padded hanger. She wandered into the kitchen still wearing her bra and half-slip, fixed herself a whiskey on the rocks. While she was there she picked up her boning knife—always razor sharp—and headed for the bathroom.

Rosa finished her drink while the tub filled with steaming water. She stripped and stepped into it, clutching the slender, sharp-pointed utensil. The water soothed yet stung as she stretched out, deciding where to slice herself.

She plunged the knife deep into her right arm, sliced from her wrist almost to her elbow, then did the same to the other one. Must have hit an artery. *Her bright-red blood fountained up, covered her throat like a ruby necklace.*

Brigitte should have waked up quicker, forced herself to crawl out of bed and rush up here as soon as Leo left. She could have talked to Rosa, made her realize things weren't as bad as they seemed. That noise should have told her something was wrong. Even if she hadn't run right up here, surely she could have come in time to help. Rosa hadn't done this much more than ten minutes ago.

But Brigitte was a selfish slug. She could have saved Rosa, who'd taught her, given her everything. But she hadn't wanted to get out of her warm bed and had dozed, oblivious to her best, her only friend.

Why had Rosa done this to her? To herself? Why?

Brigitte found the folded note in Rosa's bedroom, beside the telephone.

Darling Brigitte,

Don't think too badly of me, but I've had enough. You still have a chance, so get out of New Orleans before you end up like me. I'm leaving you everything I own. That way, you don't have any reason to stay here.

If you love me, you'll go to Paris and find someone who'll make you happy. You deserve a good life. Maybe you'll even find true love, though I still think it's a myth invented to torment people like me.

You're free. Take advantage of this opportunity and find yourself a worthy dance partner.

All my love,
Rosa

Brigitte refolded the note, smoothed her fingers across it, and called the police.

Chapter Two

Paris, France
June 15, 1972

"Where is that book? I could swear it was right here," Eva Laroche murmured to herself as she sorted through the stack she'd left sitting on the library table. She'd only been gone long enough to copy several magazine articles. The missing book was the most useful one in the batch she'd selected during her last few hours of research here in one of Paris's lending libraries.

She glanced around at the neatly positioned tables. Surely it hadn't sprouted legs and scampered under one of the thick-legged monstrosities. But then she spotted someone sitting two tables away, idly rubbing one hand over the scratched surface of the dark wooden tabletop as she perused a book—*her* missing book. She could tell because of its distinctive maroon jacket. She had to have it to research the background of several of the women she planned to include on her upcoming tour.

At first she saw only a veil of silky blond hair cascading down a head bent over the book. Then she noticed perfectly shaped hands, a long white neck—ah—and those stunning breasts! They completely filled out the blonde's black ribbed pullover. Whew. She wanted to take them in both hands and find out if they felt as spectacular as they looked. She'd squeeze them very carefully, run her fingers over hardening nipples—

Shaking herself from increasingly lewd thoughts, she strode over to where the blonde sat engrossed in her book. She didn't have time for fantasies or idle chatter, even with such a beauty. She stood on the opposite side of the table for what seemed like five minutes, but the blonde never looked up. So Eva cleared her throat, ever so softly. She waited what seemed like forever and coughed, a little louder this time.

That did it. Two cool blue eyes the color of the sea on Turkey's southern coast made her ache with desire, though the gorgeous eyes categorized, judged, and dismissed her in a single blink.

She clenched her hip muscles, trying to suppress the sudden throb between her legs, and opened her mouth to ask a question. She had to have the book the stunning blonde held so possessively in those beautiful hands.

Brigitte sat in the library trying to read about Colette's early novels featuring the sensual adventures of the schoolgirl Claudine. But she couldn't concentrate. She couldn't think about anything except Rosa's final advice: go to Paris and find somebody to love.

Well, with nothing to hold her in New Orleans, she'd taken Rosa's advice and had been in Paris almost four months now. But not much had changed. She hadn't had the heart to even think about looking for anybody. To make things worse, she couldn't go anywhere without men hitting on her, so she'd mostly stayed holed up in her luxury suite at the George V.

Now that was some fabulous hotel. Rosa had left her a pile. Added to her own considerable savings, it'd ensure that she'd never need to work again and could cut men completely out of her life.

Paris was beautiful and exciting, but she just didn't have an urge to be anywhere but here in the library or in her room, reading and relaxing. Rosa would be disappointed in her.

Someone cleared their throat, startling Brigitte from her thoughts. Why couldn't people leave her alone? This was a library, for God's sake, not a café or a bar. She wasn't interested in meeting anyone yet, much less carrying on a civil conversation with them.

She ignored whoever was trying to get her attention. Surely they'd take the hint and go away. She slipped back into the question that wouldn't leave her alone, even after this long. Why had Rosa killed herself? Those five words had Brigitte by the throat and wouldn't let go. She woke up in the middle of the night asking herself why. She wondered about it while she sat in a taxi, barely noticing the traffic that clogged the streets of Paris.

How could Brigitte ever forgive herself? She took a deep breath. Why hadn't she jumped out of bed as soon as she heard that knife drop? How could she have let sleep and dreams of being here in Paris be more important to her than Rosa's life? She could have saved Rosa.

Damn Rosa anyway. How dare she desert her? They were supposed to grow old together, laugh about the men they'd entertained, enjoy the piles of money they'd made. It'd be a long time before she'd feel like forgiving Rosa for running out on her. Besides, who would she dance the tango with now?

But that was all in the past. Maybe Rosa had killed herself as a way of pushing Brigitte out of the nest. Here she was, all alone in a strange city with no clue how to find anyone to love. What should she do? Sure, she could shack up with someone in a heartbeat, but that would be too easy, too much like going back to work. She wanted to find someone who'd see past the beautiful façade she always presented to the world, love her for who she was inside. But what was she inside? Only Rosa had ever seemed to see something worthwhile in her.

"*Ahem.*"

The intruder obviously wasn't going away, so Brigitte reluctantly raised her head, pushed back her hair, and stared up at the person who loomed over her wearing an unhappy expression.

Reddish-brown hair with long bangs half covered small ears and brushed her shoulders. "What are you doing here, and where did you get that book?" the stranger whispered in French, pointing. Her words were as clipped and blunt as her buffed fingernails.

Brigitte shrugged, then gestured to a nearby table and replied in French. "From that stack of rejects over there."

The woman almost snarled, tiny dimples bracketing a full lower lip topped by a narrow upper one. "Those are not rejects. I carefully chose each of them. The one you're holding is mine."

Brigitte hugged the book close to her chest. She didn't appreciate anyone treating her like she didn't belong here, though she herself would be the first to admit that she didn't. Should she get a special permit, pay an admission fee? She also resented how inferior this woman was able to make her feel with just one judgmental glance.

She resorted to sarcasm to drive the unwelcome intruder away. "Am I mistaken, or is this your private collection?" How dare the woman act like this? "In American libraries, we check books out for a limited period of time. Have you done that?"

The stranger stared at her, so near Brigitte could see she used practically no makeup on her flawless skin. And those eyes. How could anyone not be pulled into their intensity? Blue-green orbited a ring of yellow, circling eternal blackness.

"No. I haven't checked it out." The woman's tanned skin darkened, and her solar eyes flared. "But I intend to." She thrust her hand almost under Brigitte's nose, reaching for the book.

Brigitte pulled back a few inches and straightened her slumped shoulders. What an irritating, presumptuous person. Who did she think she was? Just because the woman was obviously a Parisian, how dare she leave a book she wanted just lying around and then waltz up and claim it?

The stranger backed up a step, but her eyes didn't dim. "I have to have it to help me prepare for an important project." Her upper lip pulled into an even tighter line, and her lower one plumped. Something about her seemed familiar, but Brigitte couldn't determine what it was.

If the woman had been gracious, had softened her tone or her expression just a little, Brigitte would have handed her the book immediately. After all, she'd picked it up on a whim. Famous Frenchwomen had always intrigued her, but the library in New Orleans didn't have much information about them. Here in Paris she'd discovered a treasure trove, and this book seemed to be the best of the lot. She needed something absorbing to help her stop worrying and wondering about Rosa's death.

Brigitte rose slowly and shoved the book into her large purse. "I've decided to check it out." She ignored the woman's panicked expression. "Don't worry. I'll return it when my allotted time's up. Excuse me."

She strolled over to the main desk. Maybe that would teach the woman not to be so rude to foreigners.

Chapter Three

Brigitte sat under a large red umbrella at a sidewalk café and, with dainty strokes, reluctantly licked the last of her bowl of chocolate mousse from her spoon. It had been a heavenly blend of rich, fluffy, oozy decadence as she'd savored each bite, which was as silky smooth as the inside of a woman's thighs. The bitter dark chocolate had been just sweet enough and textured perfectly with the rich whipping cream, meringue, sugar, and a liqueur she couldn't identify. The mousse was delicious, luxurious, even to someone like her who was used to the high life. She hadn't had much of an appetite since Rosa's death, but this mousse was like a cloud, leaving chocolate fog on her tongue.

The clink of coffee cups and the buzz of the people sitting nearby made her feel a little less alone. She had no trouble understanding the French language that engulfed her. It was the most beautiful language in the world, like birds in flight, swooping and dipping in constant melodious discourse. She opened her compact and pulled out a tube of lipstick. Removing the cap and rolling it up, she noted that she'd used almost all of it. And it was such a beautiful color red—her favorite. She smoothed it over her lips and blotted them on one of the tissues she always carried. She needed to go shopping.

Becoming restless, she shifted her weight from one hip to the other. The plastic back and seat of her chair were becoming a little hard, but the activity around her here on the tree-lined Champs Élysées made her want to stay right where she was.

People of various colors and nationalities, sporting everything from straw hats to turbans and berets, walked past her on this most famous thoroughfare in Paris. Many seemed to be tourists, scurrying in large groups behind loud-voiced leaders who pointed this way and that with an umbrella. Strange. One of the tour guides she glimpsed resembled the woman she'd had that run-in with at the library last week. But before she could get a second look, the group quickly disappeared down the street, and that would have been too much of a coincidence, anyhow. Besides, she certainly didn't want to tangle with that rude woman again.

Many of the people, especially those walking with purpose instead of following a leader or gawking at the sights on their own, were obviously Parisians. Many of the men sported dark business suits, and almost all the woman wore summer dresses or knee-length skirts and blouses. She guessed they were either on their way to the cinema or a nearby small shop, going out to eat, or headed to or from work. Some of them could even be former clients. Rosa had been proud of her international connections.

Just then, however, a man passing by on the sidewalk slowed his pace and stared at her as he puffed on a cigar. She slid her compact and lipstick back into her purse and picked up the book she'd brought along. When she finally raised her eyes, he was gone.

Whew. What a nuisance. She was so tired of having people, especially men, react to her like that. Rosa's death had severed her ties to the US, and now she could be who she wanted and do what she wanted with her life, in this city she'd always dreamed about. And away from the US she wouldn't be tempted to crawl back to her real mother. They'd quarreled right before she'd gone to live with Rosa, ages ago, and she never wanted to have anything to do with her mother—or men—again.

She kept her book open but let her mind wander to the conversation she'd had with Leo the day after she'd discovered Rosa dead. He'd said he'd miss Rosa, and maybe he had—for about ten minutes. He'd probably already found another mistress. What a loser. But she planned to forget the past now and simply enjoy herself among people supposedly more broad-minded and accepting than the ones who'd snubbed her so often back home. Though she wasn't off to a very good start. That brunette in the library had made her feel about as welcome here in Paris as a mouse turd in a fruit salad.

Feeling a little down, Brigitte rummaged around in her purse and located a medicine bottle.

She waved to the waiter, ordered some mineral water, popped an aspirin, then rinsed it down. "Thanks." She smiled at him as he pocketed his tip.

That awkward incident in the library the other day had given her a headache that kept cropping up at the strangest times. The brunette she'd quarreled with there had been so demanding, and she'd stared at Brigitte in such a condescending way. The woman's judgmental air reminded her of the self-important women in New Orleans she'd encountered occasionally. They couldn't satisfy their husbands in bed, but they clearly considered her and Rosa—and women like them— inferior because they could. Didn't make a bit of sense.

The stranger in the library was beautiful yet glacial, with none of the warmth that had always oozed from Rosa. Obviously the woman was much more concerned about her book and her important project than the feelings of others. Rosa had always been nothing but sympathetic and caring. Brigitte sighed. God, she missed her.

She rubbed tears from her eyes, then pulled a cigarette from her package of Kent Lights. As she was reaching for a match, a tall, well-built woman appeared, her hair cut short in a chic style. The stranger whisked an expensive gold lighter from an inside pocket in her tailored men's suit jacket and fired up the tip of Brigitte's long filtered cigarette.

"May I join you?" the woman asked, her Germanic accent noticeable.

Brigitte considered her briefly. The woman's air of authority was impressive. "If you want to."

The stranger settled into a white plastic-and-metal chair near her. "Waiter. Whiskey, neat," she called, then turned to Brigitte. "May I buy you another of whatever you're drinking?"

She nodded, deciding to see what this person had to offer in addition to a drink.

"Been in Paris long?" the woman asked.

"A few months."

"Beautiful weather, eh?"

Not a very original opening line, Brigitte thought, but the woman might help her get to know Paris in a whole new way. And she might be able to distract her from brooding so much. It obviously wasn't doing anyone any good. Nothing could bring Rosa back.

"Ah. The weather's glorious. Much cooler than June in New Orleans. And not nearly as humid." That was just one of the many things she wouldn't miss about Louisiana.

"So you're an American. A beautiful American, I might add."

That was better. Unoriginal still, probably fake as hell, but she could use a little reassurance right now. All these weeks of mourning had surely taken their toll on her appearance. "Thank you. And you are?"

"Mies, from Amsterdam, here to film a documentary about the jazz scene." Mies's eyes glinted like she'd just discovered a valuable ring lying on the sidewalk.

There, she thought. Those gleaming eyes said a lot more about Mies than her words did. "Ah, jazz. What an exciting subject for your film. Speaking of, I'd love to hear some of the groups in town. A lot of the big names play here, don't they? I'm Brigitte, by the way."

Mies's eyebrows shot up in mock surprise. "Brigitte Bardot?"

Brigitte took a drag on her cigarette and exhaled a long stream of smoke just past Mies's head. "Very flattering, but don't be silly. Her eyes are brown. Mine are blue. And I certainly wasn't born in Paris."

"Ah. Yes. I see that, now that you mention it. But those have to be the only differences. Are you an actress or a model?"

No way was she spilling the beans about her background. Mies might be cruising her but probably wouldn't be interested in paying for whatever happened between them. And something would, fast, the way things were already going. She'd slept by herself long enough now. A little recreational sex might give her a whole new outlook on life. "Neither an actress nor a model. Let's just say…I've had a career in high finance."

She could usually spot a con a mile away, but Mies looked relatively sincere. As Mies picked up the heavy crystal glass in capable-looking hands, she wondered if Mies would be able to take care of her, like Rosa had. She had always needed someone steady in her life, like her grandmother and Rosa.

"Why do you want to hear some jazz here in Paris?" Mies asked. "You said you're from New Orleans, didn't you? Don't you get your fill of it there?" She took a long drink of her whiskey.

"I've had my fill of everything in New Orleans." The thought of being with a woman made Brigitte's pussy twitch for the first time in a long while. Strange how she could begin to be interested in sex all of a sudden when she couldn't have cared less about it as a working girl. "I'm hoping Paris will be more my style."

Mies set her glass on the table and stared at her. "I'd like to do my best to make sure it is."

Brigitte recognized the look—knew it all too well—and this time it touched something carnal deep inside her. When Mies moved her hard-backed chair even closer, she didn't pull away.

Instead, she said, "Maybe you can show me what your best is. I'm getting a little bored being here by myself. Where are you staying?"

Mies took another big swig of her drink. "The George V. You?"

"The same." She sipped her mineral water.

"You don't say? Nice." Mies looked at her watch. "Listen. I'm already late for an appointment, but how about meeting for dinner in the hotel restaurant? Say, seven o'clock?"

Why not? Last week, the woman in the library had set off a few fireworks in her after a long, dry spell. However, the library Nazi was probably as passionless as a stalk of celery. Mies seemed like she might be able to ignite the flammable tinder that had accumulated in her.

"Sounds interesting. Maybe we could go hear some jazz sometime soon too."

"Jazz, eh? I'd like that." Mies smiled with what appeared to be either triumph or anticipation. "We could enjoy ourselves exploring Paris together."

And each other. Brigitte didn't say the words aloud, but Mies's expression said the same thing.

After Mies hurried away, Brigitte looked at her own watch. She had time to take a bath and a nap before indulging in her first real taste of Paris. Rosa would approve.

❖

Dinner had been a success, Mies charming and attentive. She'd even made Brigitte laugh several times, which was a real relief after all the mourning she'd done. Afterward, Mies had slipped Brigitte a key to her room and arranged to meet her there later.

Now she rested on Mies's bed and stretched, wide-awake, trying not to think about Rosa. She eased her hand under the robe she wore and stroked her warm stomach. Was she finally stirring to life again? But how could she even think about enjoying herself with Rosa gone? Her throat tightened, and she couldn't stop the tears from welling up.

A key rattled in the door, and she glanced at the clock radio on the Louis XVI nightstand. Ten, on the dot. Mies was certainly punctual.

"Brigitte, where are you?" Mies sounded as excited as Brigitte began to feel again.

"In here, Mies." How wonderful to hear a woman's voice instead of a man's. And how thrilling to rendezvous with someone simply because she wanted to, instead of because she was paid to. Rosa would definitely approve. She squeezed her eyes shut so she wouldn't start crying again and willed herself to forget what had happened to Rosa. Life was certainly full of surprises.

"I'm waiting for you." She arranged herself in her most seductive pose. If only she'd brought her red silk robe from her own room instead of undressing and pulling on this plush white terry-cloth one the hotel supplied. She was slipping. "Are you coming?" At least she'd dabbed some Givenchy III between her breasts as an opening attraction.

Mies sauntered into the bedroom, and a large smile spread across her broad face as she set a bottle on the nightstand, kicked off her low-heeled shoes, and unbuttoned her white shirt. After unzipping her trousers, she carefully laid them across the back of a chair, all the while gazing at Brigitte through half-closed eyes.

"Now this is what I call room service." Mies lowered herself beside Brigitte and kissed her. "Ah. I can't think of a better late-night snack than you." She slid her hand up and down Brigitte's leg, her large palm relentlessly inching Brigitte's robe more fully open with every stroke.

A river of sensation coursed up Brigitte's legs, from her calves past her knees and into the flesh of her thighs. "Mmm-hmm." She purred her pleasure.

Mies grasped the tie of Brigitte's robe, wrapping it around her strong, elegant fingers. "And what have we here?" She growled, slowly loosening the sash.

"Something I think you'll like." Brigitte's stomach quivered, and her pussy began to throb as Mies brushed it and her breasts with the coarse terry cloth.

Mies's soft kisses made the pulsation rush through Brigitte's arms, up her neck, and finally to her mouth. Her lips seemed to swell, filled with the familiar electricity that flooded her body. "*Ohhh.*"

"You're gorgeous," Mies whispered and tasted one of her breasts as if it were as delicious as the chocolate mousse Brigitte had enjoyed earlier at the café.

She liked the way Mies licked one stiffening nipple, then the other, and circled each one gently, gradually pressing more forcibly until she moved and kissed her way down Brigitte's body. As Mies massaged her thighs and buttocks, the flashes inside Brigitte became almost painful.

Mies returned to her lips, and Brigitte opened them to the thrusting tongue that claimed her so powerfully, so surely. "Ah. That feels so good," she managed to say when Mies began to inch her way down Brigitte's body once more. Silver, sparkling moments such as these teased her, promised to let her escape into a world of pure sensation. If only she could whiz past that final barrier and sizzle into the atmosphere.

Maybe this time.

Mies's forceful fingers slid over her clitoris, triggering the liquid that cascaded from her and created a tremor between her legs. "Oh yes." She gasped as Mies manipulated her tingling folds. "Your lips—down there."

Smelling of expensive cologne, Mies slid down her body and buried her face in Brigitte's thatch.

"Yes. That's it."

Mies's head bobbed up and down as she licked and sucked, tonguing Brigitte's clitoris, biting it lightly, thrusting into her.

Mies was obviously experienced, and Brigitte tried to let herself go, strained to allow herself to burst open inside.

"I'm almost there. More. More."

But the more she willed her body to relax, the more she mentally drifted away. Mies didn't give a rat's ass about her. She was probably fantasizing that she was fucking Brigitte Bardot.

Finally she sighed and pushed Mies's head away. "It's no use, tough gal." At least she'd be honest, not fake an orgasm like she always had done with her clients. "That pussy has a mind of her own. I appreciate the effort though. Maybe later." She grabbed the folds of the robe on each side of her and began to cover herself.

"Maybe later indeed." Mies sat up and licked her lips. "You just need a little time. I'll wait." She got up and pulled on a man's dark robe. "How about we crack open this bottle of Beaujolais? I'm thirsty, and I bet you are too."

Brigitte tasted the wine, trying to recapture her earlier mood of anticipation. But it immediately soured in her stomach. She pulled the hotel robe around her, let out a deep breath, and carried her clothes into the bathroom, where she slowly dressed.

Back in Mies's living room, Brigitte looked out the windows at the lights of Paris. They seemed dimmer now than they had when she'd gazed at them earlier tonight.

She stood there alone a minute, staring at the city, while Mies, at the minibar, poured them each another glass of wine, her back to Brigitte. She sighed. Being in Paris hadn't magically allowed her to let Mies take her completely. She felt more alone and unloved now than she had before she'd met Mies.

Mies turned around and held out her full glass with a grin. Brigitte straightened her back and tried to smile, but she couldn't. "No, thanks. I'm going to call it a night."

She hadn't come to Europe to be the same person she'd been in New Orleans. Hooking up with Mies had been a bad idea. Lesson learned.

Chapter Four

D o you think anyone would sign up for a tour of Paris featuring some of the famous women who've lived here, Jeanne?" Eva Laroche sat on the edge of a cushiony green chair in her aunt's travel agency, Taste Paris, and gulped some of the coffee she'd just made. "Ouch. Burned my tongue."

Jeanne gazed at her with farsighted blue eyes and shook her head. "Slow down, child. All in good time." Jeanne inhaled deeply, until the steam from her white china cup slowly dissipated. "Ah. Nothing like the smell of a rich brew. Thanks for this." She finally took a sip. "Some people will definitely be interested in the tour. This is the seventies. We're liberated."

"Are you sure?" Eva blew on her coffee before she tried it again. "You can take care of yourself. And I'm trying. But what about women like Mother?" Her mother would be content to live in the Middle Ages, when most men regarded women as either property or as a means to gaining it.

"I know." Jeanne appeared rueful. "She ignores your father's weaknesses because he looks after her."

"Weaknesses?" Eva jumped up so fast she almost spilled her coffee all over her blouse. "Is that what you call screwing prostitutes? Spending all Mother's inheritance on fancy cars and clothes to impress his women? Refusing to bail me out of jail? She should have left him years ago."

As Eva paced, Jeanne nestled more comfortably into her chair and concentrated on her morning coffee. "Calm down. Yves isn't all bad."

"Yeah. You could have fooled me." Eva's blood was as hot as the coffee she tried to keep from sloshing over the rim of her cup. "He's set the liberation of women back a hundred years, and if he had his way, he'd eradicate it altogether."

"Have you heard about that new American television series called *All in the Family*?" Jeanne asked.

"You know I don't like television, especially American shows. The few I've seen are too full of Americans and their endless shallow obsession with things and appearance. Where on earth did you hear of such a program?" Jeanne was always surprising her.

"I watched it in New York last year, while I was there on a business trip. But that's not important." Jeanne settled in as if she intended to spend the morning chatting instead of working. "The wife in the comedy series—Edith's her name—reminds me of your mother. She acts unintelligent, and everyone treats her as if she is, but she's obviously much smarter than anyone gives her credit for."

"Smart? How?" Eva walked over to the front door and peered out at the morning traffic before turning her attention back to her aunt. "Mother's pretty and charming and a great shopper, but I've never considered her particularly intelligent."

"Your mother doesn't think of herself as smart either. But she has a good heart and an open mind, like Edith." Jeanne smiled wryly, as if recalling a particularly poignant episode on the show. "The show deals with current issues such as women's lib and homosexuality, and Edith always innocently shows the rest of the family, especially her husband, how unenlightened they are."

"If you say so, but I've never seen anything particularly worthwhile in either Americans or their so-called culture." Eva finished her coffee and set her cup down on a small table.

Jeanne tapped her own forehead. "Remember what I've always told you, dear. Keep an open mind, even about Americans. Everyone has something to teach us."

Eva took a deep breath and walked over to the plate-glass window. "Yes. Thanks for reminding me. And I need to stop acting like a kid and letting Father bother me so much."

"You have to be patient. Change takes time. Your mother's not as mistreated as you think she is. She chose to marry Yves, and she continues to stay with him for reasons of her own." Jeanne took another sip, as if sorry she'd almost finished her morning coffee. "Worry about your own problems, such as this tour you've suggested. Sure, it'll attract only a small, select group of tourists. They'll have to be interested in the subject and stay here in Paris for more than just a few days."

Eva looked out the window at a bicyclist rushing by, several baguettes stretched across his basket. "You're right. Most tourists, especially the Americans, fly through here without seeing much more than the Louvre, Versailles, and Notre-Dame."

Jeanne finally emptied her cup and carried it and Eva's to a small screened-off area in the corner of the large room, where she rinsed them.

This simple act always made Eva feel cared for. That was one reason she lived with Jeanne right now, instead of with her parents. She walked over to her desk, ready to begin her workday.

Jeanne returned, her expression thoughtful. "No, this will be a gourmet tour, for connoisseurs. You should meet some intriguing foreigners for a change." She glanced at Eva with concern. "You must already be getting tired of bored teenagers and their overworked teachers."

Eva nodded, warmed as much by Jeanne's kind expression as by her coffee. "I would welcome a group of adults. And I could practice reading a varied group and persuading them to see things my way." Having to defend a case before a jury in a few years, after she passed her bar exam and became a full-fledged lawyer, made her more nervous than she wanted to admit. Well, she'd just have to get over it.

Jeanne straightened her large-lensed Lafont eyeglasses and rearranged a display of brochures praising the wonders of the South of France. "You've done well so far encouraging tourists to see things as you do. No one would ever suspect how difficult it's always been for you to speak before a large group. But you may have another problem."

Eva shuffled through some papers on her desk, sure she knew what Jeanne would say. Instead of being rude, though, she humored her aunt. She meant well. "What's that?"

Jeanne quirked her mouth into a half smile. "I realize I've warned you about this several times, but it's important."

Eva nodded, though she really didn't need to hear this bit of advice again.

"Some of the people you'll lead will want to get to know you better," Jeanne said. "After all, you're beautiful, when you take time to pay some attention to your appearance."

"And when I don't take time, I'm ugly?" Eva was only half kidding. She'd never thought of herself as attractive and didn't see why she should spend a lot of time trying to be. She had too many other important and interesting things to do. What had Mother's good looks gotten her except a handsome, philandering husband?

"Don't be silly. You're never ugly," Jeanne said. "I'd just like to see you maximize your natural good looks." She walked over and brushed her fingers through Eva's bangs. "But even if you don't, some people on your tour will treat you like their best friend. They'll even suggest after-hours activities." She backed away when Eva moved her head slightly. "Once the tour ends, though, they'll disappear and forget you completely. Why, when I began in this business, I…"

Eva had heard about the attempted seductions Jeanne had endured a million times, so she tuned them out. She didn't intend to become involved with anyone who was paying her to guide them around Paris. That would make her too much like the prostitutes her father couldn't seem to get enough of.

"I know," she said. "Why do you think so many people, especially Americans, dream of sleeping with a Frenchwoman?" The thought made her uneasy. "For that matter, why do so many people consider us sexy?"

Her aunt swiped a bleached-blond strand of hair out of her own eye. "Perhaps because we are?" She laughed. "Seriously, since the time of Elizabeth I, Anglo women have been taught that they can become powerful only by denying men sex."

Eva nodded. She hadn't thought of that.

"But, through experience, we Frenchwomen have learned that we can use sex to gain power. It's as simple as that." Jeanne looked satisfied, as if she thought she'd answered Eva's question completely.

But Eva needed to think about what Jeanne had just said. She glanced down at the list of teenage Americans she was scheduled to lead through Paris, then looked up again. "Regardless of what causes people's misplaced fantasies, I refuse to become the victim of them. I just want to try to repay you for all your help during the past few years and become a better lawyer in the process."

Jeanne gave her a quick hug. "You don't need to repay me, child. But I do appreciate your help, and I love being able to spend some time with you for a change. You were out of the country far too long to suit me." She gazed at Eva with pride. "Besides, I really do like your idea for this new tour."

Eva filled with warmth and hugged Jeanne back. If only her father made her feel this way. "I have to meet my new group. Go ahead and advertise the Women of Paris tour. And don't worry about me. I can deal with whoever signs up."

❖

Brigitte felt on top of the world here on the second level of the Eiffel Tower. She pulled off her floppy hat and large-framed sunglasses and, for a minute, let the glorious sun warm her cheeks, which she'd carefully coated with Coppertone sunscreen.

She inhaled deeply, alive with sensation, as she glanced across the Seine at the Place du Trocadero. The two long buildings at the back of the Trocadero reminded her of a woman's arms stretched wide open to welcome her to Paris. She just wished she could find that woman.

She almost wished things had worked out with Mies, but not seeing her again had been the right choice. That liaison was going nowhere fast, and she was relieved she'd ended it after just that one night. At least she'd been honest with Mies and with herself. Now she felt reenergized and ready to see Paris on her own.

Brigitte gripped the worn-smooth wooden rail. The iron fencing under it felt cold against her right knee, and a chilly breeze caressed her, so she untied her red sweater from around her shoulders and pulled it on over her shirt. She should have worn pants instead of this miniskirt, but it felt good to bare her legs to the world and know she could handle whatever attention she attracted.

She gazed at the city that stretched all around her, wishing she had someone special to share the breathtaking view with. But she didn't, so she checked her hair in her compact. Windblown—it needed some major repair work. She pulled her hat back on.

Mies had appeared to be infatuated with her, but what had they actually talked about during the few hours they'd spent together? What to eat, Mies's filming schedule, how beautiful Mies thought she was—nothing really personal, intimate. She wanted to share things with someone like she had with Rosa.

Could someone be both a lover and a friend? Those two spheres had always been totally separate for her, and she didn't know if she could bring them together. If only she could find someone who could provide her with a roaring orgasm like she'd seen lovers in the movies enjoy, as well as converse with her about music and literature and art, she'd be happy.

She meandered to another spot on the platform and spotted what she thought must be the Luxembourg Gardens in the Latin Quarter. The horse-chestnut trees were such a rich shade of green. They made her feel younger than she had in years.

A few days ago she'd strolled through those gardens and noticed some brown spots on the leaves of the chestnut trees. But from here they looked perfect. How strange that distance usually made things seem more desirable. She pulled on her sunglasses again and thought of the couples she'd noticed during her time in the Luxembourg Gardens. Some had been walking arm in arm, and others lying entwined on a blanket, but none of them seemed to care who saw them.

She was definitely no stranger to sex, but for her it had always had to occur behind closed doors. It had been a private affair she could never share with the world, an impersonal business transaction.

Having to worry about being arrested for what she was and did had certainly put a damper on things, though Rosa had always shielded her from that particular bit of reality. But she couldn't protect her from the holier-than-thou attitude of practically everyone she'd come in contact with. And for what? She was simply making an honest living.

But she reminded herself that she wasn't in New Orleans any longer, thank God. She was in Paris, where women could walk hand in hand along the street and no one would notice. That would have never been accepted in New Orleans unless the women were very young, very old, closely related, or feeble.

She stood there and continued to gaze at the faraway park. Maybe if she'd grown up here instead of in a small town near New Orleans, she'd have been able to accept sex as something natural and enjoyable. Why should she have to hide such an important part of herself?

After a while, the sun vanished behind the clouds, and the wind began to chill her bare legs. As she walked toward the lift to leave, she heard a familiar voice. "I'll give you ten minutes to look at the city. Remember how I told you the Parisians used to think this tower was an eyesore and wanted it torn down? Well, this view will show you what you would have missed if they'd had their way."

That voice. Shrill, demanding, instructing, arrogant. Brigitte had heard it not that long ago. But where?

"Don't forget. I'll meet you here at the lift in ten minutes."

And then she remembered. The striking woman at the library, the one who'd been so overbearing about that book. She hurried in the opposite direction. She didn't want the woman to see her. Maybe she wouldn't recognize her. She felt a bit embarrassed about reacting the way she had at the library and decided to return the book today. What if the woman truly needed it? She shook her head. All the brunette had needed to do was ask her nicely.

After riding the lift down to ground level, she stood at the bottom of the massive tower and gazed up at it. Its size overwhelmed her, as Paris did at times, but she tried not to gawk. She was a sophisticated woman in a sophisticated city, and she needed to look and act like one.

She grabbed a taxi to Avenue Montaigne. There she strolled into some exclusive boutiques where, with her perfect French, the clerks competed for her attention. She tried on several cocktail dresses—designed by Pierre Cardin, Vera, Oscar de la Renta, and Diane von Furstenberg—and chose a simple black number and a pair of sexy black dress sandals. Rosa would have loved this.

She also picked up some lipstick and nail polish, some matte-finish makeup, and a large bottle of Givenchy III—her all-time favorite perfume. The natural look seemed to be out of fashion here in Paris, judging by most of the well-dressed women she'd eyed on the street all week.

But it was getting late. She needed to return that library book today so she could get that abrasive yet attractive Frenchwoman off her mind. Then she'd leisurely dress for her date with herself tonight to listen to some jazz.

Chapter Five

Marian Smither grasped Eva's arm a little too familiarly. "My little darlings want to go to a club tonight. Can you recommend a good one?"

Eva had to struggle to keep up with Marian's rapid English. Her accent was different than the British English Eva had learned during several extended visits to England. Since Marian supposedly taught French in an American private school, Eva had supposed she'd welcome the opportunity to practice it here in Paris. But with only a few exceptions, she reverted to English. She wasn't that different from most Americans Eva encountered. They simply couldn't believe that everyone in Paris didn't speak fluent English.

Eva wiggled her tired feet and groaned to herself. Everyone in Marian's group, with Eva in the lead, had just finished walking up all three hundred steps to visit the Sacré-Cœur, and she'd just sat down with a cup of coffee. "What kind of club do they have in mind?" She hoped it was one that closed early.

Marian perched on the edge of her chair in the small open-air café and gazed around the famous shaded square in Montmartre, filled with painters and their easels. She looked as fresh as her students did, even though they'd all been sightseeing practically nonstop since they arrived in Paris three days ago from somewhere in the American Midwest. "They'd love to go to one of those raunchy places in Pigalle, but that probably wouldn't be suitable, do you think?"

Raunchy? What did that word mean? Probably immoral. Americans were so puritanical and assumed that everyone shared their values. Eva played along with Marian's prejudice. "I don't imagine their parents would approve of that type of outing. You should come up with a better idea."

Eva ordered a second coffee and tried to soak up the creative spirit she always associated with this square. Knowing that so many famous artists, like van Gogh, had worked and lived near here always gave her a boost. And she enjoyed its calm, village-like atmosphere, which gave her a sense of peace and stability.

"What about jazz?" Marian asked. "Some of the kids really dig it."

Dig it? Did real people actually use such slang? Judging by her vocabulary, Marian wasn't much older than the dozen or so recent high-school graduates she was escorting through Paris and Rome this summer. American women in general were so very unsophisticated and devoid of a sense of style.

Marian pressed on. "Where's the best place for that kind of music?"

Eva didn't want to encourage Marian by recommending a club, but she didn't want to alienate her. "Are you sure you want to stay out that late? You have to be exhausted. After all, we just finished walking up to the second-highest point in the city."

Eva shook her head. "Exhausted? This is their senior trip. I don't dare get tired. Their parents back home are paying all my expenses, so I have to be ready to do whatever the kids ask me to. I'll make it worth your while if you'll take us. We have a slush fund for special excursions."

Eva suppressed another groan. She just wanted to go home, soak her feet, and read a good book. Cobblestones such as the ones in this part of Paris were charming, but tiring to walk on. Besides, she needed to do some research for her Women of Paris tour, which began all too soon.

"Well, I suppose I could—"

Marian grabbed her hand, her eyes blazing with something more than excitement. "That'd be great. Could you find us a place where the locals go, instead of one full of tourists? We want to experience the real Paris."

How tiresome. Marian was flirting with her. Quite likely, she wanted to experience a real *Parisienne* as well. Jeanne had been right.

"Miss Smither," one of the students called from a nearby artist's stand. "Can you come help me pick out a painting? I can't decide between one of the Eiffel Tower or the Sacré-Cœur. I really like it. It looks like the Taj Mahal."

Eva groaned to herself. Everyone, especially the Americans, wanted to see the real Paris, instead of the artificial one constructed to rake in tourist dollars. She really didn't blame them. In fact, during her recent travels over much of the world, she'd gone out of her way to associate with the locals. She'd had some unforgettable experiences as a single woman on her own, and several she'd rather forget.

She shrugged. She could use the extra money Marian had offered. She planned to repay Jeanne every cent she'd loaned her, with interest. She'd never have been able to get out of jail and away from France without her aunt's generosity. Strange, how her father probably spent more on his women in a month than she'd needed for bail and for her entire trip, but he'd refused to loan her any at all.

Jeanne, however, hadn't hesitated. Jeanne had encouraged her to get away, to see the world while she was young instead of doing nothing but studying and trying to change the system in France. She'd told Eva that she needed a break after all the political upheaval she'd been involved in while studying for her law degree.

Marian returned with an annoyed expression, breaking Eva's reverie. "Honestly, that girl can't tie her shoelaces by herself. I wish she'd find someone else to hang on to instead of expecting me to be her friend. And some of the others in the group just told me they're ready to leave now. I swear they have the attention span of a gnat."

Eva jumped to her feet, caffeine surging through her. In the morning she'd put this group on the train to Italy. *I can stand up to this pace one more night.*

As she and Marian rounded up the teenagers scattered around the colorful square, she kept trying to persuade herself the extra excursion tonight wasn't a bad idea. After the group left, she'd have an entire weekend all to herself before another week like she'd just had arrived.

❖

Brigitte finished removing the coral lacquer from her nails and held up her fingers to inspect each one, making sure no color remained. She shook her bottle of cranberry-red polish, unscrewed the top, and grazed the brush against the inside of the bottle's neck to remove any excess polish. Images of that troublesome brunette from the library kept popping into her mind.

Imagine seeing her again, at the Eiffel Tower. Evidently she was a tour guide, most likely the one she'd glimpsed that day on the Champs Élysées, and had truly needed that book. She shook her head, trying to brush off her nagging regret at having acted so childish about the incident. At least she'd returned the book, so she could forget it had ever happened. But the woman's unusual blue-green eyes seemed to have burned a hole in her brain.

Just then, she felt as if someone were sweeping her hair to one side and kissing the back of her neck. She stiffened. A faint scent of spring perfumed the air, as it had momentarily when she and Rosa had tangoed that final time. She shook her head and banished the thought.

Instead, she concentrated on covering her right thumbnail but kept sniffing remnants of the elusive aroma. A vision of those young people making out so unashamedly in the Luxembourg Gardens kept blinking off and on in her mind, like the traffic lights in Paris that whipped directly from green to red without a yellow warning. She'd glimpsed two women sprawled on a blanket in that park, oblivious to the stares of strangers. Would the brunette at the library ever make such a spectacle of herself? She doubted it. She seemed more uptight than a married woman in New Orleans.

Mies certainly hadn't been uptight, but she hadn't been able to think about anything but sex. Right now Brigitte just wanted to go out on the town and let some good jazz help her get her mind off everything.

She stood and let her negligee drop to the floor. She didn't want to smudge her nails, so she waved her hands to speed up the drying process. Satisfied, she eased her panty hose up her legs and settled them around her waist, making sure the crotch wasn't too tight. Then she stepped into her half-slip, maneuvered it slowly up, and smoothed it over her hips.

Not too bad, she thought as she gazed at herself in the mirror. The bags under her eyes had almost disappeared, and her skin was glowing again under her light dusting of face powder. She looked ready to conquer the Paris jazz scene.

Now for her new dress. After she slipped it on and strung a pair of cords around her waist, she marveled that they were all that held the black outfit together. She pirouetted in front of the mirror, admiring how beautifully the dress fit. The skirt was so sheer it felt like Kleenex. The soft jersey hugged her closely, and the halter neck felt comfortable. Having her back completely bare always excited her. Luckily, the dress had a built-in bra and held her breasts in place, displaying them perfectly.

It reminded her of some of the outfits she'd worn while she was working, but being in Paris made it seem much more special than her old clothes had. She applied her new red lipstick and then winked at her reflection. Her hair looked like spun gold, glittering against her black dress, and at that moment Brigitte felt golden.

She improvised a few tango steps, humming a familiar tune and leading an imaginary woman whose face was blurred and who felt oh-so light in her arms. Then she grabbed her evening wrap, left her room, and walked to the elevator. She felt like Cinderella leaving for the ball.

Chapter Six

"*B*onsoir, Mademoiselle Eva*," Marian said in what she apparently considered a sexy voice and accent, then immediately reverted into English. "How's it going?" She and her two most adventurous students had been waiting in the lobby of their hotel when Eva arrived.

Eva cringed. Instead of her usual ladylike loose-fitting slacks and blouse with its Peter Pan collar, Marian wore an incredibly tight all-black outfit. "What happened to everyone else?" Eva asked.

Marian had put her long, stringy red hair up into a French twist and piled on the makeup. She'd attract a lot of attention, hopefully not the wrong kind. "The rest of them backed out." She shook her head. "Said they needed to pack and get some sleep. Kids. You never can tell with them."

At least most of the group had some sense. She wished Marian and the young couple with her had followed their example.

"These two kids adore jazz and said they'd like to ride the Metro once more. They say it's an adventure. Is that okay?"

Eva shrugged. "It's your choice. We'll have to walk a ways, and we'll have to leave the club by midnight so we can catch the last train."

As Eva led them toward the Metro stop, Marian took her arm. "This is so exciting. I've always dreamed of listening to jazz in Paris." Marian matched her pace. "And these youngsters are real music buffs. They're planning to major in it."

Eva glanced back at them, where they strolled along glued together. From all appearances, they planned to major in each other.

After an uneventful subway ride, she led them toward the new Meridien Etoile hotel.

"Wow," Marian said. "This is way cool. I totally dig the way this thing glitters. All that metal running up the front of the building's enough to blind you."

Marian certainly wasn't acting very cool, so Eva tried to lower the temperature of her little group. "Air France just finished building it. They call it the traveler's home away from home, but so far not many of the run-of-the-mill tourists have discovered it. And it's in a safe location." She didn't want to be out late in some parts of Paris with two students and Marian dressed like a common prostitute.

"Come on." Marian practically pulled her toward the towering hotel. Then she stopped, looked around, and asked, "Where are the kids?" As they waited on the steps for the young couple, who'd apparently ducked into a secluded spot for a kiss, judging by the lipstick smears on the boy's face, Marian chattered nonstop.

"That's some high ceiling," she said as the four of them wandered through the lobby. "And those geometric patterns on it are super cool."

As they entered the lounge, Eva wondered if Marian talked this way in the classroom. She'd be happy if she didn't have to hear the word *cool* again for a very long time.

In the lounge, where the featured groups were scheduled to play soon, the young couple chose a small table by themselves, which didn't seem to bother Marian. Eva found a spot near the exit. Maybe she could persuade Marian to leave early.

❖

"Drive around once more," Brigitte told the taxi driver.

The cab darted and dodged among the other small cars circling the Arc de Triomphe. They somehow reminded her of little bumper cars. Lights flashed everywhere and pedestrians lined the sidewalk, not daring to venture across the busy roundabout where twelve streets intersected. She was part of this merry-go-round of life, and she didn't want to stop or even slow.

Finally the driver peeled away from the circle of lights and dashed east on the Champs Élysées, toward the Meridien Etoile. In minutes the taxi turned onto a side street and pulled up in front of a large silver-blue building, seemingly made of shiny aluminum. This hotel's style certainly differed from the traditional one of the George V. She felt as if she were about to step from Cinderella's horse-drawn carriage into a sleek jet.

As she glided up the steps under the huge silver overhang and into the lobby, she couldn't take her eyes off the Art Deco accent pieces, though she tried to appear nonchalant about her surroundings.

The audience was buzzing as she entered the club. The warm-up group was about to begin, so she brazenly grabbed a table as near the raised stage as possible, nodded as a man standing nearby pulled her chair out for her, and draped her wrap over its back.

She glanced around the large lounge while the first band played and couldn't believe it. In the back sat the brunette from the library! Twice in the same day was too much. Was she summoning the woman to her by thinking about her? And who was that creature with her, dressed like a common streetwalker? Had the brunette hired her for the night? Yeah. Like she'd have to pay for it. But you never knew about people.

As she watched, the gauche redhead scooted her chair closer to the brunette, whispering something, then holding up her empty glass and pointing to a waiter. The brunette shook her head and looked bored. Brigitte almost felt sorry for the poor woman with the tour guide.

Although she was enjoying the music, she couldn't pull her gaze from the human drama behind her, and when she locked eyes with the tour guide momentarily, the woman's shock of recognition—and then her derisive look—hit Brigitte like a blast of heat across the room. Was the brunette judging her and questioning her right to be here? How dare she? Did she think she was better than her? And did she consider herself the owner of this entire city, including all its books, its landmarks, and now its music? Brigitte nodded curtly and looked back at the stage. She shouldn't have returned that library book. What was it about this stranger that brought out her immature self?

The warm-up group finished its set, and after a brief intermission the great Erroll Garner strolled toward the piano and perched on two thick phone books stacked on the bench. She settled in with a drink the waiter had brought, and when Garner began to play, everything but the sounds of the dreamy, romantic ballads he was famous for vanished from her mind. Even the presence of the mysterious tour guide who seemed to be following her would have a difficult time breaking through her pleasure and spoiling her enjoyment.

The screwdriver she sipped mellowed her out, and the little pianist's dramatic introduction to "Summertime" made her nostalgic, yet excited. Its steady beat carried her back to her childhood in south Louisiana, those slow, lazy days of summer when she hid from her grandmother in her favorite spot near the bayou and read romantic gothic novels. In them, raven-haired adventurers ravished fiery Southern belles, and the twosomes finally discovered they were in love. Those lust-filled novels had swept her away on a current of desire as relentless as that of the mighty Mississippi. She'd eventually begun to imagine a raven-haired female in place of the conventional male. She'd sweated away many summer hours lost in the passion those books had provoked, and her grandmother never knew that she had pilfered them from her secret stash in her old chifforobe.

She floated on the familiar melody of "Summertime" from Louisiana's bayous to Paris's nightlife. Sadly, not only was her daddy not rich, but he'd never even been on the scene. But Garner's expert performance skills impressed her. He moved his right hand freely while sustaining the song's basic rhythm with his left. Ah. Such a combination of adventure and security would please her in bed. At times the notes of the melody hit a second behind the basic beat, pushing her out of her emotional lethargy, and then suddenly Garner matched the notes to the beat again. Wouldn't it be great to find a lover who could shock her yet soothe her, the way he could on the piano? Garner's rendition of the classic song combined a sensual swing with a flirtatious tune and a steady rhythm that made her juices begin to flow.

She glanced back over at the brunette, and this time she almost felt sorry for her. Her absurdly dressed companion was ordering yet another drink, though the brunette was shaking her head again and gazing at her with clear disapproval. Just then, however, Garner's improvisation in an upbeat song grabbed Brigitte's interest again. Garner seemed so relaxed, so in the moment, so totally alive to the sounds he was weaving around her. It was like he was trying new things with each song he played without worrying that they might not work. His unique style dominated each piece he played, and his free spirit leapt out at her. She wanted her new life to resemble what his music made her feel.

She stopped glancing back and focused on the music engulfing her. All her anger at the brunette vanished as the music chipped away tiny pieces of the calcium from her petrified heart. Garner seemed to be joking and laughing with the audience through his perky, fresh renderings of old familiar tunes. With his rich, spontaneous sounds, he spoke directly to her inner being.

How could this small, mustached man with his crooked teeth and large hands make her feel so full of tenderness and passion at the same time? She wanted to be sitting here sharing this music with someone she loved. She wanted to place her hand over her dream woman's and squeeze it gently, share a look of delight in the music that surrounded them and the love that intertwined them.

She inhaled deeply and then let out a long breath. Would her dream come true here in Paris? Would anyone want her when they found out what she'd done for a living during all those years in New Orleans? Would they judge her as harshly as she did the brunette's companion, or would they see beyond her past and be willing to have a future with her?

As the performance ended all too soon, she jumped to her feet and applauded with the rest of the crowd. Two emotions she hadn't experienced in far too long engulfed her—pure joy and hope.

❖

Eva felt like hitting someone. When the striking blonde from the library had made an entrance earlier, she'd headed to one of the best tables in the club. So much for the regular tourists not discovering this place. People like the blond American were taking over her city as if they had a right to it, trying to force their inferior culture on her country. Infuriating. If they had their way, everyone in France would be wearing Levi's, drinking Coca-Cola, and eating hamburgers.

Just before Garner finished his set, someone tapped her on the shoulder. She looked up and saw one of the students, who whispered, "Miss Laroche. We've decided to go back to the hotel. Will you make sure Miss Smither gets there okay?" Judging by the student's expression, this wasn't the first time during the trip Marian had drunk too much. But what could she do but nod and mouth her agreement? They'd be gone in the morning.

After Garner finished his set and bowed to the audience's enthusiastic applause, the blonde wandered out of the room as if in a daze. Her every move suggested relaxed sensuality, and Eva was surprised that all the men and most of the women didn't follow her siren call. Hopefully that backless dress could corral those luscious breasts until she reached her destination. They were certainly enticing. Just seeing them made her teeth itch for a nip. God, was she out of her mind? That was far too much like something her father would think.

She put down her second drink. She'd had enough. She had to not only control herself but also Marian, who'd downed either four or five vodka sours. Now if she could just maneuver Marian back to her hotel, she'd be able to get home and grab a decent night's sleep before she had to meet their group early in the morning, ride with them to the station, and make sure they were all safely on the right train.

Marian stood unsteadily and clutched her arm. "Thanks for this. Now the kids have left, why don't just the two of us go to Chez Moune?"

She almost jerked her arm away but didn't want Marian to fall. "Chez Moune? Where did you hear about it?" Had Marian suggested her two students leave early?

Marian gazed at her with what she must have considered a sexy expression. "Oh, everyone like us knows about it. It's been around forever."

She steered Marian toward the exit. "And what do you mean, like us?" How had Marian pegged her as a lesbian? And how had she missed Marian's signs? Some lawyer she'd make. She definitely needed to practice reading people better. Even if Marian was so deep in the closet only a hefty dose of alcohol could evict her, Eva had to learn to see behind the masks almost everyone wore, especially in public.

Marian was definitely trolling for a tryst with a real live Parisian lesbian, something intriguing to tell her friends back home about. Insulted at being so depersonalized, Eva grabbed Marian's arm and almost shoved her toward a waiting taxi. "You've had enough to drink and enough clubs for one night. You better focus on your long train ride tomorrow and all those students you have to look after."

Marian scowled. "Damn kids." She slurred her words. "I wanna have some fun, and you're just the kind of woman I wanna have it with. But if you won't go with me, I'll go by myself." She threw open the door of the waiting taxi and flounced into it. "Some guide you are."

Shaking, Eva slid in beside her and gave the driver the address of Marian's hotel. Thank God she had a law career in her future. She couldn't stand to show many more Marians the sights of Paris. This was going to be a long summer.

❖

The traffic around the Arc de Triomphe was slower now and sparser, though the small European cars, which reminded her of little tugboats, darted past Brigitte's taxi. They made the Lincolns and Pontiacs she was used to seeing in New Orleans seem as large as ocean liners. Her cab drove halfway around the circle and merged onto the Champs Élysées on the other side, then headed west for several blocks to the George V.

She drew her wrap around herself against the chill of the evening. The sweet embrace of the jazz she'd just listened to kept her spellbound, dreaming of a future love. She felt alive for the first time in years, hopeful she could do exactly what Rosa had intended for her to when she'd practically ordered her to go to Paris.

Back at the hotel, she hummed as she undressed, then fell into her feather-soft bed totally nude. She read only a page or two of Simone de Beauvoir's semiautobiographical first novel about a ménage à trois before she tumbled into sleep and a strange dream.

Chapter Seven

Brigitte sat in an almost-deserted small café, the only other patron a gray-haired woman sitting nearby under a large chestnut tree. The woman didn't glance up from the lined tablet in front of her except to sip from her tumbler. She drank as steadily as she wrote and hurled the waiter a fierce look of appreciation each time he substituted a full glass for an empty one.

Old, with skinned-back hair and no makeup, the woman should have been invisible. But her long oval face with its full lips, well-defined cheekbones, and lively blue eyes under heavy brows made her attractive. Her eyes were clear, intelligent, full of strength and purpose.

The woman stared, then ignored her. Brigitte sat there reading Simone de Beauvoir's novel based on a sexual relationship that she and Jean-Paul Sartre had with two sisters, one of whom had been Simone's student. But Brigitte kept glancing at the woman. Was she a lesbian? The very air around her whispered yes, she loved women, or she was at least bisexual. Suddenly the woman put down her pen and spoke rapidly across the small round tables separating them.

"You are an American, alone here in Paris, yes?" The woman's accent immediately marked her as Parisian.

"Yes. From New Orleans." Brigitte was surprised. The woman seemed to know her, or at least to comprehend who she was immediately.

"You speak the language very well. I overheard you conversing with the waiter."

The stranger seemed to expect and deserve the information. "I grew up in a small town, and practically no one there spoke English, except my grandmother and the nuns who were our teachers." She shrugged. "Being exposed to Cajun French made it easier for me to learn true French later."

"You are a Frenchwoman, yes?" The woman seemed to know everything about her.

"On my mother's side." Brigitte swelled with pride. "My father was English."

"So your French blood battles your English."

She stared at the stranger. "Yes. My mother and my grandmother despised each other."

"And you were caught in the middle. Their battle should have made you stronger." The woman bent forward, her blue eyes hooking Brigitte's and reeling her closer.

"My mother left me with my grandmother right after I was born." She felt compelled to confide in this woman. "Every Christmas, Mother came to visit me and talked nonstop about her glamorous life in Hollywood. She always brought beautiful presents—dolls, ruffled dresses and petticoats. Later, rhinestone jewelry and even a mouton coat." She would never forget that coat. "I wore it to school one day, and everyone made fun of me when I walked down the hall. I never put it on again." Why had she shared such intimate details? The stranger must find her ridiculous.

The woman stared without sympathy. "You should have worn the coat to show everyone you had a mother who didn't give a damn about a conventional family life. My mother let God and my father dominate her in every way and never became a real person."

I'm dreaming, but this all seems so real—the little round white tables, the chestnut trees that shaded her and the stranger. She could even taste her screwdriver. It all appeared to be completely ordinary. She submitted to the fantasy once again.

"How did you become your own person then, with a mother like that?" She asked the woman the question that had bothered her for such a long time because the woman obviously knew her own mind. "My grandmother constantly tried to push the teachings of the church down my throat."

"Bah. Your grandmother was wrong. Religion is for the weak and for cowards."

Brigitte nodded. "That's one reason I finally adopted a way of life she'd never approve of. Is that what you did?"

The Frenchwoman tossed her head like a queen and spoke with the assurance of a judge. "No, I simply stood my ground and worked for what I believed in." She pointed to the pen and tablet that lay on her table. "We women must learn to find our true meaning in life through choosing worthwhile projects. We should satisfy ourselves instead of some God or other power outside us."

A frisson of desire shot up her inner thighs. What was happening? This woman had to be thirty years older than she was, yet Brigitte was physically attracted to her.

The stranger said, "I earned an advanced degree in philosophy and rejected everything my mother stood for." She smiled with an air of triumph. "I taught school until the Nazis forced me to quit, and then I began to write." She picked up her pen briefly and waved it as though it were a sword. "Through writing I found myself and my place in the world."

Brigitte winced as she reluctantly spoke the words that bubbled up in her. She felt strangely compelled to confess. "I became part of the world's oldest profession." She waited for the inevitable negative reaction, but the woman regarded her with an impassive expression as if waiting for more.

"At first I couldn't cope, and I gave away my power," Brigitte said. The woman frowned slightly. "But one day I realized how I despised the way men were treating me, so I outwardly took control of my life. Actually, I ran away inside myself and became aloof. That way I could keep my power for myself. And it worked."

She'd never expressed these thoughts to anyone, but this stranger nodded as casually as if they were discussing the weather and drained her glass. "It's late, Ms....?"

"Brigitte. And you are?"

"You may call me Simone."

Simone? How odd to be reading a novel by a woman with the same name as the one she was conversing with.

Simone put her pen beside her tablet and covered both with her right hand. "My greatest pleasure is to put words on paper and hope they help free others, especially women—young women like you." Simone gave her an appraising look, then seemed to reach a decision. "Would you like to visit me at my apartment, where we can have more privacy?"

Simone's invitation transformed the frisson of excitement in her inner thighs into a throb that made her clench her legs together. "I'd love to."

"Excellent."

This is the oddest dream I've ever experienced, yet I can't resist following it through.

After they reached the apartment, Simone excused herself and changed into a red silk kimono. She'd parted her hair and piled it into a crown, and she held a knife in her left hand. The pungent smell of oranges wafted from her.

"Make yourself at home," Simone said as she strode away, into what Brigitte assumed was her kitchen. She sat on a bright-yellow sofa with her back to the graveyard across the street and stared at the colorful, exotic objects that covered the tables of Simone's large sitting room/study. Books were crammed into the shelves that lined the walls, and records lay scattered everywhere. A lamp in one corner reminded her of a Giacometti sculpture.

Simone returned, carrying drinks, and placed the small tray on the table between them. She offered Brigitte a tumbler. "Here, my dear. A drink. I believe you like screwdrivers."

Amazed, she accepted the glass. "How did you know that? Are you a mind reader?"

Simone laughed, a deep, rich sound that flushed Brigitte with pleasure, and sat on the sofa facing her. Simone's dangling earrings and scarlet lipstick suggested she must have been an attractive woman before the alcohol worked on her. But she obviously hadn't been afraid to drink life to the fullest, regardless of the consequences.

"If you want to think so. But it's actually simple. I asked the waiter at the café."

Of course. The thoughtful gesture pleased Brigitte as much as the drink did.

But Simone didn't waste any time. "Now that we're in private, what do you really feel for your mother, and for the profession you chose to support yourself?"

She gasped. Simone had flung a lightning bolt at her heart. She stared at the purple carpet. "My mother? I love her and…I hate her." The contradictory emotions still pulled her apart inside. "As to my past, I worry that people will never forget or forgive me for choosing it."

Simone's expression was calm, still with no trace of judgment. "Why?"

"Almost everyone I've ever known thinks prostitutes are scum."

After a long, slow drink, Simone set her tumbler down. "Would you say you were just as much a hunter as you were prey in your work?"

She frowned. "I'm not sure what you mean."

"In your eyes, were the men you slept with as objectified to you as you were to them?"

She shook her head. "I still don't understand what you're getting at."

Simone picked up her glass again and looked as if she were addressing an especially slow student. "Let me put it this way. Did you consider yourself equal to the men you slept with? Did you recognize you were there to fulfill each other's desire and give each other pleasure?" She pushed a strand of hair back from her forehead. "You should read my essay about Brigitte Bardot. To me, she is an admirably genuine woman."

Bardot again! She took a long drink of her screwdriver as she thought about Simone's questions. "I came to consider men my equals, yes. But I never had any desire for them."

Simone looked thoughtful. "This is where you went wrong. I believe Bardot enjoyed the men she slept with and left them when she no longer wanted them."

Brigitte shook her head. "I never got any pleasure from having sex with them…except the gratification of knowing that someday I wouldn't have to accept money from anyone for anything I did for them."

Simone's blue eyes blazed. "Ah, I like your honesty. You did what you had to in order to survive. But that's past. Now you can follow your own inclinations. You can eat when you're hungry and make love when you want to." Simone took a long swallow from her glass.

A vast sense of relief filled her as Simone continued. "In other words, you can be true to yourself. And if you are, you can set your own moral codes."

"My own moral codes?"

"Yes. You—and you alone—are responsible for deciding what kind of life you want to live."

"Regardless of what people think of me?" The thought freed something inside her.

"Absolutely. What others think of you is irrelevant. It's their problem if they can't accept you and your choices."

She still wasn't sure she understood precisely what Simone meant, but she would think about her philosophy and how it applied to her. But it was her dream, and she'd seize the moment.

"Why did my mother leave me in a place she hated?"

Simone glanced past Brigitte at the cemetery. "I can only guess. Perhaps she thought you needed to grow up in a traditional way so you could choose your own life when you became old enough. She didn't want to impose her unorthodox life on you."

"Or maybe she didn't love me."

"Perhaps she loved you more than you imagine. You need to ask her." Simone looked at a grotesque mask lying on the low table between them. "We all hide behind masks. I rarely remove my disguises any longer, but when I do I'm never sorry."

She'd always worn a mask, always made herself attractive because others expected, demanded that of her. Yet Simone had stripped it from her as ruthlessly as a surgeon. Unlike Mies, and the countless men, and some women, she had slept with, Simone seemed to look beyond her beauty, to see her for who she actually was. Simone's acceptance of her as a person, as an individual, liberated something within her, which unfurled like a butterfly's wings.

Simone glided across the short distance between them, sat beside her, and stared at her with diamond eyes. "You're very beautiful, but you've hidden from life long enough." She slipped the generous slice of orange that garnished Brigitte's drink from the rim of her glass. "Taste this and describe the sensation."

She closed her eyes as Simone slid the orange between her lips. "Cool and fresh—tangy, sweet, and juicy." Several drops ran from the side of her mouth, and when she reached to wipe them away, Simone caught her hand.

"No, let it drip. I'll take care of it." The scent of whiskey mingled with the bitter spice of the orange peel, and she relaxed into the kiss, Simone's lipstick smooth and her teeth sharp as Simone nipped both her lip and the part of the fruit she hadn't tasted yet. They consumed the orange slice together and licked the juice from each other.

When Brigitte opened her eyes, Simone still wore her red kimono, and her matching scarf created a flame-like halo. She couldn't bear the thought that this dream might end. She returned her focus to Simone, whose gray hair hung slightly over one eye, giving her a sexy bedroom look Brigitte had never associated with a woman her age.

With a steady gaze, Simone guided them toward another part of her apartment, and she followed. She wanted to lose herself in the brilliance of Simone's eyes and the sweet tang of her kiss. She craved Simone's hands all over her, and she intended to memorize every inch of this incredible woman.

Simone led her to her boudoir and removed Brigitte's clothes, examining her as if she were a statue. But for the first time, she didn't feel as if a lover was appraising her. Simone seemed to be seeing her, her flaws but also her strengths. She yearned for, yet feared what lay ahead.

Simone removed her earrings one at a time and unfastened her red kimono. "My derriere was firmer twenty years ago, but my vision is clearer now. And I see a woman who needs to forget the pain in her past and grasp the love in her future."

While Simone spoke, she ran her hands up Brigitte's arms and along her shoulders. The simple touch felt like twin scalpels as Simone caressed her tingling skin with a slight pressure and then smoothed her way down her back.

"I don't want anything but the amazing woman in my present," Brigitte whispered.

With a lightning motion, Simone yanked off a red scarf she'd worn around her crown of hair and secured Brigitte's wrists together behind her, pulling her closer until their breasts met. Simone's hands moved lower and cupped her ass. "Yes, your derriere is firm now, but it won't always be. Give yourself to me today and you'll never regret what you've done."

The smell of oranges filled the room as Brigitte's juices flowed down her legs. Simone, apparently sensing the flood, quickly lowered her to the bed and thrust long fingers inside her.

She saw rainbows, their bright colors intertwining, filling every cell in her body as they exploded into tastes and smells as bittersweet as chocolate mousse. Simone plunged even deeper, and the stabbing motion became exquisite agony. It worked its way from her toes, up her instep, and through her calves, like a gathering storm far in the distance.

She struggled to free her hands, but then, overcome by Simone's probing fingers, she relaxed into the strokes and lost herself in the smell of whiskey and oranges. The sweet pain spun upward, encasing her legs, gliding past her clitoris and up inside her like a honeybee on an expedition. She buzzed inside, the ache spreading like a million pinpricks until everything inside her coalesced into a rush like Niagara. She let go and tumbled over the falls into the white turbulence below.

Rousing from what she could describe only as pure bliss, and free now from her silk bond, she shifted slightly in Simone's arms. "I feel like you stuck a knife into my heart," she murmured, barely aware of what she said. "I dreamed I was on a snowy mountain peak, where I wandered through a rosewood forest whose floor was covered with sweet-smelling flowers. There I came upon a beautiful cemetery. But the decaying bodies in the graves seemed as natural as my own live flesh, and as yours."

She touched Simone's age-spotted hand with wonder, feeling drunk. Yet she'd had only two drinks. Perhaps she was more susceptible to alcohol in her dreams? "Your hand is a miracle." She held it to her cheek, then lowered it and traced each protruding bluish vein. "I'd love to swim under your skin like your blood does." Kissing her way upward, she found Simone's breast. "I'm like a piglet."

Simone laughed—a low, throaty sound. "Does that mean you think I'm a sow?"

"But of course." She paused long enough to answer, then moved to the other breast for a long while. "And a bee, and a cow, and a lion. You're like the ancient goddess Artemis, you're life itself, and I'm drinking at your fountain." No. She wasn't drunk on alcohol, but on something more heady.

As she inched downward she heard Simone whisper, "Drink all you want," and she did. Simone was succulent and ripe, tasting of acrid spices as Brigitte pressed her tongue into her. And she had thought she had found bliss when she was under Simone.

Her thoughts vanished as she pushed deeper into the mystery of Simone. Warm liquid, strong pulsations, exploding rainbow colors— she landed on the shore of a new world, a pilgrim beginning her quest.

Simone had peeled the rind from her heart, and dream or not made little difference to Brigitte. Anything was possible now.

She woke with a start, satiated like never before, and sat up.

She ran her hands over her breasts, massaging them. They were tender, and her pussy ached. She relaxed against the pillows again. Rosa had been right. She had the strength to try to make a new life in Paris with a woman she could love and be loved by.

CHAPTER EIGHT

"Where the hell have you been lately?" Yves Laroche glared at Eva, his eyes like ball bearings.

Eva nonchalantly slid a brightly colored gift in front of her mother's antique Limoges dinner plate and sat down in her customary spot. "Working to pay off my loan." She tried but couldn't tamp down her resentment of him. Then she realized she was playing into her father's expectations, strengthening his view of her as a spoiled, ungrateful daughter. She needed to grow up.

"Huh. If you hadn't marched in those student protests and bummed around for the past few years, you'd already be a lawyer. Then you wouldn't have to lower yourself to guide tourists around the city." Yves cut into his celebratory pepper steak and removed some of the peppercorns studding it. "Lulu, put that gift down. You know you can't open it and your other ones until we have your cake."

Eva gazed sympathetically at her mother, who dropped the blue-and-yellow package as if it were on fire. "Speaking of bumming around, where's my dear baby brother?"

Yves glared at her again, his eyes glinting. "How the hell should I know? He promised to be here, but you know what Louis's promises are worth nowadays. Before he got into drugs, he was the perfect child. If his friends hadn't introduced him to marijuana—"

"So it's everyone else's fault he's disappointed you. He's a poor, helpless victim—"

"Yes, like the ones you plan to defend in the lower courts. Just wait until a good prosecutor like I used to be gets hold of you. You and your clients won't stand a chance." He picked up a crystal wineglass and swirled its contents.

Now she was glaring. Her father always affected her like that.

"I'm hungry. Can't you two act nice while I'm eating?" Lulu sounded as childish as Yves often accused her of being.

He did, however, soften his tone. "So, what do you want for your birthday this year, dear?" He took a modest sip of his wine.

The endearment sounded so false Eva almost threw up her asparagus. "Yes, Mother," she said, then repeated her father's question. She hoped she didn't sound as condescending as he did.

Her mother's brown eyes grew as animated as they ever did. "I want Louis to be here and eat lunch with us. It's bad enough that he won't be going to the seashore with us this summer."

Yves set down his glass on the white tablecloth with a thump. "Louis. How many times do I have to tell you—"

"Shhh." Eva frowned at him. "You know how independent Louis is, Mother. He likes to visit you when he wants to, so he can surprise you."

Lulu slowly nodded and her eyes dimmed.

"What about a new hat, Mother?"

Lulu seemed to consider Eva's offer as she dutifully ate the last of her potatoes au gratin. "I'm through. It's time for dessert. I'm ready to open my presents now." She gazed at Yves as if she'd never mentioned wanting to see Louis.

With a resigned expression, he laid his knife and fork carefully across his plate, his hair as silver as his cutlery. "By all means, dear. Let's celebrate your fiftieth birthday. It's a very special occasion. It's too bad your daughter has to hurry back to work. Wouldn't it be nice if she could spend a week or so with us at the coast later this summer, like she used to?"

This time she could detect a remnant of her father's affection for her mother, and perhaps even for her. She wanted to sob. She drew in a breath. No, she actually wanted to strangle all the women who'd taken him from her and her mother these many years.

But wasn't she thinking just like he did, blaming others for his failings just as he blamed others for Louis's? Other women didn't force themselves on him. He paid them good money for their services.

She remembered the affection he used to show her mother and refused to let go of her memories of him doting on her, going out of his way to please her.

Father should have thought more carefully about what it would be like to marry someone as dependent, as childlike as Lulu and live with her all these years. It had to get old, but he should have realized what kind of woman he'd committed himself to. Or perhaps Lulu had been different before Father married her. Maybe she was simply acting the way she thought a wife and mother should, the way she thought her husband and others expected her to.

She wasn't sure about her parents' mistakes, but their marriage had made her cautious about becoming romantically involved for the long term. She didn't want to make the wrong choice. And even if she did find someone to care for, she didn't want to change or try to make someone else change in order to fulfill the expectations of society or each other.

❖

"What a wonderful meal, Jeanne." Eva ate the last bite of her omelet crammed with mushrooms and artichoke hearts. How different from that horrible lunch with her parents, a few hours earlier. She pushed her chair back and gazed at the mismatched plates she and Jeanne had just emptied. The familiar glass she now cradled in her hands brought back fond memories. When she was a teenager, she'd dropped it in the kitchen sink. It was a sturdy crystal glass, but when she'd picked it up she discovered a small chip on the rim. She'd tried to hide it in the cupboard, but the next time she visited, Jeanne served her a drink in it as if the glass were still perfect. The scorch mark on the blue potholder lying near the stove told a similar story of an even earlier childhood accident. While Mother would have scolded her and replaced the cup and potholder with perfect duplicates immediately, Jeanne had never even mentioned the damage. They seemed to be souvenirs of their pleasant times in the kitchen together.

"I'll never understand how you and Mother can be so completely different," Eva said, wiping her mouth with her napkin. "You're so capable, and sometimes she seems totally at a loss, especially in social situations."

Jeanne shook her head slightly. "Lulu has always been submissive. She likes to please everyone and tries to keep the peace. She's quite intelligent, though she usually doesn't appear to be. She simply doesn't believe a woman should let a man know how smart and talented she actually is. She loves your father and feels that's the best way to keep him."

"Doesn't make much sense to me, especially these days. Here, let me help with the dishes."

Jeanne patted her shoulder. "Go into the living room and sit down, child. You have to be exhausted, leading one tour after another without a break. I just sit in the office and talk on the telephone. It feels good to get up and move around for a change. I intend to pamper you tonight. Take your wine and wait for me there."

She *was* tired, so she walked into the familiar living room in Jeanne's apartment, located above her travel agency. The worn leather chair Jeanne always favored sat in the front corner of the room. From there she could look out at the entire room and see either the street or the river simply by turning her head. The couch Eva chose stretched along one wall and had a great view of the Seine. It matched Jeanne's favorite chair, its tan leather as soft as Jeanne's and Mother's touch.

As she lounged on the couch, she thought about their differences, which went beyond Jeanne living on the Left Bank and Lulu on the Right. Jeanne had graduated from the university, set up her own business, and partnered with a series of strong, confident women, both in the office and in the bedroom. Lulu had quit the university after a few months and spent several years partying before she married Yves—a young, ambitious law student who'd apparently wanted to belong to a higher class than the one he was born into. Had he ever loved Lulu, or had he married her for her money and social position?

"What's on your mind?" Jeanne said as she entered the living room.

"Just wondering how different my life would have been if you'd been my mother instead of my aunt."

Jeanne winced, then gripped Eva's shoulder firmly. "I'd have been a horrible mother. I don't have the inclination or the patience." She crossed the room to her chair and fixed her eyes on Eva. "Lulu's done an admirable job with you, even if you don't seem to realize it. She hasn't had an easy life, no matter what others might think." Jeanne settled into her chair with a sigh and gazed out at the river. "It's actually much easier to give than to take, and much more gratifying." She sipped from her wineglass before placing it on an end table beside her. "I've been the lucky one, able to come and go as I please, with whoever attracts me. Being a parent requires a lot more commitment than I want."

Eva stretched out fully on the couch. "Uh-huh. Well, I unofficially adopted you as my other mother years ago." She saluted Jeanne with her glass. "I do love Mother, you know. But you're a friend and a parent at the same time, and most of the time you're the only one who seems to understand me." She made a face. "Father doesn't even try, and Louis is hopeless."

She lay there in silence, simply resting, until Jeanne got up and put a record on her phonograph, then headed for the kitchen. Soft jazz filled the room, reminding Eva of seeing that attractive American at the Meridien Etoile several nights ago. She had to admit that the woman had seemed to really appreciate the feast for the senses Erroll Garner had provided. She had never heard anyone evoke such passionate sounds from a piano, and the American woman had responded like a true aficionado. Her entire body had seemed to absorb the vitality of Garner's music and move with it in a way that had turned Eva on. Perhaps the stranger had more to offer than just a beautiful exterior, but Eva doubted it. She'd never known an American with a true sense of style or culture.

Jeanne placed a plate of cheese and fruit on the coffee table between them, then set a bottle of white wine beside it. "Let's just enjoy ourselves tonight. You need to relax, and I'm in the mood for your company. Okay?"

Eva glanced over at Jeanne, who sat across from her, gazing at her with such kind, patient blue eyes. "Okay." If only she could find a woman like Jeanne to share her evenings with like this, her life would be complete.

❖

When Eva arrived at the travel agency late the following afternoon, she plopped into a brown leather office chair near Jeanne's desk and kicked off her shoes. The horns of the busy traffic on the street outside the office jangled her nerves, and the unseasonably hot weather had made her irritable.

Jeanne finally finished her phone conversation, and Eva said, "My feet are killing me." She reached down and massaged one of them. "I feel like I've walked over the entire city three times this week."

Jeanne got up and fixed her some iced coffee by adding a scoop of vanilla ice cream to a steaming cup of her favorite drink. "Take it easy this weekend. Have any special plans?"

She took a sip. "Ah. That's heavenly. That recipe's the best thing you brought back from your trip to Jerusalem last year. As to special plans, I intend to hibernate and concentrate on the lives of the Parisian women I've chosen for my tour. How many are in the group now?"

"Four, so far. Two British women and an American couple."

"Is that enough?" She had really been looking forward to this experience. Hopefully only adults would sign up for it.

"I'd let the tour go if you had only one person." Jeanne shrugged. "You deserve it after what you've already done this summer."

"Thanks. Maybe someone else will get the urge to meet all the interesting women I plan to introduce them to."

The phone rang again and Jeanne said hurriedly, "Don't concern yourself about it, child. These things have a way of working themselves out. Trust me."

Eva finished her iced drink, but she was still worried, and her feet still throbbed. She certainly hoped Jeanne knew what she was talking about.

CHAPTER NINE

Brigitte pushed through the door of the upscale travel agency near the Seine and spotted an attractive older woman wearing large glasses with tortoiseshell frames. Recalling that hot dream about Simone the other night, she felt a blast of heat, which the summer sun hadn't caused.

The woman rose immediately and walked toward her with an outstretched hand. How long had it been since she'd stood near the top of the Eiffel Tower, seen the outstretched arms of the Trocadero, and daydreamed about finding a new life in Paris? Life could change so much in just a week.

But it was now time to stop fantasizing and do something, and signing up for this tour was just the thing. And already this woman's firm, lingering handshake and her soft blue eyes somehow made Brigitte believe her imaginings could come true.

"Hello. I'm Jeanne." The woman motioned Brigitte toward a comfortable-looking barrel-type chair. "How may I help you?"

She sat and Jeanne settled into her stylish green office chair. Long ago, when Brigitte was eighteen and her grandmother had just died, she'd taken the bus from her home in Des Allemands to New Orleans, where she'd located Rosa. She'd admired Rosa when she was a child and had stayed in touch with her after she'd left town. Being with Rosa had changed her life for the better, and she sensed Jeanne might do the same.

She glanced around the office, noting a blue IBM Selectric on each of the two desks in the room. A French flag and a map of France dominated one wall, and a world map covered another one. "I noticed the sign for your tour that features famous women of Paris. Do you still have availability?"

Jeanne scrutinized her almost long enough to make her feel uncomfortable, then riffled through a stack of papers on her desk. "Let me see. Yes. Here it is. I just might have a spot for you." Jeanne looked at her intently yet again. "This is a small, exclusive tour, designed for participants keenly interested in the subject and with a high level of proficiency in the French language." She studied Brigitte again. "You're certainly fluent. What about your interest level?"

Was she being interviewed for a job or quizzed for advanced standing in a university course? An American travel agent would most likely have just held out her hand for payment and called it a day. The French seemed strangely possessive of their language and culture.

"Back in New Orleans," Brigitte said, "I read everything I could about French women through history, which, sadly, wasn't nearly enough." She gazed at the posters of the Eiffel Tower and Notre-Dame that adorned the remaining wall space. "I'm here in Paris for the summer, at least, and would like to take advantage of this opportunity to learn as much as I can straight from the horse's mouth, as we say."

She smiled, hoping to ingratiate herself with Jeanne, but then pulled herself up short. She had American dollars, the highly coveted universal currency. She shouldn't have to prove herself to this…this travel agent, though she was a very attractive one. "If you don't think I'll fit in, I'll be on my way." She began to get up from her chair.

Jeanne lifted her head and pushed her big glasses back up her nose. "I'm sorry if I seemed hesitant. This is such a special tour that I wanted to be certain you'd feel at ease taking part in it." She smiled radiantly. "It appears you and this tour are a match made in heaven, as I've heard some of your compatriots say."

"Touché," Brigitte said. "Hopefully the tour guide will be as competent and charming as you are." She gave Jeanne one of her most alluring smiles. "This should be an interesting way to get to know Paris and perhaps some of its residents."

She pulled a list of questions about the tour from her purse, and after Jeanne answered all of them satisfactorily, she reserved a place for herself.

❖

At the end of the day, Eva pushed through the door of Taste Paris. "Has anyone else signed up for my famous-women tour, Jeanne?" She had led a new student group in the past week, relieved not to have to deal with another leader like Marian.

Jeanne looked up from her desk with a smug expression. "One more."

"Great. Anyone interesting?" She tossed her briefcase onto the straight chair next to her desk.

"I'll say. Makes me wish I were a guide again."

Eva sat down and glanced through her mail, then turned toward Jeanne. "You look starstruck. Tell me about her."

Jeanne held up a finger, then typed quickly, sighed, and rolled the sheet of paper she'd been working on out of her typewriter. "She's delicious. Old enough to be interesting and young enough to be full of energy. An American, but somehow different, in a good way." She folded the paper and slid it into an envelope. "She dropped by several hours ago and questioned me thoroughly about the itinerary. Then she said this tour is exactly what she's been looking for."

She had rarely seen Jeanne this impressed by a tourist. "And? Give me some details."

Jeanne licked her lips suggestively. "She's very buxom, if you know what I mean. Blond hair, blue eyes, and ripe. If she were a pear, I wouldn't hesitate to take a big bite."

"Jeanne! What's gotten into you?" She had watched many women parade through her aunt's life. Some had stayed for several years, others for just a few weeks, but none had ever captivated her for good. Maybe this was the woman Jeanne had been waiting so long for.

"She's not all looks, though. She speaks standard French with ease and seems well read. Very impressive. I think you'll like her."

Eva chuckled. "It certainly sounds like *you* do."

"You think so? Well, she did call me competent and charming." Jeanne's eyes gleamed as though she were obviously trying to appear innocent.

"Want me to keep an eye on her for you?"

Jeanne shrugged a bit too nonchalantly. "If you wish. And…"

"And what?"

"Don't forget. I saw her first."

She couldn't believe Jeanne had just said that and certainly didn't intend to compete with her. "You don't have to worry. She's all yours. I'll even play Cupid."

Maybe she could repay some more of her debt in something better than cash.

CHAPTER TEN

Brigitte glanced at her Rolex. Ten minutes after nine. Her taxi had just pulled to a stop in front of the travel agency. The traffic was swirling around her cab, and pedestrians were dashing across the street, trying to make it before the green light jumped directly to red.

"Thank you." After she climbed out, she handed several worn franc notes to the driver, who stood holding the cab door and giving her the eye. She smiled politely, pretending not to notice his leer. She was glad she hadn't left any of her buttons on her new white silk designer blouse unfastened, except the top one. She was also relieved that her blue gabardine skirt covered her knees instead of showing most of her legs, like her usual miniskirts did. She wanted to appear demure and practical, with a touch of elegance and a bare hint of sensuality. Attracting the right woman would be an artistic endeavor, and she wanted to create just the right palette.

As she pushed through the glass door of the tour company she spotted five people: a man and a youngish woman, two older women, and Jeanne. The man glanced at her legs, perhaps noticing her dark panty hose, and the younger woman, as well as the two older ones, seemed to take in her strappy Famolare sandals. They and her hose were the only hint of the type of revealing ensembles she used to wear in New Orleans. Conveniently, her shoes' thick, cushiony soles made them practical for a tour.

She'd decided to go for the strong and independent yet available look during the tour but hadn't counted on having to dress for such a diverse audience. Instead of focusing on only one person, almost always a man, like she'd been paid to do back in New Orleans, she wanted to see if she could fit into an average group of ordinary people. If she appeared normal, maybe she'd be able to attract a woman with whom she could develop a wholesome relationship. She was a virgin in affairs of the heart, but she was willing to learn.

She stood just inside the doorway for a minute, mentally preparing for her upcoming performance. Why couldn't she have been on time, especially this first day? She planned to spend most of the next week with this group, and she wanted them to accept her, not make disparaging, catty remarks behind her back like so many people in New Orleans always had.

The two gray-haired women she'd noticed stood near a rack of leaflets, their British accents apparent. "Oh, the next time we visit France, why don't we tour the Château d'Amboise? It's not too far south of here. Da Vinci's buried there." The shorter one, who'd just spoken, was dressed in a purple straight skirt and a white blouse of a soft material, with lace on the collar.

"Of course, dear. I'd enjoy seeing the replicas of his inventions." Her companion, in tailored black slacks and a green knit pullover, pointed to one of the brochures.

Both wore sturdy walking shoes. Judging by their conversation and the way the one in slacks kept her hand in the small of her companion's back, as if guiding and protecting her, they were a couple. Good. Maybe they'd be less judgmental and more accepting than the self-righteous married women back home who always gave her dirty looks.

The other twosome, engaged in conversation with Jeanne, didn't appear overly concerned that Brigitte was late. In fact, the tall, slim man's bored expression had changed immediately to one of interest when he saw her. In spite of his casual yet expensive slacks and sports shirt, he seemed accustomed to more formal attire, since his shoes resembled those of her wealthiest former customers.

His wife—she assumed they were married—was chattering with Jeanne. In her bohemian-looking yellow blouse made of some type of natural fabric and tucked into a full lime-green skirt, with comfortable-looking sandals, she reminded Brigitte of a songbird.

Apparently she was either an artistic type, or aspired to be one, and looked much younger than her husband.

In New Orleans, Brigitte had usually been able to judge immediately how a client would treat her, and she would reject him if he didn't meet her expectations. She felt good about this group. No one seemed to see anything except what she intended—a wealthy, confident, stylish widow. At least she hoped that's how they viewed her.

But shouldn't their guide have already assembled them? She couldn't rest easy until she assured herself that all-important person would perceive her the way she'd planned. She said hello to the two British women and made small talk with them for a moment. Then she strolled over to Jeanne, who introduced her to the mismatched couple, the Youngs, who were indeed married.

After a brief exchange with her, the Youngs walked to the other side of the room, where a pot of coffee beckoned, and Jeanne asked in a smooth, melodious tone, "How are you this morning, Mrs. Green? We're glad you decided to join our little group. Perhaps you'll become so interested in Paris you'll prolong your visit past this summer."

Jeanne's lingering smile indicated she might be interested in Brigitte as more than a customer, and she was about to respond when a female voice sounded from an adjoining room.

"Here's Mrs. Young's registration form. I found it in the file cabinet next to—"

That damn brunette stopped in the doorway not two feet away, and by the look on her face and her sudden silence, Brigitte suspected the shock of recognition was mutual.

Shit. The woman's spectacular eyes blazed like the reflection of the summer sun on the choppy waves of the Mississippi. And her full lower lip became almost as tight and narrow as her upper one as she stood and stared.

Jeanne lightly touched Brigitte's arm. "Eva, this is our missing guest. Meet Brigitte Green."

The yellow rings in the blue-green eyes dimmed a bit, and Eva spoke with a controlled grace Brigitte had to admire. "Welcome to our group. We were afraid you'd either backed out or forgotten about us."

Jeanne frowned, but Brigitte refused to retreat from such a challenge. "You'll find that I never back down or forget anything. When does our tour begin?" She wished she hadn't resolved to quit smoking along with casual sexual encounters. She could use a cigarette.

❖

"Our tour begins right now." Eva motioned for the others to gather around her, and she began to deliver the briefing she'd written and memorized, just as she would an opening statement at a trial. "As you know, we'll meet daily this week, Monday through Saturday, and focus on the life of several famous Parisian women."

But she could barely concentrate on her speech because of all the questions bombarding her. Why had Brigitte chosen her tour? Had she really been married? Conveniently missing husbands were a popular ruse for women traveling alone, straight or gay. If so, was she available now? Could she return Jeanne's interest? Brigitte could merely be bored and stretching her wings, but that didn't seem likely. No, that modest skirt and blouse couldn't disguise the smoldering sensuality that almost leveled Eva, in spite of her aversion to the rude American. It could be wishful thinking, but Brigitte seemed to be searching for something, for someone. Eva tried to wrench her mind away from all these thoughts, including her upsetting and most unwelcome attraction to Brigitte.

As she spoke, she tried to meet the gaze of each participant, some of whom seemed to be listening intently. But Ryan Young and Brigitte Green weren't. Ryan appeared to be there only to please his wife. And after the first thirty seconds, Brigitte's blue eyes glazed over and she seemed to vacate her luscious body.

Unfortunately, her own eyes kept straying to the top pearl button on Brigitte's frost-white blouse. Her fingers itched, but she had to control both them and her eyes. Shaking her head she tried to refocus. Some lawyer she'd make, if she allowed the sight of a beautiful woman to distract her this easily.

"Any questions?" she asked when she finished her introduction.

"Is lunch included in the price of the tour?" Ryan asked.

"Yes. Daily. I'll introduce you to a variety of fine French cuisine." She was as proud of the cuisine of France as she was of its arts.

"Will we keep to a strict schedule of departure each morning?" That from the taller of the British twosome, Leigh.

"I certainly hope so. Nothing's more annoying than having to stand around and wait for a tardy group member." She couldn't help herself. She just had to glance at Brigitte, who finally seemed to be paying attention.

In fact, Brigitte was staring at her, as if waiting for her to say something insulting.

She responded to the unspoken dare. "I've wasted a lot of time and energy because members of some of our other tours have been habitually late. But I'm sure that since you're all adults, we won't have that problem." There. She hoped she'd been tactful yet firm.

Brigitte cleared her throat, and everyone turned toward her.

Great. Of course Brigitte would have something to say. She'd probably be more trouble than an entire busload of teenagers, distracting the rest of the group.

"Do you plan to offer a series such as this, or is it one of a kind?"

Relief flooded Eva—it was a good question and one that showed real interest—and washed away her doubts, at least for now. "We'll have to see how this one goes. Taste Paris is always open to suggestions about future itineraries, and its owner will certainly be glad to listen to yours." She gestured toward Jeanne, who nodded.

There. She'd been able to direct Brigitte's attention to Jeanne without losing her temper at the annoying—though gorgeous—woman. Now she just had to keep doing the same thing for six long days.

She gathered her notes and motioned for the members of her group to follow her. "Our van is waiting outside to take us to Versailles. Most of you have probably already visited it, but let's go view it through the eyes of Marie Antoinette."

Surely she could keep her mind on the tour instead of on Brigitte.

❖

"What does the name Marie Antoinette make you think of?" The group stood in the queen's high-ceilinged royal bedchamber at Versailles as Eva asked the question.

"Let them eat cake!" Ryan Young said, without a quiver of doubt in his voice.

Brigitte regarded the queen's bed. What a prick that man was. His cocksure attitude reminded her of some of her former clients. It usually took her a long time to convince men like him that she had a brain as well as a beautiful body. They didn't want to admit their view of the world might be skewed. They owned the universe and refused to let anyone doubt or forget that fact, even after she'd halfway won them over with her knowledge of world events. She'd always let her mind drift far away into fantasyland while she had sex with customers, especially ones like him. They'd helped her perfect the art of mind/body separation.

Eva replied to Ryan, "Actually, Marie Antoinette never said that, though I'm glad you brought that common misconception out into the open." Brigitte had to hand it to her—Eva didn't mince words.

Ryan looked like he didn't know whether to scowl or smile. Brigitte's opinion of Eva slid up half a notch, but it still had a long way to go.

Eva looked Ryan right in the eye. "You can thank Marie Thérèse—Louis XIV's wife, who lived almost a hundred years before Marie Antoinette—for that famous line. And the English translation *cake* is incorrect. It should be *brioche*, which is a roll that contains butter and eggs."

Ryan opted for the scowl instead of a smile. Brigitte shouldn't have expected anything different from him.

Eva concluded the exchange in a businesslike way. "We'll discuss Marie Antoinette's political situation tomorrow, when we visit the sites in Paris where she was imprisoned and beheaded."

Good for Eva. She'd stopped Mr. Ryan Young gracefully but decisively. She might not be so bad after all. He took a step back and looked around the room as if making himself invisible, though he wouldn't stay that way long. Men like him never did.

Ryan's wife Clover seemed oblivious to how overbearing her husband was. Moving around the gilded room on light feet, she told him, "Marie Antoinette had her own painter, a woman who painted tons of portraits of her. The queen looked like she might have been tall, with a long oval face and translucent skin."

Eva's eyes lit up as she followed Clover's airy movements. She seemed delighted that Clover had done her homework. "Yes. Her portrait painter said the queen was kind, accommodating, and down-to-earth. And she adored all the arts. Later today, we'll see where she danced and put on plays and operas—"

"Isn't it true she and her husband didn't have sex until eight years after they married?" Brigitte almost clapped a hand over her own mouth. Why had she blurted out something so revealing? She'd promised herself to act demure, but instead she'd mentioned sex during their first stop. Not the impression she wanted to make on Eva or her tour mates. She searched their faces to assess the damage.

The two Brits glanced at each other with a secret smile she couldn't decipher, and Clover didn't seem to be fazed. But Ryan stared at her smugly, implying she'd made a bigger fool of herself than he had.

Eva's face revealed nothing, but she ignored the question and began to lecture about the architecture of Versailles, as if she needed to lower the temperature in the room. She obviously was a prude and would do nothing but recite boring facts throughout the tour.

Brigitte sighed. She wanted to learn more about Marie Antoinette the person, the lonely teenager married to an awkward boy more interested in making locks than in bedding her. She could read about the characteristics of the Baroque style that Eva was droning on about in the encyclopedia. As Eva continued to recite dry information about the high domes, twisted columns, and other complicated architectural shapes of Versailles, Brigitte gazed around at the bedspread, canopy, and wall hangings all made from the same fabric, which was covered with roses. The ceiling had to be at least twenty feet high, but the ornate room felt oppressive for some reason.

She slid her hand along the rail that separated visitors from Marie Antoinette's canopied bed, then wandered over to a tall window, hoping to catch a whiff of fresh air.

Suddenly, something was running down her leg, staining her lacy white nightgown red. "Tear out the windows," a voice shouted, and as the loud crash of glass sounded, someone took her arm and led her back to her bed. It was her dear friend, the Princess de Lamballe.

"She needs air," the princess called. "Clear out of the way, you gawkers. Don't you have any decency?" The courtiers milling around the room stopped chattering and stared, their right to observe the royal birth threatened. Some of them edged uneasily toward the door.

Even Marie's normally timid husband, Louis, spoke up. "This is ridiculous. My wife needs privacy. She may be bleeding to death. Bring me another doctor to replace this incompetent."

As the princess helped Marie settle into her bed and a new doctor scurried to her side, Marie breathed in the fresh air streaming from the destroyed window of her bedroom and heard the mewling sound of a newborn. She'd finally given birth to a child. *God willing, it was a son.*

"As a result of this incident, few courtiers were allowed into Marie Antoinette's bedchamber during the birth of her other children." Eva's words broke into Brigitte's consciousness and pulled her back to the present. "But the custom of letting anyone, even commoners, visit—if they were dressed appropriately and checked their weapons at the door—continued. The royal family didn't have much privacy."

What had just happened? Had she had one of her spells, as her grandmother used to call them? Her long dream the other night had seemed so real that she'd felt she'd actually had sex with Simone de Beauvoir. But it had been a dream, at night, in bed, and she'd definitely awakened from it. This…waking dream, if that's what you would call it, was different. She'd actually become someone else, someone who'd been dead for several hundred years. At least that's how it had seemed.

She shook her head and hurried to catch up with the group as Eva led them from the queen's bedchamber. She had to control herself much better than this or she'd reveal her totally unacceptable past life. If that happened, Eva would think even less of her than she probably already did. Strange, but for some unknown reason, she valued Eva's opinion.

❖

Eva rushed out of the bedchamber, anger lengthening her stride. This Brigitte person had caused her initial presentation at Versailles to become a scattered, jumbled mess. First, Brigitte had blurted out one of the most private facts about Marie Antoinette's life, one she certainly would have mentioned later, but not before she'd had time to gauge the level of intimacy this special group would be comfortable with.

She'd tried to smooth over the abrupt leap Brigitte's comments about Marie Antoinette had caused by briefly pointing out facts about the furnishings in the room and its dominant architectural features. But then she'd decided to focus on the quaint custom of allowing courtiers to view royal childbirth as if it was a drama enacted by actors, instead of a very real and private event.

However, instead of listening intently and appreciating what she'd done to salvage their visit to the bedchamber, Brigitte had tripped out, as the hippies she'd met during her travels would say. Brigitte's eyes had dulled and she seemed to have flown away—to where, Eva had no idea. Brigitte had merely stood near the window, wearing an impenetrable expression.

She had sent the rest of the group to revisit the Hall of Mirrors on their own and instructed them to meet near the large fountain behind the palace in thirty minutes. And now, Eva returned to the bedchamber to locate her stray sheep. And there Brigitte was, wandering toward her.

"Where have you been?" Eva forced her best tour-guide smile. "I was worried about you." And she was, just a bit. Brigitte had appeared so far away as she'd stood over there by the window. She'd resembled a lost lamb, innocence trying to peek out from behind her masklike expression. There was more to Brigitte than an overbearing American tourist. But Eva refused to feel sorry for her. She was still angry. "Did I bore you?" The words burst out before she could stop them. Why did she care?

Brigitte recoiled. "If you don't mind, I'd occasionally like to take time for a few private thoughts."

Eva stepped back and forced a pleasant expression. "I'm sorry. I'll keep that in mind."

Brigitte appeared somewhat mollified.

"Is this the first time you've visited Versailles?" Eva simply couldn't keep her curiosity about this woman on a leash.

"Yes. My first time in Paris, and in Europe." Brigitte glanced around at the ornate chandeliers hanging from the ceiling, which was covered with elaborate designs and studded with golden cupids.

That explained some of the innocence she'd detected earlier in Brigitte. She wasn't as well traveled as Eva had assumed.

"Then welcome to the Old World. I hope you enjoy your stay. What do you think so far?"

"I've been in Paris since late February but haven't seen much." Brigitte shrugged. "I have a lot on my mind."

Eva bit her tongue and decided to change the subject, though she was dying to continue her current line of questioning. "You've chosen the right country. Your French is outstanding. How did you become so fluent?"

Brigitte smiled faintly but still seemed on guard. "A few college courses, several sets of language tapes, and a lot of books. I love the language and challenged myself to learn it well."

Eva glanced at her watch, surprised at how quickly the time had passed. The more she learned about this elusive woman, the more she wanted to know.

"If you'll excuse me, I'd like to visit the Hall of Mirrors now," Brigitte said, obviously ready to end their conversation. "I've read so much about it I'd like to take in as much as I can."

As Brigitte walked nonchalantly away, Eva called to her, still trying to maintain an amiable façade. In fact, she didn't feel quite as on edge as she had before their little tête-à-tête. "We'll see you in half an hour at the Fountain of Latona. It's the one stacked up like a wedding cake."

Why had she reacted so strongly to Brigitte every time she'd seen her, beginning in the library several weeks ago? Brigitte must have a good reason for wanting some private time even when she was part of a group tour. And it had never bothered her this much if the members of her tour didn't find her mini-lectures enthralling. In most of the student groups she led, she was surprised if anyone paid much attention to her remarks. She was obviously overreacting to a perfectly reasonable request and needed to control herself around Brigitte.

❖

Brigitte wasn't sure why, but Eva seemed overly concerned that she listen to every word she uttered. She'd really enjoyed her time alone here in Paris during the past months. Maybe she wasn't ready to try to be sociable, but her dream had given her the courage to try to connect with a woman who might treat her like a person instead of an object.

Her clients in New Orleans had paid her handsomely to be an object. They'd wanted her to forget her own desires and focus on them exclusively. And she'd perfected that art as skillfully as a painter or a musician had polished his talent. Each client had apparently believed she regarded him as the center of her universe, as her sole reason for existing, as her only source of pleasure. But they had no idea how hard she worked to create that illusion.

Now Eva was demanding her total attention, and Brigitte didn't want to award it to anyone until she was ready to. Even—especially—a woman as haughty as Eva.

She strolled through the Hall of Mirrors and recalled reading how rare and ultraexpensive mirrors were several hundred years ago. As she stopped and gazed at her reflection in each of them, she felt ridiculously uneasy that she might fall through one of the tall looking glasses, like Alice.

In a way, though, Paris was a wonderland for her. She was determined to begin a new life. And part of starting over was to not let others watch her and judge her. She also didn't want to have to monitor her every thought and feeling in order to please them. Here in Paris she was finally free to let her emotions out in any way she pleased, with whom she pleased, within reason.

She needed to talk more to Eva in private and provide her with more insight into how she felt without alienating her. Eva had been pleasant enough during their recent conversation. Perhaps, in time, they'd become less antagonistic. Otherwise, she might as well quit this tour right now and find another way to meet desirable people.

❖

Eva stood near the Fountain of Latona and let its shooting streams of water wash away the unpleasant exchange with Brigitte. What a glorious day, with this sunshine and unusually mild temperatures for early July. She'd hoped she would enjoy this tour, but the recent incident with Brigitte worried her. She wanted to be financially able to choose those she tried to help, instead of living her life at the mercy of lustful chaperones like Marian and her indifferent charges or hard-to-handle tourists like Brigitte.

She caught sight of Clover, obviously an aging flower child, almost floating through the formal gardens that adorned the palace grounds. Strange that she'd chosen to marry someone so uptight as Ryan. He marched several paces behind her without seeming to appreciate the gardens that surrounded him, probably murmuring *Let them eat cake*, with her and the rest of their group in mind.

Hopefully, he and the others had read Jeanne's list of suggestions and worn comfortable walking shoes. Their other three stops at Versailles—the Petit Trianon, Cupid's Temple, and Marie Antoinette's hamlet—were located quite a distance from here through a wooded area. She planned for them to stroll leisurely across the huge estate, which would give them plenty of time to absorb its grandeur.

Clover ran over to her, her long red hair falling loose down her back like a schoolgirl's. "Isn't this place fantastic? We visited it on a bus tour a month or so ago, but it was cold and rainy so we just saw the inside of the palace." She glanced back at Ryan, who was trudging along as if he was enduring a forced march. "Of course the Hall of Mirrors is divine," Clover said, "but I want to see the grounds. Especially since you mentioned Marie Antoinette thought the palace was too stuffy. I can't wait to see where she let her hair down."

Ryan walked up, scowling. "Humph. Seeing this place once is more than enough for me. Just a big, overdecorated monstrosity." He looked as if he might spit on the white gravel under their feet. "I'd rather be touring northern France, revisiting the battlegrounds where

I spent several years." He sighed and looked almost nostalgic. "But Clover isn't interested in anything to do with the war. She just wants to soak up the *culture* of Europe."

Maybe Ryan wasn't quite as bad as he'd originally seemed. He simply wasn't interested in what she had to offer. At least he might help prepare her for the cynical prosecutors she'd be up against as a lawyer, so he'd serve a somewhat useful function.

Soon, Emily and Leigh wandered up, Emily stopping every two feet to snap a photo and saying, "Oh, Leigh, look at this. Isn't it beautiful?" Leigh was carrying a large bag that Emily was already pulling pamphlets and snacks from, and she also wore a large camera and a striped canteen crisscrossed over her chest and her broad shoulders.

"Do you have water in there," Eva pointed at the canteen and laughed, "or something stronger?"

"Just water," Leigh said with a grin. "We have several bottles of something stronger in our hotel room for later."

Eva nodded. She didn't care what they were drinking. They certainly weren't teenagers. In fact, they'd probably never see seventy again, but they seemed totally devoted to each other and to enjoying their stay in Paris.

"Have you seen Brigitte?" Eva asked the group as she scanned the knots of tourists scattered over the broad expanse of gravel paths, manicured lawns and gardens, and spurting fountains. "I told her to meet us here in thirty minutes." Everyone shook their head.

It had already been thirty-five minutes. She wouldn't insist on a rigid timetable for adults like these, but she had to enforce some rules. For God's sake, this was only the first day, and Brigitte had already gotten under her skin several times.

Then she saw her, sauntering toward them in her sedate outfit, a floppy white hat and Jackie Onassis sunglasses hiding her face. The annoyingly regal way she carried herself suggested she considered herself every much if not more of a queen than Marie Antoinette. The hat covered even her hair, which she wore twisted up on the back of her head. Eva preferred it long and spilling down into her face, like it had been the first time she'd seen her, in the library. But why was she thinking about Brigitte like this?

Clover waved. "Yoo-hoo. Here we are." Brigitte lifted her hand slightly and waved as if tossing them a bone. She didn't increase her speed one little bit.

What arrogance. Her every movement infuriated Eva once again. She had to grit her teeth as she stood there waiting for Brigitte to join them.

Finally she managed to say, "I hope you're all prepared for quite a hike. We'll walk down to the Apollo Fountain and along the Grand Canal for a bit, then head over there to the right, into the woods."

Maybe Ryan and Brigitte would fall into the canal or get lost in the forest.

Chapter Eleven

Clover, Emily, and Leigh hiked with Eva toward the Petit Trianon with ease. As they approached the square beige stone building, its flat roof featuring a railed walkway, Leigh said, "Too bad it isn't open to the public. It'd make a fascinating hotel or restaurant."

"Perfect for a second honeymoon, don't you think, dear?" Emily said, and they smiled at each other with a special light in their eyes. Eva couldn't help but echo their smile.

Brigitte and Ryan had lagged behind, Ryan limping even before they reached Marie Antoinette's three-story private château. Eva slowed her pace, waiting for them to catch up.

"If I'd wanted to take a walking tour of Paris, I'd have signed up for one," Brigitte remarked as they approached, her floppy white hat and large-lensed sunglasses still in place.

Brigitte obviously didn't realize how far her voice would carry in this quiet environment.

"Damn straight." Ryan sounded even more acerbic than he had earlier. "I haven't had this much exercise since I played football in college."

Eva sped up and joined the three women in front of her. To hell with Ryan and Brigitte. She couldn't waste her energy on clients who were determined to be miserable, especially when they were adults who continued along out of their own free will.

Clover interrupted her thoughts as they finally stood gazing at the building. "Oh, I wish we could go inside. How can they let something so beautiful just stand there and slowly fall apart?"

Eva nodded. France was full of treasures like this that needed to be restored. She took several deep breaths, afraid to speak for a moment. She had to calm down and concentrate on the tour instead of letting Brigitte and Ryan get under her skin.

Clover seemed carried away with the Trianon. "You said this was Marie Antoinette's personal home, and she had her own theater on the grounds, where she and others put on plays and operas? Wouldn't it be neat to have seen a performance here?"

Brigitte surprised Eva by walking up and pausing beside her, heat radiating from her flushed cheeks. "I certainly would have enjoyed seeing Marie Antoinette in *The Barber of Seville*."

Her presence and her remark warmed Eva. Maybe Brigitte had simply been making small talk with Ryan. "Ah, yes, playing Rosine. Her favorite and final role."

Brigitte took off her sunglasses, and her eyes sparkled. "I suppose she identified with the combination of innocence and craftiness."

The observation pulled Eva in. "Interesting point. You may be right." She paused, enjoying their interchange yet unwilling to be upstaged by Brigitte's knowledge. She tossed out another fact from her arsenal. "Of course it was rather thoughtless that the play satirized the nobility. That may have had something to do with their hostile attitude toward her."

Brigitte nodded. "They're supposed to have had some great machinery for scene changes," Brigitte said, then bent down and rubbed one of her calves, revealing a hint of cleavage.

Eva glanced, then looked away quickly.

"It was a long walk," Brigitte said, "but it's worth it to see the place where Marie Antoinette felt at home and really enjoyed herself. Makes her seem more real to me."

An expression of compassion transformed Brigitte's face so completely Eva almost gasped with pleasure. If the inner beauty of this woman matched the outer, *she* would be a treasure as lovely as the Petit Trianon. How could someone's behavior swing so wildly from one moment to the next?

"As reclusive as she supposedly was," Brigitte said, "it must have been awful for her to have to put up with the backbiting, the gossip, the insincerity, and the intrigue in that stuffy main palace."

Eva was enjoying this side of Brigitte, who evidently had experienced some of the negative experiences she'd just listed. Why would people gossip about her? Intrigued, and encouraged by Brigitte's participation, Eva told the group more about how the queen and her close friends had gotten into trouble because they'd performed the banned *Barber of Seville* that criticized the monarchy. She also described how well Marie Antoinette was supposed to have sung and acted.

Brigitte seemed to actually listen to her comments this time. What a welcome change. Eva warmed further toward her, almost forgetting their earlier clash, as she led them from the Petit Trianon to the nearby Cupid's Temple. Its twelve columns supported a massive dome with a coffered ceiling, but she didn't spend much time discussing such architectural features.

Instead, she said, "Marie Antoinette could see this from her bedroom. The structure's made entirely of marble. And this statue of Cupid here in the center is just a copy. The original's in the Louvre."

Ryan's eyes lit up, and he pulled out a cigarette. "I bet it's worth a fortune."

Eva shrugged. How typical. The first thing most Americans thought about, except maybe the ones like Clover, was how much something cost. They didn't seem to comprehend what art was and how the true artist considered money less important than the process of creating the work itself. Ryan was so gauche. But he and the others were paying her salary this summer and hopefully would leave her a generous tip, so she continued to try to be pleasant. Now who was being mercenary?

Ryan scowled. "Look at Cupid—like a gawky kid getting into mischief."

Emily walked closer to the statue and spoke to the group for the first time all day. "Isn't that what love's supposed to do—make you act like a kid?"

"I don't know about you, but it made me act like a damn fool." The look Ryan hurled at Clover wasn't very loving, but she didn't even seem to hear or see him. It reminded Eva of the contempt with which Father sometimes regarded her mother, and her mother's own obliviousness. But Leigh and Emily—their relationship was different, a pleasure to watch.

Leigh slid her arm around Emily's waist and spoke to Ryan as if challenging him to a duel. "Well, that's what it did to us, fifty years ago. And we pride ourselves on acting like children whenever we can." She kissed Emily on the cheek. "So-called adults have forgotten what's really important—art, nature, and being together. If enjoying things like that is childish, I say hurrah for Cupid."

Ryan looked embarrassed and slipped over to one of the dome's elaborate columns, whereas Brigitte gazed at Emily and Leigh with a clear expression of envy. Eva studied her. Had Brigitte's marriage resembled Ryan and Clover's? If so, had it been with a man… or maybe a woman? The possibility made her breathe a bit faster. She couldn't imagine Brigitte ever being as compliant and docile as Clover acted, but you never knew what lay in a person's past. Just as, earlier, she'd wanted to know what was on Brigitte's mind, now, she wanted to discover more about Brigitte's past.

After they left Cupid's Temple and were walking toward the last stop on the day's itinerary, Brigitte and Ryan caught up with her.

"We've been discussing that statue and would like your opinion," Brigitte said, her hat and large sunglasses firmly in place again.

Eva almost stumbled with surprise. "Of course. That's what I'm here for."

"You said it depicted Cupid carving a bow for his arrows of love from the club Hercules used to fight with." Brigitte seemed absorbed in whatever she and Ryan had been discussing.

"Yes."

"Could you view it as an antiwar statement? Ryan thinks I'm stretching too far."

The question delighted Eva. "Absolutely. True art is always wide open to interpretation." As she began to expound on the subject, Ryan scowled and stalked away, leaving her alone once again with the delicious troublemaker she'd be saddled with all week.

"I hope the peace talks here in Paris don't last as long as the war in Vietnam has," Brigitte said. "The French were smart to get out of that country when they did. I'm tired of losing American lives in a conflict we didn't have any business taking part in."

Eva wanted to pursue the subject with Brigitte, but Ryan had joined the rest of the group, and they were looking at her for directions. She reluctantly led Brigitte toward them.

Perhaps Brigitte *was* much more than just a pair of beautiful eyes and luscious breasts. Maybe she'd misjudged her.

❖

Brigitte followed as Eva guided them through the grounds to their next destination. Clover and Ryan were actually holding hands now, and Emily and Leigh were talking as they pointed out things that interested them and snapped pictures of them. Brigitte walked through the wooded fields by herself, tagging along alone, like she had most of her life.

Hearing Emily and Leigh defend Cupid from Ryan's dismissive comment had pierced her as surely as one of the little love god's arrows had struck the British couple. Fifty years together, and they still seemed to delight in each other's company.

Was that what she would find in Paris? She held on to the belief that she was worthy of love, but how could any two people live together happily for that long? Did she even want to find out?

Rosa's care had eased some of the pain her mother's desertion had caused her, but selling herself for all those years had made it nearly impossible for her to imagine what a relationship like the one between Emily and Leigh might be like. Would being a part of this group help her find what she was looking for? Granted, meeting Emily and Leigh had already clued her in on what she was missing, and Ryan and Clover were a wonderful example of what she didn't want. That left only Eva, pretty but prickly, with a personal agenda that Brigitte couldn't even begin to understand. They couldn't do much of anything but annoy each other, though their brief conversations had sparked her interest.

Eva was very easy on the eyes, young, and obviously intelligent and hardworking. But she was so judgmental, and many of her comments sounded like she'd given the same rehearsed speech a hundred times.

Besides, someone as attractive as Eva couldn't possibly be available. Her boyfriend, or perhaps girlfriend, was probably already at their apartment waiting for her to come home after she got rid of the tiresome tourists she had to put up with. No. Eva was a dead-end street on the relationship highway.

So why was Brigitte even wasting her time thinking about her? She'd give this tour idea a few more days, and if it didn't offer her what she wanted, she'd drop out.

❖

During their final stop at Versailles, at a village known as the Queen's Hamlet, Eva pointed out various buildings as they walked through the grounds, which were dotted with lakes and large old gnarled trees. "This is the mill, though it was never used to grind grain, and there's the farmhouse where the resident farmer and his family lived."

Emily stared at the buildings they passed. "With all these half-timbered façades, this reminds me of an old village in a Dutch painting," she said. "Leigh—look at the fences made of sticks and these rough stone floors."

"Yes, that was the model," Eva said. "And all the buildings have roofs thatched with reeds." She pointed to some other structures. "The dovecote held doves and pigeons, as well as several varieties of hens and roosters, and that tower over there that looks like a lighthouse? It was used for storage as well as atmosphere."

"Where did Marie Antoinette spend most of her time?" Brigitte asked, seeming enchanted by this fairyland for adults. She seemed more relaxed now, more childlike, and Eva enjoyed this new, softer side of her.

"She stayed in that large two-story house over there, called the Queen's House, which was where she had her parties and visited with the people she enjoyed associating with."

Clover joined in. "Oh, what did she like to do besides act in plays?" And Brigitte appeared to be interested in the answer as well.

Everyone liked to know about the personal lives of the rich and famous—or the doomed and notorious, and Eva couldn't resist giving them what they wanted. She was glad she'd read a lot about Marie Antoinette's pastimes. "Well, her harpsichord stood in her large living room on the second floor, and she could see practically the entire village from one of the six windows in the room. I imagine she enjoyed standing there and viewing her little kingdom."

"What are the rest of these places?" Clover looked like she'd love to move in if the place hadn't been so run-down.

Eva glanced around. "The barn, which was used for balls, was damaged during the French Revolution and destroyed later, but you can still see one of the dairies that was later restored. Marie is said to have enjoyed the dairy products." She pointed to direct their attention. "Oh, and that tiny building over there is her boudoir, where she went when she wanted to spend time alone."

"Or with one of her closest friends, I bet," Brigitte remarked suggestively.

Eva glanced at her with increased interest. Brigitte certainly seemed fascinated by the queen's sex life, which even she had to admit was a more compelling subject than dairy products. "Yes, you may be right. Marie Antoinette entertained mostly female companions here. The Princess de Lamballe, who was her Mistress of the Wardrobe, and Madame Polignac, the governess of her four children, were her favorites."

Leigh raised her hand. "I've heard that people at the royal court whispered about her being a lesbian, though I doubt they used that word."

Eva felt more relaxed with the group now and didn't hesitate to answer Leigh's question. After all, she had a duty to keep her customers engaged. "Yes, that was a common rumor, especially among the women who were never invited to the hamlet. It could have had some truth to it, though the Princess de Lamballe had a reputation for being very prudish, so I find it hard to picture them going down on each other." She winked at Leigh.

Everyone laughed, and Eva relaxed even more. "Apparently many people were jealous because Marie Antoinette always chose people who amused her to fill important positions. The stuffy, boring ones probably had to do something to make themselves feel better because she hadn't favored them."

"Ha! Nothing much has changed in two hundred years," Brigitte said.

"Touché," Eva agreed, "but some of us keep hoping."

Now Clover held up her hand. "What did the women do here all day? When they weren't…you know." Clearly, politics wasn't her topic of choice.

This was one of Eva's favorite subjects—how women lived when beyond the scrutiny of men. "For starters, they dressed much more simply than they did at court—in white muslin dresses and straw hats instead of colorful silks and satins. Marie was a fashion-setter, but she preferred to literally let her hair down and not have it powdered. And she hated to wear a corset. Some of the ladies of the court even wrote her mother back in Austria to report she wasn't wearing hers. Her mother reprimanded her, though she did offer to send her a new one from Austria since the French ones were so stiff."

All the women laughed this time, and Clover said with a smile, "So she was a flower child two hundred years before her time."

Eva nodded. "I never thought about her that way, but you may be right." She led them through the remains of Marie's beloved hamlet. "This was a working farm, so Marie enjoyed tending to her roses, picking strawberries, and milking her cows while she was here. Of course they washed the cows before she got here."

"Why would she do something so silly?" Ryan asked. "Playing at being a milkmaid. Why would anyone do farmwork if they didn't have to?"

Eva frowned. "Back in Vienna, she'd been used to a simpler way of life. She grew up as part of the royal family there, but her parents let their children wear casual clothes and even play with the servants. Maybe she was just trying to recapture a time in her life that felt more authentic."

Brigitte seemed thoughtful. "So that's why she preferred to live here instead of in the main house."

"Yes. Her day at the palace never varied. She had to attend Mass, eat, have music lessons, go for a walk, and play cards on a set schedule. And visiting with the older women of the court took most of her time. Apparently she didn't like many of them, and they were envious of her." Once again, Brigitte appeared sympathetic to the queen's situation. "Marie must have felt at home here in the hamlet. How would you like to be married off by proxy to the heir to the French throne when you were fourteen?"

"And wasn't she stuck in that role only because all her eligible sisters died suddenly of smallpox?" Brigitte said, and this time Eva accepted Brigitte's addition as a gift instead of a challenge.

"That's right, so I doubt she was prepared for it." She loved the way their conversation was going. Even Ryan's cynicism had helped everyone see Marie as a real person instead of a name in a history book, and Brigitte's interest and insights gratified her.

"Poor thing," Clover said. "A bird in a gilded cage, as they say."

Emily and Leigh nodded, and even Ryan didn't appear quite so scornful.

"A cage isn't a good place for any bird," Brigitte said cryptically, and Eva wondered exactly what she meant. This woman was as enigmatic as the Delphic oracle.

❖

As the group returned to the main palace at Versailles, Brigitte lagged behind again. Being in Paris was having such a strange effect on her. If the incident in Marie Antoinette's bedroom earlier today was any indication, she was beginning to lose control of the fantasies and memories she'd always used to distract herself from unpleasant situations.

Their visit to the hamlet had sparked a vivid memory of a little sex game that had made her lose her only friend long ago.

"May I touch your cheek, Brigitte?" her little friend asked.

Brigitte pretended to be thinking hard. They'd played this game before. It was their secret. "No. I can't let you." Her reply echoed her friend's Cajun French.

"I'll give you a cookie," the other little girl said.

"No. I don't think so."

"I'll give you two cookies."

She smiled but shook her head.

"I'll give you *three* cookies."

"Well, okay." The small, rosy-faced girl touched Brigitte's cheek.

"May I put my hand under your shirt?" Her little friend pointed to the tiny knots on Brigitte's chest.

"No. I can't let you."

But every time the other little girl offered Brigitte three cookies, she gave in. It was like climbing the steps on the big slide at school and then finally letting go and rushing down the steep slope.

"Can I feel inside your panties, Brigitte? I'll give you three cookies."

The place between her legs was buzzing as she opened her mouth to say yes, and—

Grandmother burst into the little deserted apartment. "What are you two doing?"

Brigitte jerked away from her friend. Why did she feel like she was doing something wrong? "Nothing. We're just playing."

"Why do you have your shorts down, and why did your friend have her hand in your panties? You two are being nasty, aren't you?"

Brigitte hung her head. "We weren't being bad." It was just their secret game.

"Oh, no? You're sinning. If you don't stop, you'll go straight to hell. I heard you speaking French too. Shame on you. Why do you think I pay the good sister at the convent to give you English lessons twice a week?"

The other little girl had tears in her eyes, but Brigitte tried to imagine she was a rock so Grandmother's words wouldn't upset her.

Her grandmother kept fussing. "You know the nuns will make you kneel on rice if they hear you speak French at school. And probably worse if you touch yourself or anyone else, like you just did. *I don't want to ever see your friend over here again.*"

Brigitte envied Marie Antoinette her Petit Trianon and her hamlet. But most of all, she wished she'd had sisters and eventually the friends that had made the rest of the French court gossip so wildly about Marie.

Grandmother had been every bit as harsh and judgmental as those courtiers, and her attitude had been toxic.

Brigitte shook her head and hurried to catch up with the others. How silly to think about something that had happened all those years ago. She needed to forget it. She was an adult and needed to act like one, but she wasn't sure she knew how. Sadly, she was afraid she was even less prepared to establish a mature, loving relationship than Marie Antoinette had been.

Chapter Twelve

"How did the first day of your tour go, Eva?" Jeanne asked. She pulled out a drawer of a gray file cabinet and inserted several documents into a folder.

Eva had been exhausted when she'd returned home the night before and turned in before her aunt got home from an evening at the theater. "It went well." She smoothed her hair carefully as she examined herself in the mirror in the back room of the office. She liked the new shaggy look her hairdresser had suggested and hoped the long bangs pulled across her forehead to partially obscure one eye made her seem mysterious and sexy. *Mysterious and sexy for whom?*

"*Well*? Is that the best you can do? You've been so anticipating this tour."

"Actually it went *very* well, especially later in the day. The flower child's husband doesn't seem too happy to be there, and at first Brigitte acted strange, but by the time we reached the Trianon, she began to become involved."

Jeanne shut the drawer with a bang. "Strange-mysterious, strange-weird, how...strange?"

Eva described Brigitte's unusual behavior in Marie Antoinette's bedchamber, her provocative questions, and her seeming alliance with Ryan.

"A troublemaker, no?" Jeanne asked, but she seemed pleased rather than concerned. Her aunt had always had a soft spot for wild women.

"Not really. Later, she actually began to listen to what the others and I said and to empathize with Marie Antoinette." The memory filled her with—what? Anticipation, excitement, enthusiasm? She couldn't pin it down, but it was a pleasant sensation, one she seldom experienced before a day of guiding tourists through her beloved Paris.

"So she has a heart as well as beauty and brains?" Jeanne began to file some documents from a nearby pile.

"Yes. And for your information, I'm not sure I believe she really has a late husband. And if she has been married…I'm guessing, but I don't think her marriage was ideal. And at least once she seemed envious of the obviously happy relationship the two Englishwomen admitted to having."

"So they are, as I suspected, a couple? Emily and Leigh?"

"Yes. They've been together fifty years."

Jeanne paused and raised an eyebrow. "Fifty years? I don't blame Brigitte. Such a record makes me envious too. And what about the others? The flower child and her bored husband?" Jeanne left the back room and walked to her desk, then absently began to tidy it.

Eva followed her, trying to control her ricocheting thoughts. Granted, Brigitte had provoked her more than any of the others, even Ryan, in both negative and positive ways, but she refused to let herself fixate on the woman she'd pledged to scout out for Jeanne. She'd certainly enjoyed seeing Emily and Leigh take such an open stand about their relationship, but they didn't intrigue her as fully as Brigitte did.

She settled in her desk chair. "Ryan and Clover. They remind me of Mother and Father."

Jeanne stopped and stared at her. "How?"

"Oh, Clover appears to be oblivious to what a boor Ryan is and how he belittles her every chance he gets. I want to shake her and tell her to wake up, but it would probably do about as much good as if I tried the same thing with Mother."

Jeanne shrugged and shuffled the papers she held. "Some people you can't change. At least you have Emily and Leigh in the group. We'll see what happens with the other three." Just then the phone rang and Jeanne said quickly, "This should be an entirely different experience today, visiting the places where Marie Antoinette's life disintegrated and ended."

"Speaking of which, I've arranged to meet the group in the Tuileries this morning." She jumped up and pulled on a light sweater. "I hope this mist doesn't turn into rain, though it would suit the mood of today's agenda." She waved. "'Bye, Jeanne. See you later."

As she hurried out the door, she kept hoping the good Brigitte would join them, not the bad one.

❖

"The Tuileries Palace that once stood here was demolished in 1883, and only these vast gardens remain."

Brigitte yawned, barely taking in every third sentence Eva uttered. Mornings weren't her best time. She was used to sleeping late everyday, since most of her clients liked to see her in the afternoons or at night. And she hadn't accepted many appointments a week, so most of her time had been her own.

Having to meet this tour group at ten o'clock in the morning had forced her to rise by seven and drink several cups of coffee to get her going. She'd changed outfits several times before finally deciding on a soft cotton blouse and long flowered peasant skirt in honor of Marie Antoinette's love for the natural look. By then she'd barely had enough time to eat a croissant. Besides being tired, she was out of fuel.

As they wandered through the formal gardens with their large fountains and basins and collection of both classical and contemporary sculpture, Eva continued to feed them the history of the Tuileries available in any guidebook. Were most tourists totally unaware of anything associated with the sights they visited, like baby birds expecting their guide to stuff them with facts and figures?

Bored, Brigitte stopped at a bronze classical sculpture of three women standing in a circle, all perfectly nude, facing each other, yet each of the three was gazing into the distance as if the others didn't exist. She could identify. And to top it off, the head of each woman was covered with dried bird shit, the white stuff dripping down one's back and coating the entire breast of another of the women. It expressed exactly how she'd felt during her working days in New Orleans.

She jumped as Eva spoke from behind her. "Marie Antoinette refused to desert France without the king," she said and explained that though the royal family did try to leave the country once, the king postponed running away from Versailles for so long, they were captured and brought back. "They took refuge in the Tuileries Palace, located right over there." Eva herded the others like sheep toward the site she'd pointed out.

Brigitte trailed behind them on the gritty, rather muddy path. She'd already read about these events. The laughs and shouts of children in the distance made her wish she could run and join them in their games instead of walk along in this regimented fashion. She'd like to stop at one of the ice-cream stands that dotted the park, feed the ducks in one of its many ponds, sit and relax in one of the green wooden chairs that were scattered about, maybe even eat lunch there later. A baguette stuffed with ham and cheese sounded good.

But Eva continued to drone on, and Brigitte had to keep up with the group. She thought Eva mentioned that though this palace wasn't as nice as Versailles, it was okay. Then Eva explained how a mob broke in and killed the royal guards, so the royal family was sent to an old accommodating prison called the Temple. "The angry crowd murdered the Princess de Lamballe, Marie's longtime friend, near there and paraded her maimed body through the streets," and Brigitte finally stopped daydreaming and thinking about food and concentrated on Eva's words instead. Somehow, standing here in Paris made Marie Antoinette's tragedy seem much more personal than ever.

She spoke up, and Eva looked startled to hear her voice. "Does the princess's extreme loyalty provide enough evidence for us to believe she actually was Marie Antoinette's lover?" Brigitte had never had a close female friend except the little girl her grandmother had made her stop playing with and Rosa, who'd been everything to her. She was trying to understand the type of feelings the queen and the princess might have shared.

Eva paused, seeming hesitant to discuss the subject today. Then she took a deep breath. "I'm really not sure what to believe. Maybe all the rumors were vicious lies. After all, the aristocracy as a whole was very repressive, and the commoners were starving, so they would naturally blame their problems on the easiest targets. A foreigner, like Marie Antoinette."

Eva's honesty made Brigitte eager to hear what else she had to say about how both the courtiers and commoners hated Marie.

"During the revolution, pornographic pamphlets showed the princess using a strap-on dildo to service Marie," Eva said, and someone in the group tittered. To Brigitte it sounded like blatant sensationalism, but part of her wouldn't have minded a glimpse of those pamphlets. She held her tongue and didn't ask Eva whether they were on display anywhere.

"Marie Antoinette was from a Germanic area, and the virtuous French were certain homosexuality was a German vice," Eva said, her sarcastic tone making it clear she didn't agree with her French ancestors' bigotry. That revelation relieved Brigitte. And she agreed with Eva's conclusion, that whether Marie ever expressed that love physically, she did seem to have genuinely loved her close female friends. Perhaps Eva wasn't a prude, as she'd first thought. Maybe she was just sincerely attempting to sift rumor and innuendo from historical fact.

"Everyone called Marie, among other things, the Austrian bitch." Eva reminded them that France and Austria had declared war on each other about the time the monarchy was dissolving.

"So Marie was everyone's scapegoat," Brigitte said.

"Exactly." Eva beamed. "I see her as courageous throughout her life, rather frivolous and a spendthrift as a young bride, but a strong woman as the situation in France worsened into the horrors of the French Revolution."

"Courageous?" Ryan scoffed. "Why on earth would you say that? She was just a silly, weak woman."

Brigitte jumped in before Eva could respond. "Can you imagine being a ten-year-old girl, raised in an informal family atmosphere in Austria, unprepared for marriage because you expected your older sisters to be married off before you, and then suddenly you become the wife of the incompetent king of a country your parents wanted to secure as an ally?"

Oh, how I'd love to tell them how it hurt for my mother to abandon me. How free she'd felt after Grandmother died and she went to live with Rosa in New Orleans. Even if Rosa could only teach her how to make a living on her back and how to tango, she always knew she was loved and wanted.

But Brigitte couldn't reveal her past. No one in this group, except perhaps Emily and Leigh, could possibly understand how she felt, just as Ryan seemed to lack any empathy for Marie Antoinette.

Eva cleared her throat. "Thanks for your insights, Brigitte. The term culture shock would certainly fit Marie's situation. When I said she was courageous, I was thinking about something I haven't mentioned yet."

The mist was turning into soft rain, and Eva led them beneath a nearby tree, where they stood while she spoke about the slow, tedious marriage transactions between Marie and her future husband and about how Marie's mother did everything she could to make Marie attractive, hoping to speed them up. She wiped a few raindrops from her arm and said, "Unfortunately, Marie's strawberry-blond curls were always falling down in her face, so her governess made her wear a wooden band around her forehead. It was so tight she lost patches of her hair."

Brigitte rubbed her own forehead, and Clover said, "Ouch. Not fun." Even Ryan looked a tiny bit sympathetic.

Eva had a beautiful smile, and it made her seem much more human than she had at the beginning of the tour. Was that only a day ago? Apparently she was delighted to have finally found a subject that interested everyone in the group. Eva explained that an imported French hairstylist created a new hairstyle for Marie, which started a new fad for the young people of Vienna.

"That didn't take much courage," Ryan said, returning to his scornful manner and lighting a cigarette.

But Eva didn't let his attitude faze her and told them how a French dentist possibly fixed Marie's crooked teeth—by using pliers to straighten them. When Ryan shrugged, Eva reminded them that anesthesia and other painkillers were probably scarce back then, but he said, "How about a good shot of schnapps, or whatever was popular in Vienna at the time?" He laughed.

Brigitte wanted to slap him. Instead, she said, "I doubt if they would have risked spoiling their valuable bargaining chip. They probably convinced her she owed it to her family and her country and guilted her into enduring the pain." She knew a lot about bargaining chips and guilt trips.

Eva smiled again, in seeming agreement. "Yes. I like to think the dentist used the other method I read about—a metal band with gold wires through it that encircled the problem teeth and gradually straightened them. Even that couldn't have felt too pleasant."

Brigitte sighed. "Yes. That would have been more humane, though still probably uncomfortable. All this reminds me of Chinese foot binding. We consider that barbaric, but women in our society will go to painful extremes to make ourselves attractive." God knows she'd been guilty of that.

Leigh spoke up in her usual blunt manner. "All this is interesting, but I'm getting wet. You were talking about Marie Antoinette's courage. Can you finish your point so we can go somewhere dry?"

Ryan nodded vigorously, though Clover and Emily didn't seem to mind the dampness.

"Sorry," Eva said. "I'll be brief. I see Marie as both courageous and innocent. We'll drive by the Place de la Concorde later today, and I want you to think about her final words before the blade of the guillotine dropped: *Pardon me, sir. I meant not to do it.* Any idea what she was talking about?"

"A clear admission of guilt if I ever heard one," Ryan said, appearing vindicated. "She was probably apologizing for saying *Let them eat cake* and ignoring the peasants' demands."

Though Brigitte chuckled along with the others, she didn't like herself for doing so. It was so easy to stomp on the underdog. "I doubt that's it. Tell us, Eva." She had to give Eva credit for trumping her in the research department.

Eva appeared satisfied, as if she'd finally won a point in a game only she knew the rules to. "After she climbed the scaffold, she accidentally stepped on the executioner's foot."

Clover and Emily looked horrified, and even Ryan and Leigh stopped fidgeting.

"If the Princess de Lamballe wasn't her lover, she should have been," Brigitte said. "She deserved the love of a faithful woman."

"Exactly." Eva gazed at her with an expression of triumph and something else, something more intimate.

"Thanks for answering my question," Brigitte said. "I think I'm going to enjoy this tour." Perhaps Eva wasn't as boring and dictatorial as she'd thought. Perhaps they could even become friends.

❖

Finally, a major breakthrough, Eva thought as she led the group toward the spot where the van was scheduled to meet them. Not only was Brigitte sympathetic toward lesbians, but possibly she was one herself. She herself had practically been born a lesbian, and seeing the way her father treated her mother had confirmed her choice long ago. She'd loved to cuddle up in the lap of her favorite babysitter and rest her head on her comforting breasts.

She ushered her charges from the damp Tuileries gardens into their waiting van and directed the driver to take them past the site of the old Temple prison, in the Marais district. Nowadays, the Metro sign was the only reminder of it. She tried to condense her comments about the Temple's history as a medieval fortress, realizing now that the group preferred to focus on the more personal aspects of the story of Marie Antoinette and her associates.

Ryan called from the back row of seats, where he and Clover sat peering out through the misting rain at the busy street. "Exactly what happened to the Princess de Lamballe?" She was surprised he recalled her earlier comment. She never knew if he was listening or thinking up nasty remarks. But she instructed the driver to take them along the right bank of the Seine, to the Rue du Roi de Sicile, before they went to the Temple.

"It's not a pretty story," she said. "Everyone up for the gory details?"

Though Clover and Emily blanched, all of them nodded as they drove through the city.

"The princess was separated from the royal family when they were in the Temple and imprisoned in La Force, a nearby jail reserved primarily for prostitutes," she said. Brigitte visibly stiffened, and Eva absently wondered why. "The other women's rough language and taunts horrified the princess, who was sensitive and nervous. However, she did have some companions confined with her—a female friend and the friend's daughter."

If that part of the story had bothered Brigitte, Eva hoped the grisly details, which she'd have to mention before long, wouldn't upset her. She provided a little background to ease into the Princess de Lamballe's fate. "Though the princess's friends were released, the princess refused to say she hated the queen and the monarchy. So the judges declared her guilty and handed her over to the mob in the courtyard."

Everyone sighed, and their van pulled to the curb. "Here's where the entrance to the La Force prison once stood," she said, and they all peered out the window.

"What did the mob do to her?" Leigh asked the question this time.

"No one knows exactly. Have any of you come across any details? Brigitte? Obviously you like to research such things."

Brigitte gazed at her, seeming startled she'd finally referred to the day they met in the library. Brigitte shook her head. "Not many I want to recall. I read that they raped her, bit off her breasts, and cut out her entrails. Yet they tried to keep her alive so she'd suffer. Evidently, they hated Marie Antoinette and took their feelings out on the princess, her supposed lover. Royal gay bashing."

The fierceness in Brigitte's tone and the agony in her eyes revealed Brigitte's distress, and Eva realized she'd added some black humor to cover her disgust. Brigitte had shown herself able to deal with gore readily, so evidently something else bothered her. Eva sighed. Maybe she'd learn the secret later in the week. One thing was certain—Brigitte really was interested in the women of Paris. How nice they had something like this in common.

She resumed her story. "The pamphleteers, who were the paparazzi of the day, took full advantage of each famous victim of the French Revolution in order to sell their scandal sheets."

Even Ryan looked like he disapproved of the way certain members of the media abused their power to form people's opinions. This group was much more responsive than any she'd led so far. She could do this. She motioned for the driver to leave the site of La Force, and they pulled out into the swirling traffic just behind a huge blue-and-white tour bus that lumbered in front of them for a while. "I doubt if we'll ever know the truth, but I did find a reputable account of a clerk who actually inventoried the contents of the princess's pockets. So at least the crowd didn't carry her maimed body naked through the streets."

Leigh frowned. "I doubt that mattered much to her at that point."

"Exactly." Eva nodded. "However, the clerk does say her head was missing, so the crowd probably stuck it on a pike and paraded it around as a victory sign. Supposedly they even carried it by the prison cell of Marie Antoinette in the Temple and held it high so she could see it."

Emily and Clover sighed again as they pulled away from the curb, and Brigitte said, "Marie Antoinette reportedly fainted when she heard what had happened to the princess."

Eva turned around to face the women. "Yes, but most sources say she refused to look out the window of the Temple prison as the mob paraded her severed head past it."

Silence filled the bus for a few moments until Emily said quietly, "It's hard to imagine such outrageous behavior, given our civilized society today."

Clover nodded, but Brigitte winced and spoke up. "Not if you live where I do."

Eva wanted to ask Brigitte to elaborate, but Brigitte seemed so upset that Eva merely nodded again and turned back around. Brigitte looked like she was taking some of her private time, here in the bus, and Eva would respect that.

What was going on in Brigitte's head, which thankfully was still very much attached to her sumptuous body? Maybe they could spend some time together so Eva could find the answers to some of her questions about this mysterious American.

Chapter Thirteen

All these prisons were making Brigitte's head spin, so she tapped Eva on the shoulder as they drove through the sloshy streets and asked her to help distinguish between the sites they'd just visited. When she touched Eva, her fingers tingled and Eva jumped. Odd. They were both as on edge as if they were the ones headed to jail. Or maybe it was something else.

What was going on between her and Eva? Could they be attracted to each other?

She had a difficult time digesting Eva's physical response. The idea of feeling anything meaningful for Eva confounded her. They didn't have much in common except their admiration for the women of Paris, their love of research, their enjoyment of jazz…Well, maybe their reaction wasn't so strange. But Brigitte wanted to find someone who *liked* her instead of antagonized her the way Eva had—until today.

She barely registered Eva's no-doubt detailed catalogue of the different palaces and prisons, ending with, "…and we'll be able to tour the Conciergerie, which is our next stop, after lunch."

Good. She needed a break from the roller-coaster feelings that listening to Eva and being so near her were causing, and she was starving.

They ate at a small, expensive café near Notre-Dame cathedral, where Brigitte sat back and observed how easily Eva talked with the others. Eva was very attractive, and as she held her glass of pinot noir to her lips, Brigitte had a sudden urge to take Eva's plump lower lip between her teeth and taste it.

But she ordered another glass of merlot instead.

By the time they reached the Conciergerie, she felt warm and content, despite the cold rain pelting them as they drove up to the huge gray building. But her mood instantly changed. The medieval towers loomed over her like giants wearing gray-slate dunce caps, their mottled brown-stone exterior magnifying the gloom of the day.

Once they were inside, Eva took charge. "When the members of the royal family were imprisoned in the Temple, they were constantly exposed to damp, cold conditions, but the Conciergerie was much worse," she said as she led them down a narrow corridor. She explained that some of the royal family members became ill in the Temple, especially Marie Antoinette's son, who was sickly anyway. "But Marie," she said, "suffered even more than before from the harsh conditions, as you can imagine just by being here." She explained that the royal family had been able to live together in the Temple, unless a hateful jailer kept them apart temporarily. They'd even had a maid, books, writing material, decent furniture, and some privacy. "Here," Eva said, "Marie was isolated in the small cell you'll see in a minute."

As they entered a claustrophobic hall, quite a change from the openness of Marie Antoinette's elegant Trianon and farm-like hamlet, Brigitte shivered. She suddenly longed for the summer heat of New Orleans and the warmth of Rosa's smile. Eva's voice began to fade into the distance.

Brigitte touched the cold wall of the hall they walked through and then found herself forced to bow her head in order to walk through a low door. A rough-looking man sneered at her, and a deep sense of mourning filled her. Her husband was gone, beheaded, and the new French government had taken her beloved son and sent him to live with a shoemaker.

She examined her loose-fitting black dress, made of a much-cheaper fabric than she was accustomed to, and ran her hand through her hair. It was unaccountably thin, and the lock of it she drew in front of her was white, though it didn't feel powdered. Ugh. It was filthy, and something crawled in it, making her want to claw at her scalp. She blinked—she could see out of only one eye! What had happened to her, and where was she?

Coins clinked, and she looked up with blurry vision at two leering men who stood outside staring at her through her barred door. They moved on after an eternity, and then a vile-looking couple gawked at her through her open door. She felt like one of the wild animals the nobility customarily kept for entertainment and spectacle. The couple taunted her, yet finally left her alone. Hopefully the wretched viewing hours had ended.

She coughed—or, rather, hacked—repeatedly, which made something gush from between her legs and trickle down them. Rather than embarrass herself by letting what she knew instinctively was blood stream onto the floor, she tottered to one of the two rickety chairs in the small room. At least her dark dress wouldn't show the stains, and she had a window to look out of, a crucifix on her wall, and a prayer book.

After she regained a little strength, she wet a rag in her stone water basin and retired behind her privacy screen to attempt to clean the sticky mess from herself. Then, exhausted, she trudged to her small trestle bed and lay down in her tiny kingdom. Only her plum-colored, high-heeled slippers, which rested at the side of her lumpy bed, remained—her sole reminder of her once-extravagant wardrobe.

As the light faded in her cell, the prisoners in the ones nearby began to moan, their groans keeping her awake. At least she had a bed and a blanket. The other prisoners slept on straw and used it to cover themselves. She'd once had a life of extreme luxury, but now it had ended. Oh, how she missed her poor Louis, *and her two remaining children, and her faithful Lamballe.*

"Modern scholars believe Marie Antoinette may have had uterine cancer."

Brigitte shook her head at the sound of Eva's voice, trying to refocus. She glanced around the small, dark cell in which she and the rest of their group stood.

Damn, she'd slipped into the thoughts of Marie Antoinette so completely, for a few minutes she'd almost become her. Why couldn't she control her fantasies like she used to? Her vivid dream about Simone seemed to have affected her in a drastic way, let loose a coping mechanism she'd always been able to use for her own purposes.

She trembled. What a terrible place to stay. How Marie Antoinette must have suffered. She gripped the cold stone wall to steady herself.

Eva stopped talking long enough to glance at her with a mixture of alarm and concern.

Wonderful. Brigitte shook her head once more. Now she'd set Eva off again. And they'd been getting along so well.

❖

Every word Eva tried to roll up her throat and out of her mouth seemed like a boulder that might fall back down and crush her internally. She tried to describe how horrible the conditions here in this stone cell had been for Marie, but she couldn't think of anything but her father's eyes aimed at her during lunch.

Why hadn't she remembered that café was one of his favorites? Was she purposely putting herself in his way? But by now he and her mother should be enjoying themselves away from the hot, crowded city.

Seeing him there with one of his *women* had unleashed murderous thoughts about him. Why wasn't he at the seashore with Mother, like he was supposed to be? He must have driven her there and dumped her. But he was definitely back in Paris and had sat there smoking, his eyes constantly flitting over at Brigitte.

Thank God he didn't seem to have seen Eva. She hadn't greeted him because she didn't want to be forced to introduce him to any of her group, especially the alluring Brigitte, who was just his type. And she certainly didn't want to meet the woman he was with. Oh, he and Ryan would have seen eye to eye immediately, and she'd have gladly sent them off together. But she didn't trust him around any woman.

To make things worse, Brigitte had just zoned out again, like she had in Marie Antoinette's bedchamber at Versailles. Did she have an aversion to bedrooms? Eva should have felt like laughing at her own idea, but she didn't. Instead, she stood there heaving words from her throat and trying to lob them at those few members of her group who appeared to be listening.

She should have been excited to be here in this ancient, revered building. Someday she hoped to serve here as part of the Bar Council.

She'd have to spend long apprentice years as a lawyer before that. Maybe eventually she'd become a member of the French Court of Cassation, the highest court in the land. She'd have more prestige than her father, who'd sold out by accepting a lucrative job as a corporate lawyer.

She stopped and caught a breath. Here she was, in a narrow cell, trying to leverage words out of her mouth for a tiny audience, yet she dreamed of being a member of the highest court in France. How ridiculous. If Brigitte would just shake herself out of her stupor, return from wherever she'd gone, and show even a flicker of interest in the presentation, maybe her words would stream out like they had yesterday afternoon at the hamlet.

But why did she let Brigitte have such an effect on her? It was almost stronger than her father's power over her, and she resented both of them.

Emily and Clover seemed focused on her, their eyes kind. Leigh and Ryan appeared restless, occasionally walking over to the one window in the gray cell or staring at the meager furnishings, but they did seem to be covertly listening. However, Brigitte stood near the bed like a stone, apparently caught up in her own inner drama. In other words, she was bored, even though she'd refused to admit it even when Eva had questioned her directly yesterday. Well, she'd merely asserted her own rights, not commented on Eva's ability to maintain her interest.

If Brigitte were like this consistently, it wouldn't bother Eva so much. She'd write Brigitte off and concentrate on the other members of the group. But yesterday afternoon and this morning, Brigitte's careful attention and probing questions had made Eva toss words around like pebbles skipping over the surface of a lake.

She needed to learn to ignore Brigitte's mysterious disappearances and disregard her as a viable member of the tour. But that meant she'd have to also ignore her vibrant presence, her questions that sparked Eva's brain like steel on flint.

She gazed out the window at the rain that had started to pepper down. It was time to head to Revolution Square, where Marie Antoinette's story ended. If only the entire tour were scheduled to end today. Brigitte's erratic behavior was driving her crazy.

❖

As the group filed onto the street outside the Conciergerie, the sight of the sun beginning to peek out mitigated some of the chill Brigitte had experienced in Marie Antoinette's cell and helped her return to her normal self. They paused there on the street and huddled together, looking back at the grim building as Eva described the final stage of Marie's life.

Eva spoke so quietly Brigitte had to strain to hear her, and she appeared so upset and almost defeated that Brigitte wanted to grasp her arm and reassure her that the tour was going just fine. She wanted to explain to Eva that her presentations didn't bore her, that these unexpected hauntings were preoccupying and worrying her. That is, if Eva had even noticed her strange state in the cell.

"They sentenced Marie to death after an hour's deliberation, which was quite long for the time period," Eva said.

"What on earth did they accuse her of?" Clover seemed outraged.

"Conspiracy, treason, and allying herself with the enemies of France both in and out of the country," Eva explained. "But they eventually dismissed several of the charges, including the one that accused her of having sexual relations with her eight-year-old son."

"How ridiculous." Brigitte spoke up, and everyone nodded.

"I agree," Eva said. "Marie stood up to the Tribunal, beginning her defense with these words: *I appeal to all mothers.* She even convinced the market women who despised her that she was innocent on that count."

"Good for her," Clover said.

As Eva told them about Marie Antoinette's final hours, Brigitte looked back at the Conciergerie and envisioned them. Someone had helped the doomed queen down a steep spiral staircase and finally allowed her paper and a pen and ink. Exhausted from her trial, which had concluded late that evening, she wrote a letter to her sister-in-law and, at four thirty in the morning, left a note for her children in her prayer book. Neither was ever shown to the intended recipients, which saddened Brigitte.

Her heart clenched as Eva recited the words of the note. Brigitte had never had children, never wanted them. But clearly Marie

Antoinette was a devoted mother to have written the words they never got to read: *My eyes have no more tears to cry for you, my poor children; adieu! adieu!* Having your mother beheaded would be as difficult as having her desert you as a baby. No. Worse. She could always fly to California and try to reconcile with her own mother. Marie's children had lost her forever.

The breeze cooled by the recent rain gave Brigitte goose bumps as Eva asked, "Would you like to walk the route Marie would have traveled to the guillotine? It's a little more than a mile and a half and would be a fitting way to end our time with the queen."

Ryan glanced down at his shoes; he'd chosen more sensible ones today. Though he nodded reluctantly, Brigitte and the others readily agreed to the plan, so they headed over the bridge from the island where the Conciergerie stood and walked along the Left Bank.

Brigitte strolled alongside Eva, who looked almost gratified when she asked a question. She tried to act extra enthusiastic. It bothered her for Eva to appear so downcast. "So we're returning to the Tuileries, where Marie Antoinette began her horrible downward spiral after leaving Versailles?"

"Yes." Eva glanced at her. "You seem to have mastered the geography of Paris."

She nodded. "I have a lot of spare time and love to wander these streets. They're so full of history."

"I wasn't able to visit New Orleans when I traveled in America. Does it resemble Paris?"

Brigitte grimaced. "In some ways. The street names, the French heritage of many of its residents, the food, the appreciation for the arts. I'd say it's one of the more liberal cities in the US in some ways, but it's much younger and cruder than Paris."

Eva took a deep breath and smiled, her mood seeming to lighten. She appeared sincerely interested in the differences between the two cities. "I'm glad you like Paris so much, though I'm sure New Orleans is worth a visit."

"Yes. A visit. But it can be a difficult place to live and work in. Old streets like these take me into another time, almost another place, and you're helping me paint a much fuller picture of this wonderful city and its past."

Eva flushed. "Why, thank you. I'm still wondering if, at times, my presentations bore you. You never answered my question yesterday at Versailles, but today at the Conciergerie you acted like you did there—almost...absent."

The blood rushed to Brigitte's face and warmed her in spite of the chilly wind blowing across the Seine. She wasn't ready to confide in Eva, but strangely, she was relieved that Eva had observed her lapses of attention and pleased by her concern that something strange was happening to her. The remarks made her feel almost like Eva cared about her, and the very thought transfixed her. "Absent? The queen's drastic change in status overwhelmed me. I have quite an imagination, so don't worry if I seem to get caught up in my own little world at times." She was embarrassed that Eva had perceived her unwelcome fantasies. Had the others noticed too? As always, she was different, though she was trying so hard to be normal. She sped up and joined Emily and Leigh, who were strolling hand in hand.

As they continued along beside the river with its constant boat traffic, she began to worry. She'd thought she'd learned to control herself, but for some reason, here in Paris she couldn't keep herself from suddenly inhabiting the thoughts and feelings of a long-dead person. Hopefully Eva wouldn't say anything to the others about her peculiar behavior. After all, her ability to withdraw from her body had been a real plus during her career in New Orleans. She didn't want it to harm her chances of creating a new life here.

❖

Eva chatted with Clover and Ryan, who was beginning to sweat as they strolled beside the river, filled with barges and sightseeing boats. Clover asked about a pungent-smelling metal *pissoir* that they passed and nodded in seeming surprise after Eva explained that public urinals were common in Europe and kept men from peeing on the sidewalk or in the gutters or the street. Ryan pulled out a cigarette and puffed on it as they walked along, then flicked the butt into the ornate iron grate encircling a tree growing in the sidewalk. Eva was glad none of the women on the tour smoked too. As they finally neared the Place de la Concorde, they all lapsed into silence.

What had just happened with Brigitte? The word *absent* had caused her to react visibly, but Eva didn't know how to interpret her reaction. She'd blushed, half smiled, and obviously lied, then appeared almost frightened before she dashed away. What was going on? Surely she wasn't being coy. Something real was troubling her, and that possibility affected Eva more than it should.

She shook her head. They'd almost reached their final destination for today, so she tried to clear her mind and sped up her pace. After four more days together, she and Brigitte would never see each other again, so she needed to step back and be a tour guide, not a counselor. It was time to bring down the curtain on the first third of their tour.

She gathered the group near the Luxor Obelisk and explained that approximately thirty thousand guards had been stationed throughout the crowd that mobbed the route they'd just taken. Friends had tried to rescue the queen while she was in prison, and the Tribunal that had sentenced her to death were determined that wouldn't happen.

"I bet she had to duck a lot of rotten vegetables and eggs on the way here," Ryan remarked, "if the people had any food to spare." He rubbed his hands together, almost seeming to enjoy himself, until everyone else glared at him. "Hmm. Sorry. But the French people were obviously really angry at her. By the way, how many people were beheaded here?" He lit another cigarette.

There's always one in every group, but Eva threw a few figures from her storehouse of statistics at him. "The estimates range anywhere from thirteen hundred in one month to between eighteen and forty thousand during the entire French Revolution. No one kept exact records." There. That should satisfy him.

Brigitte seemed to have recovered her composure after her sudden retreat, because she asked, "Marie Antoinette would have been able to see Tuileries Palace from here, wouldn't she? What do you think went through her mind as she took her last look around?"

Eva appreciated her intervention. "Reputedly, she acted very calm and dignified and didn't ask for help when she climbed out of the demeaning cart and up the steps to the guillotine." As she pointed to its approximate location she noted that Brigitte was paying strict attention to her words now.

Emily looked around the site with sad eyes. "Marie Antoinette was a lady until the end, wasn't she? If I'd been around back then, I'd have tried to rescue her too. She wasn't guilty of anything but wanting to have a good time and some privacy, though she evidently was quite a spendthrift."

"Aren't we all?" Brigitte murmured, and everyone chuckled.

Eva was grateful for the change in mood. She led them to their waiting van. On the way back to the tour office, even Ryan seemed subdued, which made her think maybe she'd shared the life and death of one of the most famous women of Paris successfully. She looked forward to tomorrow, when they would begin to become acquainted with their next famous figure, George Sand.

Perhaps her work with this group would enable her to communicate effectively with a jury, someday. And during the rest of this week, maybe she could figure out what was wrong with Brigitte and help her instead of constantly alienating her. She felt as noble as the queen had been when she faced death.

After they returned to the office, Eva told her charges, "Don't forget we're leaving at eight in the morning to drive four hours south of Paris. Bring your toothbrush, sleeping clothes, fresh clothes for the next day, and, as always, comfortable shoes. I think you'll enjoy visiting Nohant, George Sand's estate."

She was looking forward to the peace and quiet of the countryside after two days of trekking all over Paris. And maybe the fresh air would help Brigitte cope with whatever her mysterious problem was.

Chapter Fourteen

Eight o'clock! In the morning? Brigitte was worried about how early she'd have to get up to be ready to leave Paris at such an ungodly hour. Why had she signed up for this tour?

When her alarm rang at five thirty, she'd felt like Marie Antoinette being awakened to prepare for her final hours. Well, maybe that was an overstatement, but she wasn't pleased.

By the time she'd showered, carefully applied her makeup, fixed her hair, and pulled on the casual clothes she'd chosen the evening before, it was already seven fifteen. She ate only a croissant at the coffee shop downstairs in the George V, but it took three cups of coffee to wake her from what felt like a bad hangover. By then it was twenty minutes till eight, so she dashed upstairs for her overnight bag. It was so heavy she had to call a bellhop to carry it for her and place it beside her other piece of luggage, then arrange for a cab…and she was late.

The group members were already seated in their idling minibus, and Eva, waiting outside it, glared at her. Damn. If Eva was going to be such a tight ass, why had she signed on to be a tour guide? People were late all the time, especially this early in the morning, and this was supposed to be a vacation, not a job.

The driver left the minibus running and took Brigitte's bags from the cabbie, then finally managed to wedge them into the back on top of everyone else's. Fortunately they hadn't needed to pack as much as she had.

"We're just planning to be gone overnight, Brigitte," Eva muttered, as if to herself. Judging by Eva's appearance, she'd simply run a comb through her hair, jerked on the first pair of slacks she saw, and slung on a shirt. And even then, she looked charming.

"Just because we're going to the country doesn't mean we shouldn't be fashionable," Brigitte murmured back out of spite, just loud enough for Eva to hear her and tighten her upper lip and shoulders like a prissy nun. Only that full, plump lower lip redeemed her in Brigitte's eyes.

To make matters worse, Ryan and Clover had claimed the seats in the very back, with Emily and Leigh in front of them. Damn. Brigitte had wanted to sit in the rear of the bus and perhaps sneak in a small nap or two on their way south, but now she'd have to sit beside or behind Eva. Either way, she'd be forced to pay attention and pretend to participate in whatever discussion or lecture Eva had planned for this morning.

Not that she hadn't enjoyed the tour so far, but when she was sleepy like this she definitely preferred to let her mind wander.

Eva started talking as they wove through a sea of blue, white, and gray cars, with an occasional red or black one for color. "Aurore Dupin was born here in Paris in 1804, just eleven years after Marie Antoinette was beheaded. Many people consider her the first modern liberated woman. When she was thirty-one, she successfully divorced her husband and managed to maintain custody of her children, which was almost unheard of during her day."

Who the hell is Aurore Dupin? Brigitte wondered. How could such a significant figure have escaped her notice?

Eva continued her presentation. "If you're wondering why you've never heard of her, during her life, she was known simply as Aurore, though today we recognize her by her pseudonym, George Sand. She'd already written two famous novels when she was in her twenties and continued to be a prolific, popular author until her death at seventy-one."

That explained it. Some of the information Brigitte had read earlier in the library was coming back to her. George Sand had scandalized Paris by wearing men's clothes because, as she said, they were better made and more comfortable than women's. But had that been before or after she took a man's name?

Brigitte snuggled back into the comfortable plush seat. She'd let Eva worry about that. She was sure Eva would reveal all soon enough.

She closed her eyes and let Eva's words about Sand's great-grandfather being a Polish playboy who fell for an actress wash over her. Perhaps she'd take a nap after all, though all that caffeine should have wired her. Why would Eva think they wanted to know anything about George Sand's great-grandparents?

She focused on the sound of Eva's voice. Sometimes it had a pleasingly deep, rich tone, especially when Eva was discussing a subject she seemed to care about. But right now it sounded almost strident, strained and higher than usual. It was shredding Brigitte's nerves. Why didn't Eva calm down and focus on Sand herself, instead of providing such detailed background information about Sand's childhood spent mostly on her grandmother's elegant country estate, Nohant?

She sat up and stretched her back. The old planation house she'd lived in with her own grandmother had probably been elegant a hundred years ago. But when she was growing up, the carpet on the grand staircase inside was worn almost through. Her grandmother had done everything she could to keep up appearances, but it was never enough.

Eva glanced around at her, gauging her attention level with those blue-green eyes, so Brigitte closed her own eyes while Eva continued to lecture. All right, so she did find it rather interesting that George Sand's grandmother had first married when she was fifteen—a bastard son of Louis XV who died and left her some money—and that she later married a man twice her age, who spent most of her money. Eva's voice quality had lowered a tinge, as if she was beginning to lose herself in her story, forgetting she was onstage.

Brigitte listened more carefully now. She wanted to discover how her own grandmother compared to the great George Sand's. It sounded like they had quite a bit in common.

"Tall, fair, slender, calm, aristocratic," Eva said about Sand's grandmother.

Amazing. Hers had been somewhat similar. Her great-grandfather had owned the plantation and passed it down to her grandmother, even after she married a handsome speculator. Of course, her new husband had squandered her inheritance and sold off most of the surrounding acreage. After he left her and her infant son, her grandmother had managed somehow to pay the taxes and raise her only child, only to have him marry a lower-class woman from New Orleans and then get killed.

Brigitte opened her eyes and gazed out the window at the ivy-covered buildings they were passing. With their dark roofs, cream-colored exteriors, and wooden shutters, most of the structures she saw on their way out of Paris looked similar. Were most people's childhoods similar too? Her mind strayed to her own father. Would her life have been different today if he hadn't been killed when she was an infant?

She came to attention when Eva mentioned that Sand had lived with her parents in Paris until her father died in a riding accident when she was young. Odd coincidence. At least George Sand had known her father for a while.

Then Eva explained how different Sand's grandmother and mother were and how the future novelist had lived with her grandmother in the country more often than with her mother in the city, and Brigitte impulsively put her hand on Eva's shoulder and asked, "What was her mother like?" It was almost as if she were hearing her own life story.

Eva flinched from her touch as if from an electric shock, and Brigitte jerked her hand back, though she'd enjoyed touching Eva. Her shoulder felt strong yet delicate, rather like Eva herself.

"Her mother grew up in poverty and had a fiery temper and a practical approach to life," Eva replied. "Her mother and grandmother hated each other completely, and her mother's visits to the estate usually ended with her leaving in a rage. Sand grew up afraid her mother would forget her."

Brigitte could still hear her own mother and grandmother quarreling on the few occasions her mother had visited from Hollywood. She hurt inside as she remembered how she'd run outside and wandered along the banks of the bayou under the huge overhanging cypress trees every time after her mother left in a rage. Even the mosquitoes that had swarmed her couldn't drive her inside until it was almost dark.

Eva's voice grew deeper, more confident as she described how Sand's grandmother had told her, when she was just thirteen, every despicable thing about her mother she could dredge up, that she was a whore and that no one was sure who Sand's father was.

Brigitte didn't want to interrupt again and draw attention to her personal interest in this story, but she couldn't keep quiet. She whispered, "Did she turn against her mother and side with her grandmother after that?" She shot a furtive glance at the others. It was almost as if she and Eva were having a private conversation now. The rest of the group members had either closed their eyes or were staring out the window. Would Eva understand if she confided in her about how similar her childhood was to this famous woman's?

"She sided with her mother, even though they rarely saw each other," Eva said. "This pattern is reflected throughout her life, when she supported the commoners against the nobility and did everything she could to defend the underdog in her writings." Then she lapsed into silence.

Brigitte gazed at well-kept farmland and an occasional château in the distance as they sped south, trying to let the constant road noise and steady hum of the motor of the minibus calm her. She'd never forget her own grandmother telling her when she was a teenager: *Your mother is no better than a prostitute.*

Those words had felt like acid dripping on her heart. If Sand had been as hurt, no wonder she'd favored her mother over her grandmother. During the rest of their trip to George Sand's country home, Brigitte thought about how that one sentence had scarred her for life.

Chapter Fifteen

"Oh, no," Eva told the hotel clerk. "I specified four rooms, not three. Don't you have another one?"

"Sorry, but your reservation here at La Petite Fadette is for only three rooms." He held out his reservation book. "See. Here it is. And now we're completely full."

"Someone must have made a mistake. Let me speak to your manager."

"A thousand pardons, but I *am* the manager. If I could change the situation, I would do so gladly. But my hands are tied. You will, however, find a nice fruit basket and a bottle of wine in each of your rooms in recompense."

She shrugged. "Thank you. Since we're staying only one night, I suppose we can manage."

"At your service. Here are your room keys," he said, then turned to the couple standing in line behind her.

She hurried back to the waiting minibus, where the members of her tour group were milling around on the gravel driveway outside it.

"Bad news, I'm afraid, Brigitte. You and I'll have to share a room tonight. There's been a mix-up."

Brigitte appeared distracted. She'd been staring at the estate next door, as if she could hardly restrain herself from walking over to it. "That'll have to do, I suppose," she said. "I hope I don't snore—or that you don't."

Brigitte seemed to be in a strange mood, but at least she hadn't objected to the new sleeping arrangements. And maybe this would give them the chance to really talk.

❖

"George Sand's grandmother bought this estate the year Marie Antoinette was beheaded," Eva said as they finally stood in front of the Château Nohant. Two stories tall, it stood like a solid taupe castle. Columns of stone worked into the surface reinforced its severe appearance, and only the white shutters on its numerous windows made it seem welcoming.

Brigitte laughed to herself. Her grandmother would have felt right at home here.

According to Eva, the solidly built house made Sand's grandmother feel safe. Brigitte's grandmother had had similarly strong feelings about her plantation. She'd grieved because she couldn't afford to have her house repainted as often as it needed it. At the time Brigitte had thought her grandmother was being silly, but that old house must have embodied the values she saw slipping away. In fact, as a child, Brigitte had enjoyed running a fingernail down the big white columns on the front porch and stripping off the slivers of paint that curled up in the hot Louisiana sun. It was like peeling the bark off a crepe myrtle tree. Her grandmother had spanked her several times before she'd left the paint alone.

"Sand's grandmother died and left her this estate," Eva said, "and when she lived here, she opened it to the artistic giants of the day: novelists Balzac and Flaubert, the painter Delacroix, and musicians Liszt and Chopin."

Brigitte's mind was wandering, so she stayed as far away from Eva as she could so she wouldn't upset her if she had another weird psychic experience. How different Sand's adult life had been from hers. She gazed around, wishing she could have been one of the famous guests invited to stay here. How thrilling that would have been. After her grandmother died, Brigitte had sold the run-down plantation. Now she didn't even know if the new owners had torn it down or restored it. Perhaps visitors were touring it right this minute, speculating on its past occupants. *A well-known call girl from New Orleans was its last owner*, she could hear the guide whispering to tourists with a gleam in her eyes.

But all that lay behind her. She followed Eva through the large living room where so many famous figures had gathered. Then they toured the spacious kitchen and climbed the stairs. "This was George Sand's bedroom," Eva pointed out, "and there's the suite she had soundproofed for Chopin to compose in."

Sand had obviously known love, even if it hadn't lasted a lifetime. Brigitte ran her hand across the author's writing desk. Why couldn't she find someone who would take her to the emotional heights George Sand had obviously conquered?

But Sand, despite her numerous romantic affairs, had reputedly never had a lasting relationship with a man either. Had her numerous affairs ultimately been as unsatisfying as Brigitte's professional life? How could Brigitte avoid such emptiness?

❖

"What did you do this afternoon after we toured the château?" Eva asked her group as they ate dinner in the hotel restaurant.

"Leigh and I walked through the grounds and admired the flowerbeds and vegetable gardens," Emily said. "In fact the flowers on all the tables here are probably freshly picked." She took another bite of her pâté and smiled with clear delight.

"And the fresh salad they just served that group over there most likely came straight from their vegetable gardens," Leigh said. "This place is a real jewel, Eva. Emily and I plan to come here for a longer stay next year."

"What's the main course?" Ryan asked as he eyed the dish the waiter had just placed in front of a guest at a nearby table. "I worked up an appetite inspecting the outbuildings with Clover."

"If you like fish and potatoes, I think you'll enjoy this dish. It's called *brandade de lieu* and contains a lot of cream along with the broiled fish and potatoes."

"I should be gaining weight," Clover said, "eating all these rich sauces. But I suppose we're getting more than enough exercise to prevent that from happening."

"Sorry I'm late." Brigitte slid into the empty chair next to Eva. "Nice. Limoges china and crystal vases full of roses."

For a change, Brigitte's tardiness didn't bother her. She smiled indulgently as Brigitte took a bite of pâté. "We've been discussing what we did this afternoon after the tour of the house."

Brigitte took another bite, then lowered her fork. "I walked up the road toward a nearby village, to the spot where George Sand's father supposedly had his riding accident and died."

"How did you know where it happened?" Clover asked. Eva wondered too.

Brigitte looked resolute. "I just knew. And I read everything I could about it in the information in the hotel lobby before I left here."

Eva half listened to the conversation that picked up again after a lull. Brigitte didn't explain why she'd gone off on her own, and Eva didn't ask. She simply ate her dessert in silence. She'd ask Brigitte about it later, perhaps when they were alone in their room. Another mystery about her soon-to-be roommate.

As she finished her fruit and cheese, she felt slightly breathless. Had the sharp yet sweet flavor of her dessert made her feel so giddy with pleasure? Or was it the thought of sharing a room with Brigitte? No, it couldn't be that. But she had to be honest with herself. She couldn't ignore the fact that she'd already spent more time and energy thinking about Brigitte than she'd ever done with anyone else. She was obviously attracted to her and maybe even willing to risk asking if she felt the same.

As Eva wiped her hands on her white linen napkin, a bit of information about George Sand as a child tickled the edges of her mind. Though some people found it strange that such a young girl would sit for hours and simply stare into space, her mother had always insisted she was simply a dreamer and not to worry about it, because that was her nature. Maybe that type of tolerance—no, respect and acceptance—had made Sand prefer her mother to her grandmother.

Perhaps Brigitte was like that too. Once again, she resolved not to take Brigitte's strange lapses of attention personally and also to try to have an intimate conversation with her tonight.

❖

After they finished eating, Brigitte strolled to the lake and skimmed through one of George Sand's pastoral novels, *La petite Fadette*, which she'd picked up in the hotel lobby. It focused on the fairy-tale story of a girl, deserted by a disreputable mother and reared by a wicked grandmother, so of course she had a hard time putting it down. The heroine finally found true love, which made Brigitte hope she could do the same. And after sitting out there and reading by the quiet lake, so unlike the constant noise and confusion of New Orleans and Paris, she felt rejuvenated as she wandered back to the hotel.

Now she sat in front of the mirror attached to the antique dressing table in the room she and Eva were sharing. Behind her now, Eva spoke in a rather shaky voice. "So, how are you enjoying the tour so far?" She sounded almost nervous. Why on earth would she be, unless…

Had Eva been staring at her with lust just now? Brigitte had caught the barest glimpse of her in the mirror as she'd crossed from the door to her single bed next to the wall. Unless Brigitte was imagining things—which was certainly possible after the strange visions she'd been having lately—Eva had looked like she wanted to walk up and put her arms around her. She couldn't decipher Eva's expression, but she'd definitely felt some strange energy coming from her. Interesting.

"Oh, the tour's fine." Where had she put her jar of Vaseline? She tried to ignore her suspicions about Eva being interested in her as she rummaged around in her overnight bag, finally locating the container.

"Just fine?" Eva's voice resonated with disappointment. Evidently she wanted to have a real conversation, and one-word responses wouldn't cut it.

Brigitte unscrewed the lid of the small jar, slid her index finger into the opaque, sticky substance, and rubbed it across her right upper eyelid. She couldn't let Eva know how nervous even the possibility of being desired made her. But wasn't this what she wanted? The possibility of a real relationship, finding love? Life was confusing.

She half turned toward Eva, who sat cross-legged on her bed, appearing dejected yet determined. Eva had spent less than five minutes brushing her teeth, splashing water on her face, and pulling on lightweight shorty pajamas. It must be nice to look beautiful in such a short time. Eva was so appealing sitting there like a fresh-faced schoolgirl, Brigitte conceded that she could be attracted to her.

"I'm enjoying the tour a little better than fine, I suppose." Brigitte turned away again and concentrated on herself in the mirror, beginning to remove her heavy eyeliner and eye shadow with her Kleenex. What was the use of encouraging Eva? This was a one-time situation. They'd be back in Paris tomorrow and would never see each other after this weekend, when the tour ended. Besides, much of the time Eva didn't seem to even like her. Eva had probably given her that look a few minutes ago only because they were alone together in a romantic setting.

Brigitte relented, though. "Seeing all the places associated with Marie Antoinette's life and death made her story seem a lot more real than reading about it. But hearing about George Sand's childhood and actually being here at Nohant…" She refolded her tissue and wiped the remaining black and brown gunk from her eye. Then she applied Vaseline to her left eyelid, and when she gazed at herself in the mirror, she looked at the reflection of Eva in it.

Eva shifted on the bed and coughed, seeming eager for Brigitte to say more. And when she pulled her bed pillow onto her lap and wrapped her arms around it, Brigitte felt drawn toward her.

She tried to decide whether she should say what was on her mind. She glanced Eva's way again. "It's just that I see so many parallels between my life and Sand's. I haven't read everything about her—just skipped around. You're filling in a lot of gaps." Good. She hadn't said anything very revealing. That was enough. "What you said earlier about the differences and the conflict between her mother and her grandmother brought back a lot of unpleasant memories I'd rather not talk about right now. I need to sort them out. Do you mind?"

"Actually, I do," Eva said. "I know you must be tired, but something about you has puzzled me since we met."

That wasn't the response Brigitte had hoped for. She cleaned the other eyelid and gazed at the results. She looked naked, ugly without her eye makeup. Could she expose herself emotionally as well? Still speaking to Eva's reflection, she asked, "And what's that?"

Eva sat up a little straighter on her bed. "Are you really a widow?"

Brigitte pulled out a small bottle of astringent before she spoke. Another surprise. "Why do you ask?"

"Oh, it's just a feeling. Somehow you don't seem like you've ever been married."

"A *feeling*? How do I seem?" Damn Eva. She was getting too close.

Eva unclenched her pillow and put it to one side. "Like a woman with an unconventional past. I'm a lesbian, and I'm attracted to you in a way that tells me you're one too."

Brigitte gasped and turned around. What the hell? She stared at Eva directly now. She'd certainly underrated her courage. Brigitte took a deep breath. "I just might be one. In fact, I probably am, but I haven't spent much time exploring that side of myself."

Eva reached for the pillow beside her again, but before she had a chance to protect herself with it, Brigitte said, "If you really want to know, I told the group I was a widow because I didn't want to let them know what I used to be."

Eva stopped mid-reach. "And what was that?"

Brigitte hesitated, but Eva had asked for it. "A very well-paid prostitute."

Eva's top lip pulled tight, and Brigitte was immediately sorry she'd opened her mouth. "Please don't tell anyone in the group. I'm here in Paris to start over."

❖

The harsh alcoholic smell of the astringent Brigitte was using on her face stung Eva's nose almost as much as the word *prostitute* did. The news numbed her, but she'd try to think through that revelation later. It was too much to comprehend on the spot. Right now, however, she didn't want to miss this chance to find out more about Brigitte.

"You have my word." But could she accept Brigitte for who she was? For who she'd been? She forged ahead. "Why did you want to see where Sand's father had his fatal riding accident?"

Brigitte lowered the wet tissue from her cheek. "Because mine was killed in a fight while he was gambling in New Orleans. I was just a baby."

Eva's throat constricted with compassion. At least her father was still around, though a lot of times she'd wished he wasn't. "So you never knew him."

"No. Only through the idealized descriptions of him my grandmother kept up until her dying day. According to her, he was perfect until he fell for my mother and had to marry her because she was pregnant."

"So I take it that your grandmother and your mother didn't get along very well."

Brigitte crumpled her tissue and dropped it into the wastebasket beside the dressing table. "That's an understatement if I ever heard one. They despised each other." She screwed the cap on her bottle.

Eva couldn't believe Brigitte was opening up so much, but she couldn't stop herself from asking questions. With her face stripped bare, Brigitte was even more beautiful than she was fully made up. Eva suppressed her urge to walk over, throw her arms around Brigitte, and kiss her senseless. Brigitte seemed to want to keep some physical distance between them, but Eva had never felt closer emotionally to anyone than she did right now.

"Mother was in town for Christmas," Brigitte said suddenly, as if reliving the experience. "It was her yearly visit, and I was fifteen. I didn't know whether to be as enchanted by her as I had been when I was younger or to believe only a fraction of what she said."

"Why wouldn't you believe her?"

"Why do you think? Grandmother had poisoned my mind against her for years, and I didn't know who to side with." Brigitte rammed her bottle of astringent back into her makeup bag.

Eva tried to calm her. "That makes sense. What happened that Christmas?"

"It was the night before Christmas, and we were in the kitchen. Mother asked if we'd seen the movie *Singin' in the Rain*."

"That was a reasonable question," Eva said.

Brigitte's smile was tight. "I thought so, but Grandmother said, *We don't have the time or the money to go watch frivolous musicals*. Those were her exact words. I'll never forget. All the light went out of Mother's face, like she'd been slapped."

"Rather judgmental, eh?"

"Yeah." Brigitte looked like she'd eaten something rotten. "That's another understatement. Then she told us that she was in five scenes in that movie and even got to say one line."

"How exciting. I bet your mother was thrilled and couldn't wait to tell you about it."

"That's what I thought too. But Grandmother just stood there at the stove stirring a big pot of dirty rice and reiterated that we couldn't afford to go see movies. She was using every penny she had to send me to a private school, so we had to keep ourselves on a strict budget."

Eva lay down on her side, keeping her eyes on Brigitte. "I bet that set your mother off."

"You better believe it. She wanted to know why I couldn't go to a public school instead of wasting money on a snobby Catholic one. I can still see Mother sitting at the kitchen table painting her fingernails. She said I needed to find out what the world was really like instead of having nobody but Grandmother and the nuns for company."

"Why would she say that?" Eva asked. "Surely you had friends."

Brigitte reddened slightly. "I'd told her earlier that the girls at my school were all rich and wouldn't have anything to do with me."

"That sounds about right. Kids can be so cruel."

"Yes, and I really appreciated her standing up for me. Growing up without friends, especially as a teenager, is hard."

Eva nodded. "You must have felt pulled between your mother and your grandmother."

"You can say that again. Mother had left Grandmother to feed and house me all those years, and it sure didn't help when Mother said that if we were really so broke, she'd give us the price of a movie ticket."

"Uh-oh."

"I remember Grandmother slinging down her wooden spoon and spinning around to face Mother. She demanded to know where Mother got all her money to throw away on trash like that. She was in full high-and-mighty mode, like she usually was when Mother visited, so I left and went to my room."

"Oh, Brigitte. That's terrible. Especially at Christmas."

Brigitte put away the rest of her toiletries. "That was my life. As soon as my grandmother died a few years later, I went to live with someone who cared for me and wanted me with her, and that's how I got into my line of work. End of story." She climbed into bed and clicked off her bedside lamp.

Eva lay there stunned. She'd had questions, and Brigitte had answered them. Wow. What could she say to all that? "Good night, Brigitte. Thanks for confiding in me." Dumb. But with all the feelings Brigitte had provoked in her, that's all she could come up with.

"Good night, Eva. Thanks for listening. I hope we can be friends after this."

Eva's throat was too full to respond, so she merely said, "Of course we can." Surely they could be that, and maybe something more.

Chapter Sixteen

Eva rose with the sun. After pulling on her fresh outfit and creeping down the hall to the bathroom, she tiptoed downstairs. There she discovered a silver thermos of coffee just outside the breakfast room. As she laced her steaming coffee with sugar and cream, a rare indulgence for her, she recalled her last sight of Brigitte this morning.

Brigitte had been lying on her back, and her untouched skin had looked as rich and smooth as the heavy cream swirling around in Eva's cup right now. Why would Brigitte want to cover such beauty with makeup? Eva had reached out to stroke her cheek this morning before she realized what she was doing and jerked her hand back. Brigitte was obviously a very private person, and she didn't want to catch her off guard. Last night might have been a once-in-a-lifetime moment.

A prostitute. The word still shook her every time it rang through her head like someone hitting a gong. That was the last thing she'd expected. Brigitte wasn't a widow. Check. She might be a lesbian. Check. She'd never known her father, and her grandmother and her mother despised each other. Check again.

But a prostitute! Of course, now it made sense. Her polished beauty, her imperious ways. She was larger than life, which was one reason Eva had suspected that she'd never been married. Not that married women couldn't be strong women, but too often women married to gain power from their male partner or to be the proverbial power behind the throne. But that usually backfired and they ended up giving all their own power away. However, Brigitte didn't seem like she'd need to gain power from anyone outside herself, except maybe from another woman whom she could consider her equal.

Still stunned, Eva shook off her observations about Brigitte. She needed some air, so she grabbed several pieces of bread from a nearby basket, evidently left over from dinner last night and intended for guests who wanted to feed the birds.

As she strolled down pebbled paths past rose-covered arbors and an herb garden, their amazing fragrance soothed her. How could she reconcile the disgust she felt for her father and his frequent liaisons with his women with her—yes—admiration for Brigitte?

Eva wandered into an English-style park and sat on a concrete bench under some trees near a lake. The wind felt cool as it blew across the water, and various waterfowl fed along the shoreline, twittering and tweeting. France was so beautiful, a much better place to live than any of the countries she'd visited during her lengthy trip around the world.

She stared at the surface of the lake for quite a while, replaying her frank conversation with Brigitte, until a pair of white swans glided into view. Their beauty made her catch her breath, so she got up and slowly walked toward them, crumbling the bread in her hand as she approached.

"Hello there." She addressed the swans as if they were her best friends, and they eyed the bread she held. "You're as beautiful as Brigitte, and you know it, don't you?" She held out a bit of bread and one of the pair grabbed it instantly.

"Are you magic swans, appearing out of nowhere to answer all my questions?" she asked, then looked around to make sure no one was nearby. If they heard her they'd think she was crazy.

As the swans floated lazily in front of her, eyeing the bread, she said, "I have only one burning question for the pair of you. Okay?"

They seemed to nod, though her imagination was obviously working overtime. "Can I accept the fact that Brigitte has been a prostitute yet condemn my father for being attracted to women in the same profession?" she asked.

The swans didn't make a sound.

"You're named mute swans for a reason," she said as she threw each one a bite of bread.

"Let's try again. What's the difference between Brigitte and Father's women? And what's the difference between him and me?"

The swans dipped their orange beaks in the water as if taking a drink.

"You two aren't much help."

Eva couldn't believe she was being so fantastical. Brigitte's odd mannerisms had to be rubbing off on her, but she shrugged. "Okay. Let's change the subject slightly. Why is Brigitte so caught up in her appearance when she's truly beautiful without all that makeup?"

The swans floated toward each other and put the tips of their beaks and their throats together to form a heart, their white bodies shining against the blue water tinted pink by the early morning sun. After staying in that position for a few seconds, they separated. Then, seeming tired of her foolishness, they took one last bit of bread, turned their backs on her, and swam away.

Eva stood watching them and thinking about her future. She wanted to help the needy people of France, especially the poor women and children who couldn't defend themselves. If she could do that as a lawyer and find a woman to fit with her, someone she could form a heart with like these two swans just had, she'd be content. But she was a long way from achieving either goal. She'd just learned some major truths about the woman who'd captivated her more than anyone she'd ever met.

"But can I accept those truths?" She still spoke to the swans, though they were far away now, swimming toward the sun.

As the swans disappeared from sight, Eva tossed the rest of the bread to a nearby flock of ducks. And could she live with those truths if she and Brigitte became involved?

❖

Eva was finishing her third cup of coffee when Brigitte came hurrying down the hotel stairs into the restaurant. The others had completed breakfast and were about to go up to pack before they visited George Sand's grave and the small church nearby.

Though Brigitte's makeup was securely back in place, she appeared a little more relaxed than she had so far on the tour. Maybe the country air agreed with her. But perhaps it was because she'd had the courage to share some of her real self. For the first time, Brigitte wore pants—a pair of trousers that zipped up the front—and a loose-fitting plaid blouse buttoned up so high that Ryan didn't give her a second glance.

But Eva did. Brigitte exuded a new confidence. Eva imagined her in control, strong, taking what she wanted and giving pleasure... She felt a pull toward her that was almost too strong to resist.

But Brigitte also seemed somehow younger, and her face didn't appear to be covered with quite as many layers of foundation and powder as usual. The hint of vulnerability made Eva want to wrap Brigitte in her arms.

"Sorry I'm late. I'll just have a croissant and a cup of chocolate. I've already packed," Brigitte said as she sat down at the small table with Eva.

Eva nodded. "I wish you could have tried the French toast. It's delicious."

"Too fattening, though I'd love to indulge myself."

Eva shivered at the double entendre. Was Brigitte teasing her?

Brigitte slowly stirred her chocolate, which their waiter had brought immediately. "George Sand was truly an enigma, especially for her time, wasn't she?"

Eva wasn't sure what she was talking about. She put down her empty cup and wiped the side of her mouth with her napkin. "Are you referring to her dressing like a man, sleeping with whomever she pleased, or what?" She needed to go pack and review her notes for the lectures she'd prepared for the rest of the trip, but she couldn't force herself to move. This was a different Brigitte, and she liked the change.

"Both." Brigitte picked up her spoon and resumed stirring her chocolate. "She was such a mixture of grand dame and street urchin, with a big dose of spirituality thrown in."

"Yes. Attending a convent school as a teenager supposedly helped her reconcile the confusion the conflict between her mother and grandmother must have caused." Eva placed her napkin beside her plate. Maybe she could get some answers to the questions she'd just asked the swans.

Brigitte stopped moving her spoon and whispered, "Having your grandmother tell you your mother was a whore and implying you might be a bastard instead of her flesh and blood had to have affected her as much as it did me. Especially someone as sensitive as she seemed to be."

Obviously Brigitte identified strongly with George Sand, which pleased Eva. If nothing else came of this tour, at least part of it had made a difference in someone's life.

Just then, Clover reentered the breakfast area. "Beautiful morning, isn't it? What time do you want us to meet for our final walk around the grounds?"

Eva tried to shake herself out of her reverie and act like a guide responsible for five people instead of just one. But Brigitte drew her in like the rosemary in the estate's garden called to the bees buzzing around it. She wanted to light on a tiny purple bloom, lick nectar from its depths…No. Time to forget the poetic language. She blew out a long breath. "Nine thirty," she told Clover. "That should give us a chance to visit the grounds and the church, as well as the grave. Then we can load our bags and leave before noon."

Clover grinned and gave them a knowing look. "Sorry if I interrupted something."

Eva shook her head. "Of course not. We were just chatting. I need to do something anyway."

She really did have to go get her lecture notes and review them. Right now, she felt safer sticking to them than swimming into deep, foreign waters with Brigitte.

"See you both at nine thirty, in front of the hotel," she said and almost dashed back up to their room.

❖

Brigitte broke off a bit of her croissant and smoothed a tiny portion of butter onto it. Eva was rather cute, but so uptight. She'd obviously had a privileged upbringing and never had to face much unpleasantness. How had her revelations last night affected Eva?

She'd really been uneasy about facing Eva this morning. When she'd first come awake, she'd thought about how one minute she'd been taking off her makeup and the next she was pouring her heart out to Eva. Funny, but as soon as she'd seen her in the breakfast room this morning, she'd wanted to head to another table and avoid her. She'd felt as shy as a schoolgirl with a crush on a teacher, wanting to be close to Eva yet afraid of how Eva would react to her.

As she stared out the window at the solemn château across the way, she still couldn't believe she'd told Eva all that stuff last night. Talk about feeling vulnerable. It was as if she'd walked into the breakfast room stark naked. But though she'd been apprehensive, she'd also loved how attracted she was to Eva. Who would ever have thought she'd feel this way about her? Giddy, aware of Eva's presence every minute she was in the same vicinity, nervous if Eva was thinking about her as much as she was thinking about Eva. Amazing. Her life had taken a new, exciting turn for the better, thanks to these famous women of the past and especially to Eva.

Brigitte drained her cup of chocolate and glanced at her watch. Two minutes till nine. She'd be on time for a change and surprise Eva.

❖

In their room, Eva pulled a sheaf of notes from her briefcase and riffled through them. Where were the ones she'd prepared for this morning? Surely she'd just overlooked them. No. They weren't here.

She stuck her hand into her briefcase again. Were they in the bottom of it? Finally, she turned it upside down and shook it. Damn. Where were they?

Before they'd left Paris, she'd pulled the folder neatly labeled GEORGE SAND from her file drawer, planning to double-check its contents after everyone arrived. But then Brigitte had been so late, and Eva had become absorbed in that drama and forgotten to make sure all her lectures were there. The ones about Chopin and Liszt and the other famous men in George Sand's life were missing.

She looked around the room. Usually she reviewed her notes the night, or at least the morning, before she needed them. But last night before bed she'd been bowled over by Brigitte's revelations, and this morning she'd spent more time walking around and downstairs at breakfast than she'd planned, again distracted by Brigitte.

She needed to pay attention to her job, not let a beautiful woman make her look like a fool in front of the others. At least she had her notes about Sand's passionate affair with the famous actress Marie Dorval.

Well, she'd simply have to improvise when she talked about Sand's liaisons with all those men. Maybe the group wouldn't notice, though if anyone did, it would be Brigitte. But Eva couldn't think about her any more right now. She had a job to do.

Brigitte made sure to be at the meeting place a few minutes early. Eva appeared uneasy as she gathered the group, but at least she seemed to notice *them* instead of constantly referring to her notes. In fact, she chatted almost conversationally as they all strolled through the landscaped grounds of Nohant one final time, then sat together on stone benches in an out-of-the-way spot.

After Eva finished describing Sand's numerous friends and lovers, she grew uncharacteristically silent. The lull calmed Brigitte and gave her time to come up with several questions. "Who do you think was the love of George Sand's life?"

Eva didn't hesitate. "Marie Dorval."

Brigitte had been so sure the answer would be Chopin, she didn't know what to say. "Why do you think so?" she finally managed to ask.

"She seemed to view Dorval as a kindred spirit, someone who felt as deeply and strongly about the same things she did."

Right now, Brigitte viewed Eva like that. Last night, she'd trusted Eva with part of herself, and so far Eva seemed trustworthy.

Eva continued to talk for a while, sitting beside Brigitte on one of the benches under a tree in the garden. And as Eva spoke, Brigitte began to drift away, like one of the fluffy clouds she was staring at.

Brigitte looked down, startled. She wasn't wearing the loafers and chinos she'd put on this morning. Instead, she had on tight pants and high boots with tassels, and she pulled a top hat off her head.

Instead of sitting quietly under a tree in the country, she stood in a noisy theater to the rear of the orchestra, surrounded by women dressed similarly to her. Many of the men crowded together nearby glared at her and her companions.

"Damn impertinent females," one of the men muttered. "Invading our territory here at Porte Saint-Martin. They need to marry a man and stay shut away like other respectable women. That so-called George Sand is the worst of the lot, *taking a man's name as well as dressing like one.*"

Brigitte sighed, unable to fight the strange sensation that overcame her. Evidently she'd somehow entered the consciousness of George Sand, back in Paris. Instead of fighting her mysterious flight of fancy, she gave in and let it roll through her like a movie.

In the Parisian theater, the curtain opened onstage, and the lead actress spoke. The actual words rushed by Brigitte, but the actress's tone hit her full force. Throaty, with a slight rasp and filled with pure seduction, the voice made the tassels on Brigitte's boots quiver. The perfect diction drove every word the actress spoke straight into Brigitte's heart, filling it to overflowing, like a glass of champagne.

This woman—she quickly glanced at her theater program— this Marie Dorval was expressing emotions that until now had lain hidden inside Brigitte. Each gesture wonderfully conveyed a variety of feelings—anger, surprise, wonder, jealousy. Dorval's emotional range stunned Brigitte so fully that after the performance ended, she pushed her way from the theater and strode home through the streets of Paris, determined to reach her writing desk.

The words poured from her pen, *and she decided to post her letter to Marie Dorval immediately.*

"Oh, our driver's finally here." A hand shaking Brigitte's arm roused her from her trance. Eva was gazing at her with a strange expression—part concern, part exasperation. Brigitte's arm burned from her touch.

Brigitte jumped up and hurried toward the hotel. "I just need to grab my overnight bag from the room. My suitcase is in the lobby."

When she finally reached the room, she splashed water on her face and gazed at herself in the mirror. Had she actually become part of the spirit of George Sand, or had she merely imagined her first glimpse of Marie Dorval? Could Eva be her Marie?

❖

Eva was perturbed. She'd finally overcome her nervousness about speaking without her notes and surprised herself by remembering practically everything she'd planned about George Sand's numerous affairs. But as she'd answered Brigitte's question about the love of Sand's life, Brigitte's eyes had become unfocused, and she'd sat there gazing into the distance like a statue while Eva talked on and on.

This had happened three times now, and Eva wanted to know what was going on. If it were a medical condition, she needed to know in case she needed to help Brigitte somehow. If it was psychological, which Eva suspected it might be, she wanted to try to understand so she could help by not taking these lapses of attention personally and by somehow helping Brigitte through what had to be rather frightening experiences.

Since Brigitte had been so honest about her past last night, Eva felt reasonably sure that she'd open up if Eva approached her with concern instead of anger.

CHAPTER SEVENTEEN

D rop us off at the Montparnasse cemetery, division six," Eva directed the driver as they arrived at the outskirts of Paris late that afternoon. Brigitte glanced at her. This stop wasn't on their itinerary.

In the crowded cemetery Eva led them to an ivy-covered plot, then showed them a metal plaque on a weathered wooden cross that had *Morte de Chagrin* carved on it.

"*She died of sorrow?*" Clover asked.

"I'd interpret that as *a sad death*," Ryan said, and then the rest of them offered their translations.

"I recognize Marie Dorval's name, but who are these other people listed under her?" Leigh asked.

Eva pointed to Georges Luguet first. "That's Marie's grandson, who broke her heart when he died at only four. And the others are her daughter, her son-in-law, and her two granddaughters." Eva gestured toward each name in turn.

"I wonder if they named the baby Georges in honor of George Sand," Brigitte said, and Eva brightened, as if she hadn't thought of that possibility.

"I hope they got along well." Ryan laughed, and took a drag of his cigarette. "This is the most crowded grave I've ever seen."

Eva's tight smile stretched her lower lip and was barely polite. She didn't even acknowledge Ryan's remark. "Evidently, Marie and George Sand had a close connection until Marie died. Sand and Victor Hugo helped Marie financially, and Sand reportedly gave large sums to help support Marie's two granddaughters. One of them lived until about ten years ago."

Brigitte spoke up. "I've seen similar grave markers in some of the old cemeteries in New Orleans." However, she found it hard to imagine her own family being buried in such close proximity to her. Even in death, her mother and grandmother wouldn't have reconciled their differences, and her father? He'd have still been missing in action.

"Hmm." Brigitte studied the date on the weathered stone below the cross—1849, then did some mental math. "Marie Dorval was fifty-one when she died, and George Sand was forty-five." She turned to Eva. "They were friends for sixteen years, weren't they?"

Eva nodded. "Yes. In the beginning they were probably lovers, and evidently they loved each other until the end."

Brigitte sighed. Marie had been almost the same age as Rosa when Sand lost her.

"Listen to this line from one of Sand's early letters to Marie," Eva said. *"There is nothing stronger in me than the need to love."*

The quote resounded like a golden bell in Brigitte's heart. She'd never said anything like that to Rosa or to anyone else, but she could have written it. She'd needed to love her mother and her grandmother, but evidently neither of them had been able to accept her without reservation.

Without Rosa, Brigitte would never have been able to experience the emotions Sand had written about to Marie. Now Rosa was gone, though, and more than ever Brigitte recalled Rosa's final note: *Go to Paris…maybe you'll even find true love there.*

Maybe she would fall in love here. The prospect both frightened and exhilarated her. Was she beginning something with Eva that might eventually lead to love? So far Eva hadn't seemed judgmental after Brigitte's confession last night. That surprised her and made her feel better than anything had in a long time. To love and be loved—what would that be like?

The sun began to set, and a mild breeze drifted among the exposed stones that stretched in solemn rows as far as she could see. She hugged herself. At least Marie Dorval had lived a full, exciting life and ended it with people she loved. Could Brigitte do the same?

Standing there in the setting sun, Brigitte listened to Eva recite another line Sand had written to Marie: *I wish someone loved me the way I love you.* The way Eva said it made it seem as if she could be speaking to Brigitte. She hoped it wasn't just another of her weird experiences.

She caught her breath. She'd been longing for what George Sand and Marie had found in each other for longer than she could remember. But she hadn't recognized her urge until last night. Strange how admitting all those things to Eva had freed her to realize what she really wanted.

Her physical appearance, the lure of raw sex and the power it seemed to give her over men, as well as the lavish lifestyle her profession as a call girl had provided—all these temptations had distracted her until now. She'd been with all kinds of men—old, young, overbearing, shy—all wealthy, all adoring, some even professing love. She'd had sex in every conceivable way, but no one had ever made her feel like Marie and George Sand had for one another. Until last night.

Had Rosa sacrificed herself so Brigitte would be forced to go to Paris to find a soul mate like Sand and Marie had recognized in each other? They both were long dead, their bodies dust or ashes, but their love and passion for one another lived on in their words.

Brigitte gazed at the sunset, and a stray beam of light almost blinded her. Her past life was going down too. Tomorrow the sun would rise and a totally new world would begin for her. If Eva could accept her, maybe together they could discover the type of love Sand and Marie had found. If not, she'd continue to search for it. She deserved it.

❖

Jeanne's apartment was dark as Eva let herself in and dragged herself to her room. She felt like she'd been gone a week instead of only overnight. Being with Brigitte, especially sleeping in the same room with her, learning about her past, and spending so many hours near her in the minibus had drained her.

Usually she could control her emotions, but recently they'd begun to control her, especially when Brigitte was nearby. She unpacked her small bag and lay down on her single bed. Before she knew it, the sound of a door closing awoke her.

"Eva, are you here?" Jeanne called.

Eva struggled to her feet and swiped at her eyes. How long had she been asleep?

"I'm in here, Jeanne," she called. "Be right out." She must have slept longer than she'd realized because suddenly she was ravenous.

"I've been to the movies. How was your trip?" Jeanne held out a wineglass with a question in her eyes.

Nodding, Eva headed to the small refrigerator and pulled out a hunk of cheese. Adding a handful of grapes, a generous slice of bread, and a ripe pear, she sat down at Jeanne's small table and began to eat.

"Fine. Exhausting. Confusing." Where had that last word come from?

Jeanne set a glass of pinot noir in front of Eva and tasted her own. "Hmm. Not bad. Now tell me all about it."

Eva didn't spare a detail about her own growing attraction to Brigitte, though she didn't reveal any of Brigitte's secrets. She wanted to come to terms with them on her own.

Jeanne sat quietly, nodding occasionally and refilling their glasses.

As Eva told her story and devoured her food, Jeanne watched her thoughtfully. At last, she said, "I warned you to avoid becoming involved with your clients. Why haven't you taken my advice?"

Sighing, Eva swept the crumbs from her crusty bread into a small pile. "I can't help myself. Just when I think I can keep my distance from her, Brigitte does something to either infuriate me or intrigue me or endear her to me."

Jeanne didn't say a word.

"When she's aloof and far away, I get so angry I feel like asking her why she doesn't just quit the tour. I'd gladly refund her money at times like that."

"I know what you mean. I've had several clients that made me react like that," Jeanne said.

Eva thought about Brigitte's final question this afternoon at the cemetery about how long Marie and George Sand had been intimate. "Yes, but then she asks a question that makes me realize she's paid attention and considered what I've been thinking about on a deeper level than I have. At times like that my heart aches because of the sadness in her eyes and voice, and I want to be close to her."

As they'd all stood at Marie's grave, Eva hadn't been able to ignore the play of various emotions over Brigitte's face. What had been going on behind that gorgeous façade?

Jeanne swept the pile of crumbs into Eva's plate and carried it to the sink. As she returned she squeezed Eva's shoulder. "Sounds like you may have a problem. Do you want to become involved with her?"

"I'm not sure. I need to find out where she goes during those blank spells she has. I've planned my life, and until now I didn't intend to let anyone derail me." She sat up straighter in her hard-back chair. "I really need to finish school so I can get a position and repay you…and show Father I'm able to take care of myself. I can't stand the thought of asking him for any type of support, financial or emotional."

Jeanne grinned. "Obviously Brigitte has plenty of money. She could be your sugar momma, or whatever the Americans call such a person. You're intelligent, talented—"

"And you're my extremely biased aunt." She touched Jeanne's outstretched hand briefly. "I feel like such a fool. I know next to nothing about the woman, except that she's a wealthy American, so beautiful she makes me catch my breath every time I look at her."

Jeanne's grin widened. "Yes. I can understand that."

Eva slumped slightly. "She opened up to me quite a bit last night, and it was one of the most powerful things I've ever experienced. But I want to make sure that wasn't a fluke. I also want to make sure I can handle being with someone like her." Eva rested her head on both hands and propped her elbows on the table. "What would you do? Are you still interested in her?"

Jeanne stroked her own cheeks with her fingers, her grin fading. "Absolutely not, and I'm not qualified to offer much worthwhile advice. After all, I'm still single." Jeanne stood and returned to the sink, where she began to wash their glasses and utensils. "If I were in your position, I'd probably become politely distant and try to focus on the others in the group. I'd try to mentally discount Brigitte as unavailable and unattainable and will the rest of the tour to pass as quickly as possible."

Jeanne left the glasses to dry and wiped her hands on a cloth. "But that's just me. You're on your own. This isn't a skinned knee I can bandage or a headache I can give you an aspirin for. You'll have to wrestle with it by yourself, and no matter what you decide, you'll learn some valuable lessons from it." She stood next to Eva and rested her hand on Eva's head as if blessing her.

"Gee, thanks, Jeanne." Eva put her hand on Jeanne's briefly. "You're a fountain of wisdom."

Jeanne chuckled. "I warned you I'm no help. You're an adult. You'll have to act like one."

Eva got up, briefly hugged Jeanne, and headed toward her bedroom. "You're right. Brigitte's my problem, so I'll just have to deal with her as best I can. Good night."

As Eva prepared for bed, she was certain she wouldn't get much sleep that night. Her head was as full as her heart, though talking to Jeanne had made her feel better.

❖

Brigitte slowly pulled the false lash from her left eyelid as she examined her smeared makeup and mussed hair in the dressing-table mirror. How long had she been asleep? The brief trip to Nohant had exhausted her.

Tap, tap, tap. The soft knock on the door made her jerk more fully awake, even though she was expecting it. She hurried over to the door. "Who is it?" she whispered.

"It's me, madam. I've brought your sandwich, as you requested."

"Just leave it there outside. I'll take care of your tip tomorrow."

The bellboy's footsteps faded, so she opened the door just wide enough to angle the tray into her room and carried it to her small breakfast table overlooking a street so near the Champs Élysées she could hear the noise of its constant traffic in the distance. Before she opened the curtains she flipped off the lamp she'd been using so no one could see her.

Some of the excitement she'd felt earlier today at the Mont-parnasse cemetery surged through her again as she listened to the faraway hum of voices and cars. It had been almost a century and a half since George Sand had met Marie Dorval, and they'd both been dead a very long time, but the words they'd written to each other when they first met were as alive today as they'd been back then.

How unhappy to lose a day of my life when you could have been there. The phrase from one of George Sand's letters to Marie kept running through Brigitte's head like the melody of a popular song.

She bit into her sandwich. What would it be like to feel such passion for someone, both emotionally and physically? So far she'd never actually felt alive. Instead, she'd tried to numb herself to her constant loneliness by losing herself in books, music, or her imagination. But no more. She'd try to start really living instead of simply existing.

She peeled back the top of her sliced baguette and examined the filling of her sandwich. The ham was thick and tasty, and the ripe tomatoes, lettuce, and sliced hard-boiled egg looked fresh and colorful. Even the mayonnaise smelled good. Delicious.

But how much more delicious it would be to fall as deeply in love as George Sand and Marie Dorval had been.

She finished her meal, shut the curtains, and returned to her dressing table. After she removed the rest of her makeup, she got ready for bed. How could she make that dream come true?

She had absolutely no idea, but maybe after a good night's sleep she could somehow figure it out.

CHAPTER EIGHTEEN

Eva led the members of her group down a street near the busy Boulevard Saint-Michel and stopped in front of a small plaque. Ryan had left a message this morning that Clover wasn't feeling well and they wouldn't be able to make it, so only Emily, Leigh, and Brigitte were here. Eva didn't mind Ryan's absence but hoped Clover was all right. She would miss her quirky remarks. With the sounds of bicycle bells and car horns in the background, she said, "Sarah Bernhardt, born in Paris in 1844 and died here in 1923, was one of the greatest actresses of all time." She pointed at the marker, then swept her arm around the area, indicating the entire neighborhood. "She and her thirteen brothers and sisters grew up in this neighborhood, in poverty."

Being this near the Sorbonne took Eva back to her years as a law student. But she forced herself to stick to her subject matter and told her group that, strangely, Sarah hadn't wanted to be an actress. She'd wanted to be a nun. She glanced at Brigitte, who stood quietly in the small group bunched close to her. Did Brigitte regret confiding in her yesterday? She wrenched her mind back to Sarah Bernhardt and told the group that when Sarah was young, she was too shy to appear in front of an audience. She'd also clenched her teeth when she spoke, so it was hard to understand her.

Emily gazed at her and nodded, as if she understood what it meant to be timid. Eva understood too. She'd been a serious student, reading her assignments and writing every essay her professors required. She'd rarely spoken up in class, and when she did, she'd considered every word carefully before she said it. What kind of student had Brigitte been?

"Sarah Bernhardt's one of my favorite women of Paris, by the way," Eva said. "If she could overcome her shyness enough to become one of the most acclaimed actresses in history, surely anyone can overcome their fear of public speaking."

A sudden understanding sparkled on Brigitte's face, and Eva felt like she'd seen right through her. Wanting to learn to feel comfortable speaking in a courtroom wasn't a crime, but it embarrassed Eva to admit to anyone how much she lacked confidence in that area. Surely Brigitte wouldn't think less of her for being nervous in front of a crowd. Of course getting involved in the student protests a few years ago, and even being arrested, had helped her convince herself she wasn't as timid as she'd always thought.

She jerked herself back to her topic again. She was supposed to be sharing information about France's greatest actress, not thinking about Brigitte and herself. She explained that Sarah's mother had a lot of children and didn't care what Sarah wanted to do. So when one of her mother's admirers, a duke who most likely helped pay Sarah's expenses, recommended that she attend the Paris Conservatory, Sarah's mother readily agreed. Eva glanced at the three women in the group today and said, "And that's why Sarah didn't get to be a nun."

Brigitte had been cooperative and communicative all morning. She'd shown up on time for a change, saying she'd fallen asleep as soon as she returned to her hotel yesterday evening and waked up only long enough to undress and eat a bit. She'd also offered trivial yet intimate details about herself all morning, which pleased Eva. Maybe their conversation in Nohant had helped Brigitte feel more relaxed around her and the group, more accepted. Ryan's absence might have helped too.

Eva led them down the street a bit farther, toward Boulevard Saint-Michel, lined with trees and bookshops. It was crowded with tourists sitting in the sidewalk cafés that dotted it, talking loudly and taking photos. Why they would want to crowd into a hot, noisy city in the summer eluded her. Most of the Parisians who could afford it had already fled to the countryside or the seashore. She stopped her group for a minute. "Sarah's mother was a successful courtesan."

She stole a look at Brigitte, who was listening intently. She hoped the remark hadn't upset Brigitte. She wanted to announce that the mother of one of the most admired women in France had been a prostitute, but look how her daughter turned out. Then it hit her. Not all women of the night were sleazy manipulators, which was the way she'd always viewed her father's women.

Eva explained to the group how Sarah never felt her mother loved her and agreed that she might have been right. Brigitte certainly had to feel like that about her own mother. As they continued their stroll through Sarah's old neighborhood, Eva couldn't stop thinking about what Brigitte had revealed about her feelings for her mother and her grandmother.

She glanced at Brigitte, who was walking beside her, a look of compassion on her face. She could possibly be identifying with Sarah Bernhardt, as she had with George Sand, and the thought warmed Eva. Even she could relate. Mother had always idolized Eva's brother Louis but had never shown much interest in her. So she and Brigitte had that in common, though Eva did have Jeanne, thank God.

The group stopped again, and Brigitte raised her hand instead of blurting out a question, as she usually did, asking what Sarah Bernhardt looked like. "I can't visualize her as young and shy and wanting to be a nun," Brigitte said.

Eva didn't miss a beat. "She was short and skinny, with a pale oval face, blazing eyes, a large nose, and frizzy red-gold hair."

"Not too attractive, eh?" Leigh said. "Though I do fancy short women." She put her arm around Emily and squeezed her shoulder.

Just then a group of laughing teenagers pushed past them and continued down the sidewalk.

Eva nodded, gratified that Leigh seemed to be interested in their discussion too. "No. She was sick a lot and afraid she'd die young, so at fifteen, she bought a silk-lined coffin and slept in it. When she toured worldwide later, she took it with her."

Brigitte had a knowing look. "I thought she did that to get in touch with whatever character she had to play onstage."

"Yes. That was part of it. I'm glad you've done your research, Brigitte. This could almost be a seminar instead of a lecture tour. Much more cozy."

Eva was surprised that her attitude toward Brigitte had changed so completely after their private conversation. Instead of feeling threatened, she was glad to have a companion to bounce information back and forth with. This tour was turning out even better than she'd hoped.

She spotted their van idling in the next block yet paused to describe some of Sarah's methods of really getting into her characters and how she seemed to have willed herself to become a famous actress. "She was so determined to succeed that when the critics gave her bad reviews early in her career, she deserted the Comédie-Française, the premier training place for actors in Paris."

As they hurried along the street now, Emily pulled up beside her. "Why would she do that?"

"She said they didn't give her enough time to rehearse. She blamed them for her subpar performances."

"That was pretty gutsy, wasn't it?" Brigitte said. "I like her even more now."

And with that, Eva ushered them into their waiting van.

As they headed across the Seine toward the area where the Louvre stood, Eva stared out the window at the traffic. It seemed to be so much thicker than it had several years ago. But of course this was summer, and tour vans and buses full of foreigners eager to see her city filled the streets this time of year. Just then, Brigitte tapped her on the shoulder. "I read Bernhardt physically fought with several other actresses on her way to the top. Is that true?"

The question made Eva think of the violence she'd become caught up in during the student protests at the Sorbonne. Twenty thousand students, teachers, and their supporters marching toward the Sorbonne, the police attacking them, paving stones and tear gas flying. She'd never forget that day. Sarah Bernhardt would have fit right in.

"Yes. She was feisty and tough," Eva said. "She slapped one actress here in Paris, near the beginning of her career, and was fired for it. Later, after she became world famous, she slapped another actress in South America and got away with it." Just then they arrived at their destination, and the four of them climbed out of the van.

"Interesting person," Leigh said, as they walked through the doors of the Comédie-Française. "I'd like to have seen her perform. What do you think that was like?"

"Most of the people who saw her said her voice was amazing, like a golden bell." That was one of the things Eva admired most about Sarah Bernhardt. She'd love to be able to speak so beautifully that people would strain to hear her lovely voice.

She led them into the main hall, with its gold trim and high ceiling, and they all stared at the rich decorations. As she motioned toward the stage she said, "Bernhardt performed only in French, and audiences worldwide still flocked to her performances."

"Even if they didn't understand French?" Emily asked.

"Yes. She said that sometimes the sound of the audience turning the pages of the translation books they bought distracted her."

Leigh smiled. "That reminds me of going to the opera in Milan. Remember, Emily, those little books we used to buy so we could follow the libretto in English."

Emily nodded, evidently remembering their shared experience with pleasure. Eva was so glad these two women had joined her tour. "Bernhardt usually played passionate women such as Phaedra and Cleopatra. Her favorite role was the heroine of *Camille*. She was an expert in expressing the emotions of dying women." If Brigitte were an actress, she most likely would have chosen similar roles. She had something tragic about her that attracted Eva, similar to the qualities that must have drawn mass audiences to Bernhardt.

After they finished touring the theater, with its many paintings and sculptures, they all walked to a nearby café for lunch.

They chatted for a while, and then Brigitte abruptly said, "I read that Bernhardt loved costumes so much that when she traveled, she and her entourage carried eighty trunks, with an entire one just for their shoes." Brigitte laughed. "Now there's a woman I can relate to."

Emily glanced at Brigitte shyly, and Leigh slapped her on the back. "Yes. After our trip to Nohant I can see what you mean."

Brigitte looked surprised for a minute, then seemed to relax into the group's newfound camaraderie. "I also read she wore pants even though it was against the law in France to wear men's clothes. She and George Sand were certainly trendsetters."

"But Sarah didn't wear them in public, like George Sand did," Eva said. "She usually did it when she painted or sculpted."

Leigh responded, "You don't say. I didn't know she dabbled in the other fine arts."

"Why, yes," Brigitte said before Eva had a chance to respond. "She was supposed to have been an excellent sculptor. She specialized in portrait busts, which she exhibited in Europe and the States. She also designed dresses, directed a theater company, and supervised the sets and costumes for her productions."

"Amazing. She was quite a woman, wasn't she?" Leigh said.

As Brigitte continued to talk, Eva sat back and relaxed. She really liked this new, vivacious version of Brigitte. She was as intimate and charming now as she'd been distant and off-putting when they'd first met. Maybe Americans weren't so bad after all.

Eva warmed her hands in front of the emotional fire radiating from Brigitte. What incarnation of this strange woman would she encounter next?

❖

Brigitte sipped her merlot as Emily and Leigh shared their impressions of Sarah Bernhardt.

"What an exciting woman," Emily said.

Leigh took Emily's hand and held it gently. "And so strong to have established such a long and successful career as an actress."

Brigitte admired Leigh's open show of affection. "I'm interested in Sarah's personal life, as usual," she said. "Do you think she liked women too? You know, like the other women we've been getting to know?"

Emily and Leigh glanced at each other, and Eva suddenly became very interested in the passing crowd. Then Leigh dropped Emily's hand, plunked her elbows on the table, and rested her face on her fists. "Oh, come off it, everybody. We're among friends, aren't we? And we're in Paris, for Christ's sake. Surely we can talk about what we're all dying to know. We've skirted the *L* word long enough."

Leigh gazed at Brigitte and Eva until Eva finally looked at her and sighed. "I'm in, ladies," she said. "What about you, Brigitte?"

Emily took Leigh's hand again, and Brigitte slowly sipped her wine. "My history's as spotted as that of Marie Antoinette, George

Sand, and Sarah Bernhardt, but I could probably bat for your team if I wanted to." She glanced down at her perfectly manicured nails. "Figuratively, at least."

Leigh raised her glass of dark German beer. "All right, Eva. Do you think the Divine Sarah was a lesbian?"

Eva held up a warning finger. "I don't think she'd want us to discuss that point too loudly in public."

"And why not?" Leigh asked. She evidently had strong feelings about the subject.

"Well, come to think of it, I don't suppose she'd mind. After all, she's been dead almost fifty years. She'd probably be glad that we're still this interested in her, and no one's paying any attention to us." Eva cut off a small bite of brie and seemed to savor its creamy sweetness before she spoke. "Sarah was very secretive about her personal life because she didn't want to give the theater critics any ammunition to use against her. She had to please her public in order to support herself. Also, she valued her independence almost as much as her privacy."

Brigitte could relate to that. In her profession, she'd hidden her preference for women. Most of her regular male customers wanted to believe that she lusted after them as much as they wanted her. It was definitely an ego thing, and she didn't care for voyeurs who would gladly pay to watch her with another woman. No, she'd enjoyed her occasional liaison with an adventurous woman, but her affection for Rosa had satisfied her emotionally. She hadn't wanted to complicate her life by committing herself sexually to a woman she truly cared for, if she'd even been able to find one. Until now...

"Okay," Leigh said. "I get your point, but back to my question, Eva. Was Sarah one of us?"

"She had flaming affairs with such men as the Prince of Wales and Victor Hugo, yet she was close friends with Oscar Wilde for twenty years," Eva said. "To me, that friendship indicates that she accepted homosexuality as a viable lifestyle."

"But what about Louise Abbema? Didn't they supposedly have something going on?" Brigitte asked, giving them a knowing look, and Emily and Leigh stared at Eva expectantly.

"Yes. She's the biggest possibility I can come up with. Especially since we're certain Rosa Bonheur influenced Abbema to become a painter."

"That's rather confusing. Who's Rosa Bonheur?" Emily asked. "I recall hearing the name, but I don't know anything about her." She took a bite of the strawberry that crowned her napoleon.

"Just the most out-of-the-closet female French painter of the entire nineteenth century." Leigh seemed almost smug. "Remember that painting called *The Horse Farm* you admire so much, love?"

"Oh, yes. Now I recall a little about her." Emily finished the strawberry and forked a raspberry. "Bonheur cut her hair short and got written permission from the French government to wear trousers. She wore them when she dissected horses in the slaughterhouses to study their anatomy. Isn't that correct?" She glanced toward Leigh as if for confirmation.

Brigitte could have lived happily without discussing horse dissection during lunch, but Eva joined in, appearing elated with the turn the conversation had taken. "Absolutely. Bonheur had two long, successful relationships with women, with whom she openly lived as partners. She was even able to force the French legal authorities to recognize her right to leave her property to her second partner, who was much younger than she."

Brigitte didn't know much about Bonheur and listened intently as she toyed with her wineglass. "Do you think that's why Bernhardt enjoyed her artistic pursuits so much? Bonheur blazed a trail where at least a few talented women could be themselves instead of traditional wives and mothers. What do we actually know about Louise Abbema and Bernhardt? I've read only rumor and innuendo."

Eva put her finger in the handle of the cup of coffee the waiter had just set in front of her. "Abbema met Bernhardt when she was barely in her teens, and five years later she painted a famous portrait of her and became Bernhardt's official portraitist. She also sculpted her in various media, and they were reputedly lifelong friends."

Brigitte felt a bit let down. "That's not much evidence of any romantic attachment between them. Not like the letters of George Sand and Marie Dorval. Those don't leave any doubt."

"I've seen Abbema's self-portrait," Eva said, "painted when she was in her thirties or forties. She appears to be very reserved—with her black hair piled on her head, her pince-nez and penetrating dark eyes, and her royal-blue tailored suit complete with tie, stick pin, and high white collar. Her tie and the matching handkerchief in her jacket pocket are purple, which are the only softening touches." She looked thoughtful for a moment as she picked up her cup and blew on her hot coffee. "She was making her living in a man's world and couldn't afford to flaunt her intimate relationship with a famous, flamboyant actress like Bernhardt. That's my theory, anyway."

Emily nodded in agreement, as did Leigh.

The thought of the Divine Sarah making love to a reserved, professional-looking woman with dark hair made a shiver run through Brigitte. She glanced at Eva, but she was evidently focusing on their topic of conversation.

"I've heard rumors of a painting by Abbema that showed her and Bernhardt riding in a boat on a lake near Paris," Eva said. "She supposedly painted it on the anniversary of their love affair, but I have no idea if those rumors have any substance. I've also heard they were together for about five years." She looked almost wistful.

Brigitte drained her wineglass. "Let's say the rumors are true. If so, all the famous women we've visited so far on our tour have had more meaningful and satisfying relationships with women than with men. Would you agree?"

"Of course," Leigh and Emily said in harmony, and held their clasped hands up.

"It seems like a logical conclusion to me," Eva said, with a half smile.

Suddenly Brigitte wanted to know more about what lay behind the missing half of Eva's smile. She'd revealed quite a bit about herself to this young woman who'd introduced her to a world she'd glimpsed only in tiny bits and pieces before she came to Paris. But Eva had said little about herself.

The blue sky of Paris seemed to brighten as Brigitte relaxed in her chair and listened contentedly to the hum of life around her. She and Eva had time to get to know each more fully, and Brigitte planned to take advantage of it.

Chapter Nineteen

That afternoon, after they visited Sarah Bernhardt's white marble sarcophagus in the huge Père-Lachaise cemetery in the west of Paris, Eva led them to the nearby spot where Gertrude Stein and Alice Toklas lay.

"Since we're here, we might as well pay our respects to these two. After all, they were probably the most famous female figures here in Paris during one of its most memorable eras, the twenties."

"Weren't they both Americans?" Emily asked.

Eva spread her hands wide. "Yes. But they adopted Paris, and Paris adopted them."

"*America is my country and Paris is my hometown.*" Brigitte beamed with obvious excitement. "Stein certainly knew how to produce memorable quotes." She sighed. "The twenties. That's my favorite time period. I'd love to have been around during those exciting years. We women really started coming into our own then."

Leigh took Emily's hand as they strolled down the cemetery's gray cobblestone road, and in a while they stopped and nodded to each other in a kind of signal. "If you're really interested in the twenties, Brigitte, we'll tell you what it was like. You see, Paris was the first foreign city we visited together. You might say it was where we spent our honeymoon."

Brigitte stopped and stared at them. "Oh, my God. You don't look that old. I mean…I didn't even stop to think you might actually remember what it was like then. How fabulous."

"Let's sit over here," Eva said, pointing to some benches. "You can give us a living history lesson, if you would."

Leigh settled onto a bench, her arm around Emily. "In 1921, we'd both just turned twenty-three."

Brigitte strained to imagine them as young lovers.

"We met during the Great War, when we both were serving in the clerical division of the WAACs," Emily said and gazed at Leigh as if seeing her as she must have looked way back then.

Leigh returned her gaze. "The war gave us more independence than we'd ever dreamed of. We learned enough skills during that time to both get good jobs as secretaries after the war ended. But enough of that. You're interested in Frenchwomen, not us Brits."

Brigitte could have listened to more of their stories of wartime England, but Eva looked a bit impatient to hear about the women of her own country. "So, what was Paris like in 1921?"

"It was chaotic. And cheap. And wonderful," Emily said.

Brigitte prompted her. "Wonderful…how?"

"We'd thrown our corsets away during the war, but afterward, here in Paris, we cut our hair and began to smoke in public. Everywhere we went, everyone wanted to forget the war, and we all had a little too much to drink, too often."

Brigitte laughed. "I can relate to that. It sounds like you're describing New Orleans."

Leigh leaned back, as if seeing those faraway years once again. "The boulevards weren't nearly as full of traffic as they are now, but we knew the automobile was here to stay. People seemed to drive around just to be seen, as if proving how modern they were."

Eva nodded. "And the traffic has mushroomed. Sometimes I wish cars had never been allowed in the city."

"What about the women's fashions?" Brigitte asked.

"Oh, dresses were already beginning to inch up and become looser." Leigh looked thoughtful. "We women wanted to keep our newfound independence, so we believed if we could look like boys, people would think we could take care of ourselves instead of be clinging vines, like we were considered before the war."

Emily looked Leigh up and down. "I never went to the extreme Leigh did."

Leigh blushed but then pushed out her chest. "I've never had large breasts so it wasn't hard for me to have the slim, tall boyish look everyone was beginning to want. I never thought about it at the time, but looking back, I suppose that was what was in our minds."

"I wish you could have seen her in her secondhand suits and bright-colored ties. She was one handsome woman." Emily beamed as she took Leigh's hand. Leigh's blush deepened.

Brigitte winked. "She still is." Then she took pity on Leigh and returned to the story. "You mentioned earlier that it was cheap in Paris at the time. How inexpensive was it?"

Leigh was silent a minute, as if calculating. "I do recall someone saying they could live on the equivalent of a thousand dollars a year in 1921."

"That's probably one reason so many artistic types moved here," Emily added. "And of course the city was wide open with energy."

"So, did you ever meet Gertrude and Alice?" Eva asked, evidently still trying to focus on the theme of the tour.

"Oh no," Emily said. "We were never invited to their salon, though we saw them occasionally. We were mere secretaries—not painters, or writers, or artists."

Leigh interrupted Emily. "But we did get to know one couple you may have heard of, mainly because we both loved to read. Remember them, love?"

Brigitte couldn't believe she'd already spent several days with these self-effacing women and never suspected what they'd experienced. "Who was it? Tell!"

"Sylvia Beach and Adrienne Monnier," Emily said proudly.

"Amazing. I've read about Sylvia Beach," Brigitte said. "She was an American who helped launch the careers of T. S. Eliot and James Joyce." The past was coming alive for her.

Emily frowned. "And James Joyce treated her shabbily after he became famous."

"Yes, so I've read," Eva said. "But what were Beach and Monnier like?"

Brigitte was glad to see Eva was as absorbed in what Leigh and Emily were saying as she was.

"Ah, Sylvia was shorter than I am, and very slim," Emily said.

"She had excellent legs, wore her hair straight and pulled back from her face, and smoked far too much," Leigh said.

"Watch it, dear." Emily hit her arm playfully. "But I agree. Sylvia's legs were something else. During the war she'd worked either with the Red Cross in Serbia or in the wine country south of Paris. I never did get that story straight. Maybe she did both or—"

"Adrienne was dumpy, with a pretty heart-shaped face," Leigh said.

"And Sylvia wore trousers or straight skirts and tailored jackets. She was rather butch. At first I even had a little crush on her, but nobody could compete with Leigh."

Leigh gave a laugh. "Well, I never fancied Adrienne. She always wore floor-length peasant skirts and little fitted velvet vests."

"That's right. How did you remember that, Leigh? I bet you did fancy her. I'd forgotten her little vests. I can still see them, side by side, as if it were yesterday, and we were all young and silly." Emily sighed.

"But how did you meet them?" Brigitte asked, and Eva nodded like she wanted to know too.

Leigh scratched her head. "As I recall, they'd just moved in together. Adrienne had owned a French-language bookstore for several years and taught Sylvia the business. So Sylvia opened her own bookstore, the celebrated Shakespeare and Company, where so many famous American and British authors got their start." She took Emily's hand. "Remember it, Em? It was actually more a lending library than a conventional bookstore. Sylvia and Adrienne believed you had to read a book before you could know if you wanted to buy it. Gertrude and Alice had one of her store's first library cards."

A squirrel skittered up a nearby tree, and though Eva looked at her watch, Leigh kept talking.

"Though we didn't actually attend Gertrude's famous salons, we did hear the gossip in Paris and observed her and Alice the few times we saw them at the bookstore. As a new couple, I suppose we were looking for someone to model ourselves after, and we didn't know that many lesbian couples back in England."

Emily broke in. "Gertrude seemed to value men more highly than women, and we thought she treated Alice like a conventional wife."

Leigh nodded emphatically. "But Sylvia and Adrienne appeared to be partners in the true sense of the word."

Leigh put her arm around Emily and pulled her close. "They were friends who shared common interests and didn't seem to rely on the customary heterosexual roles. We admired their independence and tried to follow their lead. And it's worked for us, don't you think, love?" She squeezed Emily's shoulder, and they smiled at one another as if they were still in their twenties and visiting Paris for the first time.

Suddenly their gray hair and wrinkles vanished, and Brigitte glimpsed two fresh-faced young women, deeply in love and trying to plan their future together. At that moment anything seemed possible. In fifty years, she and Eva would be old, but maybe they'd be sitting on this same bench in this cemetery reminiscing about a couple they'd met when they first got together. That could happen. She just had to hold on to what she was beginning to feel for Eva.

Their future together seemed like an iridescent bubble blown from a child's plastic ring, and she wanted to enjoy its colors and its glow forever. Her life could be like theirs if she believed in herself and Eva.

Something inside Brigitte opened, and she breathed in the fresh air that surrounded them. How wonderful to glimpse what her life could be like.

❖

Eva sat in her small bedroom that night, gazing out the window at the passing boats on the Seine and thinking about Brigitte.

There was a brief rapping on the door, and Jeanne walked in without waiting for a response, juggling a tray filled with a pitcher of fresh lemonade and two glasses. "You've been in here brooding long enough," she said. "You need to talk about what's on your mind, and I'm here to listen. I won't take no for an answer." She set the tray on a small table next to Eva's bed and began to pour the lemonade.

"Thanks." Eva took the glass Jeanne handed her and scooted over to make room for her on her small bed. "You're right, as usual."

Jeanne settled beside her with a no-nonsense expression. "Tell me what you're thinking about."

The lemonade tasted tart yet sweet, and Eva hadn't realized how thirsty she was. "Umm, good."

"Quit stalling."

Eva took another sip, then eyed the sliced pears Jeanne had arranged on a saucer.

Jeanne shook her head. "Not a bite until you spill the beans."

"Spill the beans? Where in the world did you come up with that saying?" Eva laughed for the first time all night.

"You're not the only one who associates with Americans or watches American movies. I find some of their expressions colorful, even if they do sound a little strange in translation."

"Americans and their language *are* colorful," Eva said. "I've been thinking about one of them so much lately my head feels like it's about to turn into a rainbow."

"And that's why I'm here. Talk."

Eva glanced out the window again, then turned to face Jeanne. "You'll think I'm foolish."

"I already do. But I wouldn't recognize what you're doing if I hadn't been there myself. You're not going through something we haven't all experienced, if we're lucky."

"Lucky? You've got to be crazy."

"Crazy? Maybe. But it does help to discuss it. Trust me."

Eva reached for a pear slice but Jeanne tapped her hand. "Talk first, eat later."

She sighed and allowed her shoulders to relax a bit. Jeanne wouldn't let up until Eva told her something. "Fine. Be that way. I was thinking about Brigitte and how she looked this afternoon. There. Satisfied?"

"How did she look?"

"Like a morning glory."

"A morning glory? I've never heard you describe anyone that way."

Eva stuck out her tongue at Jeanne and took another drink of her lemonade. "All right. Today Brigitte and I were talking to Leigh and Emily, who were describing their visits to Paris during the early twenties and how they met some of the women I've only read about. It was so—"

"Interesting, but you're stalling again. You were about to tell me something about Brigitte and a morning glory."

Eva sighed again, a long drawn-out sound that released something inside her. "When our conversation began, Brigitte looked as closed as a deep-purple morning glory. You know, like a spiral bud, furled tight around herself, her color muted."

"Hmm. I get the picture. *Uptight*, I believe, is the term I've heard some of the American teenagers use."

"Yeah. That's it. But during the course of the conversation, Brigitte actually admitted she was attracted to women, and after that, she gradually uncurled like a blossom and seemed to open completely, for the first time since I've known her. The color of the bloom I imagined her to be was so intense it almost blinded me. I could almost see the water droplets on it, its pinkish veins guiding me down into its light-pink throat."

Jeanne draped her hand around Eva's shoulder and squeezed. "Oh, you've got it bad, don't you, child. Using poetic images like that usually indicates feelings too large and complex to express with ordinary language."

Eva put her hand over Jeanne's and squeezed back, her throat aching with gratitude. "I'm afraid you're right. And I'm not sure what to do. I've never felt quite like this."

"I wish I could help. But don't worry. It'll work itself out."

Eva shook her head. "I talked to a pair of swans about Brigitte while we were at Nohant. *Swans*. Can you believe that? I never do silly things like that. You know I prefer facts. They're so reliable."

Jeanne gave her shoulder a small pat, then pulled her hand away. "Yes, but facts can become rather dull. Sounds like Brigitte is adding some color and excitement to your life."

"In India, during the first year of my travels, I spent several months in a Buddhist monastery. I sent you a postcard from near there. Remember?"

Jeanne nodded.

"There in the monastery, I learned to let my mind roam, then gradually focus intently on the sensations around me. Many of the travelers I met on the road used drugs to do the same thing, but I preferred that method. It was more natural, though I really had to work at it. Maybe that helped me begin to expand my perception of the world."

"Maybe. Sounds like a good break from your usual logical self."

"But what could Brigitte have been thinking about? Why is she so closed most of the time? What's she hiding? Who is she? How can I help her open up more often?" She paused. "And why do I even want to?"

Jeanne held up a hand, then took a slice of pear and handed one to Eva. "Hey. That's a lot of questions. I can see why you've been spending so much time thinking lately."

The boat traffic slowed and a few of the lights winked out as Eva munched her pear and stared outside. Jeanne sat quietly beside her.

"The thing is, I'm not sure I want to be drawn to Brigitte like this. The tour will end tomorrow, and Brigitte will disappear, just like all the other tourists I've become acquainted with."

Jeanne nodded. "Don't give up so easily. You've only known her a week. If your feelings for her last, and even grow, maybe she'll come to trust you enough to answer your questions." She took a bite of her slice of fruit and chewed it slowly. "You talked to me, didn't you? Be patient and, when the time's right, listen to what she has to say. And if that never happens, someone else will come along."

Eva already felt better. What would she do without Jeanne? "I'm sure you're right. And if I don't find someone, the law's steady and dependable. It'll provide me a good living, a profession to be proud of and involved in. And I'll have a chance to prove I can be a better lawyer than Father ever thought about being."

Jeanne finished her pear and wiped her hand on a damp napkin, looking at Eva like she used to when Eva threw a temper tantrum.

Eva took a deep breath and tried to let her adult side take over from the child in her that tended to break out when she was under pressure. "But maybe I'll allow myself this one indulgence this summer. I think I'll let myself be pulled toward Brigitte and see where the attraction leads. Hmm. And when I have that fling out of my system—if it ever comes to that—I'll be ready to pour all my energy into preparing for my career. What do you think?"

Jeanne shook her head and arranged the empty glasses on the tray. "I *think* you need to stop thinking so much about this. Don't worry. I'll always be here for you, no matter what. Good night." She got up and kissed Eva's cheek.

"Thanks for listening. I really appreciate it," Eva said, and Jeanne merely smiled and left the room.

Whatever I decide, at least I'll always have one person in my life I truly love. She stood up and glanced at the boats on the river one more time.

CHAPTER TWENTY

Eva said her good-byes to her tour group. "I've enjoyed introducing you to some of the many interesting women in Paris and hope you enjoy the rest of your stay in my city." They had just climbed out of their van on the Right Bank, near the Pont des Invalides. "It's been a pleasure to meet each of you," she said and gladly accepted the tips they pressed into her hand.

As she turned to walk across the bridge, Brigitte joined her, though Eva knew her hotel was on the Right Bank. "This has been such an enjoyable week," Brigitte said. Running a hand quickly through her long blond hair, she seemed uneasy.

"Thank you. I've tried not to bore you."

"Oh, you haven't. I haven't missed a word."

They walked a short distance in silence, and then Eva looked at her watch. "Did you want to discuss something?"

A slight blush colored Brigitte's smooth skin. "Yes. No. I mean, do you have plans for tonight?"

What did Brigitte have on her mind? Eva decided to find out. "No. I—"

"In that case, would you like to go hear some jazz with me? I noticed you at the Meridien Etoile a couple of weeks ago. You do like jazz, don't you? I don't know many people in town and thought…"

Eva stopped in the middle of the bridge and stared at Brigitte, who stood in front of her like she'd just committed a crime. Taken off guard, Eva blurted out, "Sorry, but my company doesn't like for us to fraternize with the clients, even after a tour ends. I adore jazz, but I try to adhere to our policies. It's best for everyone involved." She smiled to try to soften the rejection. "Thanks for the invitation, though. I'm sure we'd have a good time." She looked at her watch again. "Excuse me now. I need to get back to the office. Maybe we'll run into each other at the library again."

But after she took several steps, she stopped and turned around. What was she doing? Just last night she'd promised herself a summer fling, so why had she told Brigitte no? She strode back to where Brigitte still stood in the middle of the bridge, motionless, her rigid shoulders betraying her mood.

"I'm sorry. All of a sudden I don't give a damn about our company policies. I'd love to listen to some jazz with you tonight. Do you want me to meet you at the Meridien Etoile about nine?"

Brigitte brightened, her hair as golden as the dome of the nearby Les Invalides museum. "Why don't you drop by my room at the George V a bit earlier than that, if it's not out of your way? Then we could walk. It looks like it'll be a beautiful evening." She waited expectantly, as if hoping Eva might continue the conversation. But Eva simply nodded, and Brigitte turned and strolled back toward her hotel.

Eva stood there, dazed. What had she gotten herself into? Brigitte might not even be attracted to her, but tonight would be a good opportunity to find out one way or the other. Energized, she headed toward the Left Bank.

❖

"Come on in. The door's open," Brigitte called. "I'm almost ready." The door clicked closed. "I'll be right out. Help yourself to whatever you want to drink."

Brigitte checked herself out one last time in the full-length mirror, recalling how excited she'd been when she'd dressed up to go hear Erroll Garner. Tonight, she'd dressed differently. She liked the way her chunky gold necklace glittered against the simple black turtleneck she wore. And her black flared skirt and dark hose covered any remaining flesh. She wanted Eva to find her attractive but didn't want Eva to think she was coming on to her, like that horrid woman had when Brigitte had spotted them in the club.

She'd decided to wear her hair down and patted it one final time, then dabbed some perfume on her wrists and behind her ears. She liked this more natural look and hoped it would appeal to Eva.

Eva was sitting on the couch sipping chardonnay as Brigitte entered her small living room as unobtrusively as possible. She glided to the minibar and poured herself a glass of pungent merlot.

"What a beautiful necklace and earrings," Eva said.

Brigitte wondered how she could see them in her forest of hair and stroked her mane back to give Eva a better look. "Thank you. I've had to dress well for so many years that it's a habit."

"Ah, yes. Your necklace almost blinded me. But the earrings are the perfect final touch."

Obviously Eva appreciated subtlety, so Brigitte was glad she'd chosen this outfit. "Where did you get your unusual necklace?" she asked.

Eva fingered the exotic assortment of shells that shone on the soft background her white blouse provided, and Brigitte couldn't resist touching them. "In Hawaii. They're called puka beads. I hope these aren't the imitations that are beginning to pop up everywhere in tourist spots abroad. With the real ones, the hole in each of them has formed from wear instead of being drilled by a machine."

"How interesting. So you've traveled a bit?" Brigitte stepped back, regretting that she couldn't touch the smooth, tanned skin that lay under Eva's necklace. The puka beads revealed more about Eva than she realized. She was as natural and authentic as her jewelry.

"Oh, yes. Travel's one of my passions. It's so easy to get caught up in the small space where you've grown up and either fear or ignore the rest of the world."

"I can certainly relate to that. When did you see the world, and where did you go?"

Eva's eyes shone. How beautiful she was. "Oh. Well, I'd almost studied myself into a coma here at the university, so I broke away and circled the globe for two years. Didn't miss a single continent except Antarctica."

"Impressive. So you just needed a break?"

Eva shook her head. "That too, but I was arrested during the student protests here during my final year in school. That really unsettled me, so I decided to take a break away from my routine life for a while."

"I can relate to that too." Rosa's suicide note flashed through her mind. "It's part of what brought me here to Paris."

Eva smiled and set her glass on the coffee table. "Your break is my quotidian. Now I'm back, ready to settle into my rut again." Then she glanced at her watch. "Shouldn't we go? The hotel's a little more than a mile from here, and I don't think we want to rush down the Champs Élysées on such a nice night, do you?"

Brigitte finished her own wine and stood up. "Oh no. I want to enjoy every minute of our time together. I feel special, spending time alone with my guide. Rather like being the head nun's pet back in school. Which I never was, by the way." She flashed Eva a grin. "And don't think you'll get away without telling me more about getting arrested."

Eva returned her grin, and her anticipation—and desire—only grew.

Chapter Twenty-one

Eva grasped Brigitte's arm as Count Basie's orchestra played its final notes in the smoky jazz club. The hard-driving, fast-paced sounds of the music died away, replaced by a thunder of applause and then the clink of glasses and bottles and the noise of people scraping their chair legs on the floor. Throughout the session Brigitte had been moving her entire body to the rhythm of the drums and the piano. Eva couldn't decide which she'd enjoyed more: watching Brigitte listen to the music or hearing it herself. "Are you tired, or would you like to explore the nightlife of Paris a while longer?"

The house lights came up, and Brigitte turned to her with an almost dazed expression, as if the music had transported her to another dimension. The saxophone and trumpets had affected Eva too, made her better understand what the word swing meant.

"What did you say?" Gradually Brigitte seemed to realize where she was. "Oh. What nightlife are you talking about?"

Eva squeezed Brigitte's arm, then let it go and bent closer to her. "We could go over to Chez Moune. It should be heating up by now." The crowded, hazy room was noisy as people walked up to the stage to chat with the musicians or headed for the exit. The musicians were taking their music from their stands, packing their instruments, talking among themselves and to fans.

Brigitte's blue eyes sparked. "Chez Moune. Isn't that a club for les—"

"Yes. It's for lesbians. If you'd rather not go…" Eva pulled back. She didn't want to push Brigitte into anything she wasn't ready for.

Brigitte tossed down the last of her screwdriver and nodded. "No. I'd love to. This music really revved me up. I'm in the mood for a little adventure."

Outside the Meridien Etoile, Eva hailed a taxi. She gave the driver the address and held the door open for Brigitte. "We're heading toward Montmartre, in case you'd like to get your bearings."

Brigitte was staring out the window and smiling, especially when the taxi took the Avenue de Villiers at top speed. She looked like the music was still running through her head, her entire body, as if it had loosened part of her that she usually restrained.

"Have you been to Pigalle yet, Brigitte?"

Brigitte's shoulders stiffened infinitesimally. "No. I'm focusing on the cultural centers of Paris. You know, the museums, the palaces, and the cathedrals. A place like Pigalle doesn't interest me much, at least not for its own sake."

"Yes, it does look rather shabby during the day, but at night, the bright lights and crowds change it into a busy, exciting place. Though I didn't get to New Orleans on my trip, it still intrigues me. I imagine the French Quarter there must be a lot like that too."

Brigitte's shoulders dropped. "You're right. That area draws a huge crowd looking for a good time. I've heard a lot of good music on Bourbon Street and seen some tasteful drag shows. But the drinks are overpriced, and usually the crowds seem a little frantic, like they're trying too hard to enjoy themselves."

"Do they have any gay bars there?"

"Not many. There's always Cafe Lafitte, which has been around forever. But it's mostly for guys, and the men I…went out with weren't very interested in other men."

"I don't venture down to Pigalle often, but once in a while it's fun to let go. Everyone's heard of the Moulin Rouge, but my favorite's Chez Moune. It's the oldest bar for women in the city." Eva grimaced. "Sorry. My tour-guide persona took over." Garish flashing lights and noisy crowds signaled their arrival. "Okay. We're here," Eva said. "Hopefully we won't have to wait in line too long."

They finally made it into the large basement establishment, teeming with laughing women wearing every style of clothes imaginable. As they shoved through the noisy crowd toward a vacant table, Eva caught their reflection in the mirrored tiles covering the walls. Brigitte looked right at home here, as beautiful as the women painted on the huge angular bar that dominated the club. Her blond hair and gold jewelry glowed richly in the subdued lighting.

"What a babe," someone whispered as they passed, and Eva was sure they weren't talking about her.

"I'd love to take her home with me," someone else said. Again, the observer had to have Brigitte in mind.

Eva put her hand on the small of Brigitte's back, steering her through the crush of ogling women and laying claim to Brigitte's attention, for tonight at least.

Almost every woman there stared at them, clearly admiring Brigitte, but quickly shifted her attention back to her own date when Eva glared. Brigitte moved through the crowd as if barely aware of the desire she provoked.

Finally they were seated at a small round table, and the women nearby settled down. Their knees were touching, and the feel of Brigitte's sleek hose against Eva's bare leg made her want to run her hand under Brigitte's skirt. She took a deep breath instead. *Control yourself*, she inwardly chanted. "Another screwdriver?"

Brigitte nodded as she gazed around at the women pressed close together on the dance floor. She didn't seem offended or surprised at the lesbian scene or at the way most of the women had stared at her with obvious lust. Instead, she sighed. Then she slipped off the pointed-toe high heels she was wearing.

Eva began to relax too.

Brigitte leaned forward. "Do you come here often?" Her voice had dropped at least an octave, taking on a sultry tone that made Eva's cheeks grow warm.

"No. Only on special occasions. When I'm lonely or want to blow off a little steam."

"And are you lonely or ready to blow off steam tonight?" Brigitte's voice became impossibly lower, and her eyes drew Eva in.

"Uhh—"

"Would you like a drink?" a waitress asked Eva, and she swallowed her unformed response to Brigitte.

"But yes. Thank you. A Pernod absinthe with water for me, and a screwdriver for my friend."

After the waitress gave Brigitte a lingering look and left, Brigitte shook her head and smiled at Eva. "I'd never have taken you for an absinthe drinker. I'm impressed. I've never tried such a notorious liquor."

Eva glowed inside. She'd impressed Brigitte! "I told you I felt like letting go. But don't worry. The modern version of absinthe isn't a hallucinogen like its ancestor used to be. I won't do anything bizarre tonight and embarrass you."

Brigitte flinched. "I'm not worried about you, Eva, and you couldn't embarrass me if you tried." Then she began to watch the crowd.

Eva wondered what was going on in Brigitte's head. She'd somehow upset her, but for now she kept quiet, not sure what to say. Instead, she let the noise of the women and the music and the nearness of Brigitte overwhelm her.

Finally Brigitte inclined her head slightly toward her and whispered, "Look at that couple over there." Her sultry tone had disappeared, and the intimate moment Eva had wished for dissipated into the banal.

After their drinks arrived, Eva sipped her absinthe and tried to retrieve their closeness. "So, Mary Brigitte, how do you like Chez Moune?"

Brigitte flinched again, her eyes sharp, even through the heavy smoke. "How do you know my full name?" Her hand trembled as she slowly set her glass on the table, staring at Eva as if she'd revealed a carefully guarded secret.

"Your passport, of course. Jeanne made a copy of it when you signed up for the tour."

Brigitte toyed with her napkin. "That's right. I forgot." She sat in silence for a while, then wadded her napkin into a ball. "My mother named me Brigitte and always called me that. The few times she showed up." She glared at Eva. "My grandmother refused to use the name. She said it sounded foreign and vulgar."

The force of Brigitte's angry expression hit Eva almost like a blow to the chest. "Why would she say that?"

"I told you she hated my mother, and Grandmother said she drove my father to his death. She named me Mary—called me Mary Brigitte when she spoke with my mother, and with everyone else she never called me anything but Mary. I hated it, but what could I do?"

Eva fed on the anger that sparked in Brigitte's blue eyes.

"After all, she clothed and sheltered me," Brigitte said. "When I started school, my teachers always insisted on calling me Mary Brigitte, and the other girls in my class giggled behind their hands, told me it sounded like a nun's name, just like our teachers'."

Eva was so lost in the pain Brigitte's eyes expressed, she almost didn't hear her final words on the subject.

"It took me a long time to convince everyone to call me just Brigitte, though my grandmother called me Mary until the day she died. Please don't use it again. I hate that name."

"I won't." Eva spoke so softly she wondered if Brigitte could even hear her.

Brigitte took a long drink of her screwdriver and shrugged. "Enough about me. Is Eva your given name?"

Eva's heart began to thrum. "No."

"Well? I told you my story. Let me hear yours." Brigitte sat up straighter, her eyes still flashing.

"My real name's Yvette, for my father, Yves. He apparently wanted a boy but had to settle for me. But when my brother Louis came along several years later, he treated Louis even worse than he did me." A rush of anger gripped her now, but Brigitte's satiny knee against her leg helped her keep her seat.

She told herself to calm down. "I started calling myself Eva when I was in my teens and heard Father talking to someone on the telephone. He had his hand in his pocket, jangling his loose change. When I walked by he lowered his voice and hung up almost immediately, glaring at me like I was the one who was doing something wrong."

"Most likely talking to another woman in a way he shouldn't have." Brigitte's voice was as soothing as a glass of milk to an ulcerated stomach. "And you didn't want him to." Brigitte draped her arm around Eva's shoulder and squeezed it.

"How did you know that?" Eva had never told anyone about that day and had no idea why she'd just shared it with Brigitte. But she was glad she had. Brigitte's hand siphoned off some of the pain she'd felt since then. What a difference from the distant, unreasonable woman she'd encountered in the library not that long ago.

The music changed to a Latin beat, and Eva took a risk. She'd noticed Brigitte watching the dancers and had seen how she responded to an occasional tango tune by moving her upper body. "By any chance, do you know how to tango?" she asked, and held out her hand.

Brigitte simply nodded, slipped on her high heels, stood up, and grasped Eva's hand as if dancing the tango with another woman was second nature to her.

❖

Eva held Brigitte's hand briefly, then dropped it and walked to the crowded dance floor, leaving it up to Brigitte to follow her. After turning, she paused and then stood still. Brigitte let the beat of the music embrace her, pound through her, fill her with its insistence, wrap her in its longing, its call for her to become one with it. Slowly, when Eva opened her arms and invited Brigitte into them, Brigitte felt only the music and Eva's presence. She accepted with her right hand, sliding her warm palm against Eva's cool one, and let her hand drift into Eva's.

They faced each other as still as statues, sighed, and now Brigitte waited for the pulsating music to wrap around both of them. But too quickly, Eva led Brigitte in the first step, rushing them into the dance instead of gliding toward her in slow motion, as Rosa used to do. Eva's dark hair brushed her cheek, a red mottled patch appeared on Eva's throat, and her heart pulsed in the hollow of it. Brigitte sighed as waves of heat rushed up her legs to her breasts and down her arms. Being with Rosa had never made her react like this.

Eva seemed to preen, as if aware the crowd had begun to watch them. Was Eva excited about dancing or about being close to her? The ambiguity made the shock of their initial embrace subside a bit. Then she inhaled the fresh scent of Eva's soap, with its hint of flowery perfume. Could she live with this smell for the next three minutes? For a lifetime? Eva's breath was rushing in and out like a winded boxer's. Did Eva notice Brigitte's heart racing too, like that of a fighter about to enter the ring?

Keeping her expression blank, Brigitte tried to slow her heart's pace, to pretend she wasn't about to throw herself into the excitement of the tango and the thrill of being near Eva. With a new partner, could she execute the difficult steps it had taken her so long to master, or would she make a fool of herself on the dance floor? Eva's hands trembled slightly, suddenly lost their coolness, and became warm and damp. Was she concerned about the dance, or did she tremble for some other reason?

Eva kept her at a safe distance, their breasts barely touching, and neither of them spoke. Finally, Eva smiled as she would at a stranger, but they didn't look at each other as they began to perform the elementary yet challenging steps of the tango. The distance and their pretense of indifference were part of the dance, but under the façade, Brigitte burned with questions.

Can Eva lead me, determine what I'm capable of, what steps I prefer? Eva held her as if she knew what she was doing and appeared to be analyzing Brigitte's every move. Each time Eva introduced a new step, she paused for a second, as if silently asking if Brigitte felt comfortable. So far so good.

Will Eva demand too much of me? She did her best to respond to each move Eva initiated, uncertain if she could keep pace with a woman ten years younger. Rosa had been so much older that Brigitte hadn't had to worry about that. But as the music continued she realized she wasn't even breathing hard, at least not from the dancing itself.

She relaxed into the physical aspects of their tango, but old insecurities lingered. *Is Eva dancing only to impress the crowd that's gathering to watch us?* Brigitte had come to hate having people stare at her every time she appeared in public, and right now she felt almost onstage. Yet Eva didn't even appear to be aware that anyone else was in the bar as she led Brigitte around the small dance floor. How amazing, how flattering to have someone focus so completely on her.

Just then, they almost collided with another couple on the floor, and Brigitte caught a whiff of spring rain. Startled, she stared at the two women, who'd just whirled on, faceless, into the crowd. She'd smelled that scent during her last tango with Rosa. Could she have found the woman for whom she'd come to Paris?

Eva faltered, made a wrong step, and Brigitte held her breath. *Will Eva scold herself for her mistake?* But Eva merely paused, then smoothly changed their direction, her calm expression never wavering.

Brigitte really wanted to know how Eva would feel plastered against her, their legs entangling and brushing one another, their bodies moving as one, their breath mingling to create a fog of heat, their lips coming near enough to explode into flame. To hell with the rules of the tango. Brigitte wanted to push Eva into a dark corner and run her hands and tongue over every inch of her.

Yet, in spite of the music and her own throbbing heart, she kept hearing Rosa's steady voice. *During the dance you and your partner must keep apart, yet depend on each other and stay connected.* It would be too easy to ravish Eva right here, right now, while the music pulsed through them, made them mindless. But she wanted to stay connected to someone, not dissolve into mindless lust.

This was the first time Brigitte had danced the tango with a woman other than Rosa, and when the passionate music ended all too soon, she let Eva lead her back to their table. She and Eva had danced their first tango in Paris together, and if Brigitte had her way, it wouldn't be their last.

❖

Eva returned Brigitte to their table, and they both dropped the mask of indifference the tango required. Brigitte's eyes sparked like blue topazes as she asked, "Who taught you to tango like that?"

"Jeanne."

"Jeanne, your aunt?"

"Yes." Eva beamed with pride. "She may not look like it, but she gets around." Eva savored the memories Brigitte's question had stirred up. "About ten years ago, she became involved with a professional dancer, so when Jeanne learned various dances from her, she practiced them with me."

Brigitte nodded and wrapped her hands around her drink, seeming more at ease than she had on the tour.

Eva thought about Jeanne's affair with the dancer. "I liked that woman, but unfortunately she enjoyed switching partners without informing her steady one about it."

Brigitte quirked an eyebrow. "What do you mean?"

"Jeanne caught her doing a literal belly dance with a good-looking redhead in Jeanne's bed, and that ended my lessons. I'm glad we covered the tango before that happened." Eva laughed. "What about you?"

Brigitte's smile faded. "My best friend in New Orleans, Rosa, was from Argentina. Her parents moved to the States when she was a child. From what little she told me about them, they fought a lot and separated several times. Rosa danced with whichever one she was living with at the time, so she learned not only to follow but to lead, and she taught me to do the same."

Eva leaned close to Brigitte, inhaling the floral, citrus fragrance that seemed to be an integral part of this enchanting woman. Eva's lips were centimeters from Brigitte's when she heard herself ask, as if in a dream, "Were you in love with her, your best friend Rosa?" She couldn't ignore the stab of jealousy that suddenly attacked her. "Did you do more than dance with her?"

Brigitte recoiled, and Eva woke from her dreamlike state. "No. Oh, I admired her. She was her own person, except when it came to a certain kind of man." Brigitte looked almost distraught as she spoke about Rosa. "She protected me the best way she could and gave me everything she had and knew." Tears sparkled in Brigitte's eyes. "But she was much older and like a mother to me. I loved her, yes, and she loved me. But not in the way you think."

Eva would have given anything to withdraw her impulsive question, but she burned to know more. "I'm sorry. I didn't mean to upset you. So you're no longer friends?"

Brigitte rested her head on her hand, covering her eyes, and sighed. "Rosa's dead."

Eva set down her glass, unsure what to say. "I'm sorry. I won't mention her again." They sat in silence, Brigitte's apparent sorrow washing over them with the same intensity the tango music had earlier.

Eva finally whispered, "The next time we dance, you can lead."
She sipped her absinthe, then ran a finger along the edge of her glass.

Brigitte looked up and wiped away her tears, a sad smile
beginning to appear. "I'd like that. But we'll need to wear our tango
shoes. I brought mine with me in hopes of finding someone like you
to dance with."

Eva ventured a smile. "Somehow I'm not surprised, about the
shoes, I mean. Just let me know when you want to tango again, and
I'll be happy to follow your lead."

Brigitte finished her drink. "Thanks for a wonderful night, but
I've had enough for now. Is it okay if we leave?"

"Of course." Eva stood and held out her hand. Just when she'd
felt she might begin to really connect with Brigitte, her past had
intervened and pulled them apart.

They said good night outside the hotel, and she pulled Brigitte
close for a moment and luxuriated in the feel of her body, which she'd
only flirted with during the tango. But she forced herself not to kiss
her. Brigitte seemed too sad, and Eva didn't want to intrude. She'd
wait until the time was right.

CHAPTER TWENTY-TWO

B rigitte spent the next morning in bed, reliving her date with Eva. Their tango had given her a taste of what she and Eva might have together as lovers, but she didn't want to rush it. It would be easy to fall into bed together, but she wanted so much more than that. She wanted to fall in love and stay there. That was a huge step for her, though, so she decided to spend a little time alone and let her feelings for Eva sort themselves out.

By that afternoon, however, she felt like enjoying the warm summer day, so she caught a taxi to the huge cemetery where they'd visited the graves of Sarah Bernhardt and Gertrude Stein.

Fields of graves stretched before Brigitte. Cast-iron signposts pointed her down the gray cobblestone street to her right, where she picked up a map in the conservation office. Then she sat nearby and plotted her course. On her earlier visit, she'd noticed several women she wanted to pay homage to.

As she strolled through the grounds and enjoyed the solitude, she stopped each time she saw a familiar name, until finally she reached a large, plain granite tomb with only one simple engraving: HERE LIES COLETTE, 1873–1954.

No cross, no religious symbol.

Colette had divorced two of her three husbands, so the church wouldn't participate in her official state burial, the first one that had ever honored a Frenchwoman.

Running her hand over the cold, smooth granite, Brigitte tried to contact Colette's spirit. 1873-1954. If Brigitte had visited Paris when she was seventeen, she could have actually met Colette.

Brigitte sat on a marble bench near the grave, concentrating on what she knew about this remarkable woman. What would such a meeting have been like? Her strange experiences here in Paris didn't frighten or upset her like they had when they first occurred. In fact, she'd begun to find them interesting and wondered if she could somehow call them up at will. She sat there as if meditating, and finally, slowly, the sun dimmed, and she seemed to mentally hurtle back through time.

She strolled down the street near the Louvre and noticed two women wearing dresses with midcalf full skirts over petticoats, emphasizing their tiny waistlines. And hats—large ones that completely shaded their faces. She really was back in the fifties, she thought as she entered the quiet, secluded gardens of the Palais Royal. There, she headed for the most famous restaurant on the grounds, the Grand Véfour.

The maître d' seated her at Colette's customary table with a flourish. She looked around at her elaborate gold and red surroundings, ordered a glass of Burgundy, and watched Colette arrive in her wheelchair, her sea-green eyes sparkling.

"Ah, you're drinking wine from my part of France. Nothing like it," Colette said.

"Yes, it's delicious."

"Of course. Wine is the drink of the gods." She held up her glass in a toast to Brigitte. "But let's eat. I recommend anything with truffles."

"Truffles? I've never had them."

"Of course not. You're an American, aren't you? You know nothing of fine food."

Brigitte wanted to mention the creoles and étouffées she loved but restrained herself. This woman was rather awe-inspiring.

"Then try the lobster medley in wine sauce and lamb chops and finish with some ice cream and pastries." Colette's spirits seemed to rise as she mentioned each item, and Brigitte admired her joyful attitude.

"What can I do for you, my dear?" Colette asked after they ordered. "You must have arranged this unusual meeting for some reason."

Brigitte scrambled for a reply. She didn't want to miss this opportunity to talk freely with someone like Colette. "I wanted to ask, did anyone ever reject you?"

Colette propped her heart-shaped face in her hands and looked thoughtful. "Do you mean in a personal relationship or in a public situation?"

"Both."

"Yes. My first two husbands rejected me." Colette's gaze was direct and serious, yet seemed somehow playful and flirtatious.

"Why? And how did you cope?"

The waiter quickly returned with their meals, and Colette forked a duck-liver ravioli covered with a truffle emulsion cream. "Mmm. Delicious."

Brigitte took a bite of her lobster, which was as appealing as Colette had promised.

Colette glanced up after she'd taken several bites. "Oh, sorry. I was a very unpolished country girl, and my manners haven't improved much. What did you ask?"

"About rejection."

Colette grew thoughtful. "As I'm sure you're aware, when my first husband finally discovered my talent for writing, he encouraged me to pen my series of Claudine novels, based on my schoolgirl years, and to spice them with lesbian sexual adventures."

Brigitte nodded. "I've read every one in the series."

"He introduced me to the literary society of Paris and taught me a lot, but he couldn't stop having affairs with other women." She popped another ravioli into her mouth. "During the last years of our marriage, he practically pushed me into a liaison with an older woman, and he finally moved in with a much younger one." She sighed. "I could write a book about rejection, and probably have."

Brigitte finished her lobster while Colette polished off the last ravioli on her plate and motioned for the nearby waiter to take it away.

"But why would you ask me such a question?" Colette looked around expectantly at another waiter, who was approaching with their main course.

After the waiter set a plate down in front of her, Brigitte said, "I've felt accepted by only a few people in my personal life, but in my profession, I've always been extremely popular." Brigitte toyed with the piece of lamb on the plate in front of her.

"And? Colette looked at her, clearly impatient to begin her main course.

Brigitte felt silly. "Since I began working, no one ever turned down an invitation from me, because I'd never asked anyone to do something with me. Until recently. And when a woman did turn me down, I didn't know how to act. The rejection almost devastated me, even though she later agreed to spend the evening with me."

Colette lowered her fork and grasped Brigitte's hand in her doughy one. "Life happens, my dear. Let each of your experiences strengthen you. That's what I did."

But Brigitte couldn't accept such advice easily. "Don't you regret marrying your first husband and living with him, just to have him treat you so badly?"

"Heavens, no. We married when I was twenty and divorced seventeen years later. But with him, I learned I could write and that I had to be myself." She looked thoughtful. "Becoming independent was the hardest thing I've ever done. Without being rejected, I'd never have learned how to be on my own." She took a bite of her own lamb chop and, after she finished chewing, quirked her small lips with contentment.

They ate in silence, and eventually Colette looked up from her plate and put down her fork. "You asked me about public rejection too. I have a theory about that. After we separated, I continued my affair for a number of years. I'd decided to become an actress to support myself, and my lover wanted to act in a play with me. I suppose you've heard how she appeared onstage at the Moulin Rouge as a male archaeologist and slowly unwrapped me."

"Oh yes, the performance is infamous. You played a mummy she'd discovered, and after she removed your bandages, there you stood in a scanty Cleopatra costume."

Colette guffawed. "That's right. My curly hair was frizzed out like a burning bush, and she and I kissed long and passionately." Her green eyes sparkled with mischief. "The audience erupted, and the police shut down the production. Talk about public rejection."

After they'd had a long laugh together, Brigitte finally sobered enough to ask, "How did that experience affect you?"

"I was about your age when it happened, and later I realized that, for women, sex is one of the only ways we can truly assert ourselves."

"What do you mean?" Rosa had once said nearly the same thing.

"Men have seen us as the objects of their desire for so long, the only way we can convince them we aren't what they expect is to turn the tables on them." Colette sounded defiant and unapologetic. "By pursuing my own desire for a woman, or for whomever I craved, and by expressing my own sexual instincts, I discovered and won my own independence."

"And that was enough to satisfy you?" Brigitte knew she was being presumptuous, but this was a once-in-a-lifetime opportunity.

Colette didn't falter, yet her expression softened. "Throughout all my experiences, all I ever wanted was someone to love, who would love and accept me in return."

"And your third husband does all that?" This woman, one of the most famous people in France, wanted exactly what Brigitte did, which gave Brigitte hope that perhaps she could find the kind of love Colette had.

The dessert course arrived, and Colette stared at it with appreciation. "Yes. He and my writing make my life worth living. Don't be afraid to be rejected, and someday you'll come across someone to love who will accept you for who you are. Never hide yourself." Colette dipped a spoon into her ice cream. "And now it's time for you to leave. Thank you for keeping an old woman company. *And enjoy your time in Paris.*"

Brigitte emerged from her trancelike state and shook her head to clear it. She admired Colette's will to survive and envied her happiness with her third husband.

That night in Nohant, when Brigitte had confessed what she'd been before she came to Paris, she'd expected Eva to reject her. But Eva had surprised her, just as she'd surprised her by accepting her invitation to go listen to jazz last night. And their tango together afterward had made her hope Eva might grow to care about her. But was that simply lust and pride of possession on Eva's part?

When the tango music and their dance had ended last night, Brigitte hadn't wanted to sever their connection, even as distant and seemingly cool as it had become after Eva had questioned her about Rosa. The pair of them had been so separate and remote, like twin Eiffel Towers, standing side by side. But would they be able to move any closer to each other than they had last night? If Eva truly had been able to accept Brigitte's past, they just might be able to follow their mutual passion to a satisfying end.

Brigitte felt optimistic as she blew a kiss of thanks toward Colette's tombstone and left.

Chapter Twenty-three

"What time does the flea market open this Saturday?" Brigitte twisted the telephone cord through her fingers as she lounged in bed and talked to Eva. They'd spoken on the phone several times during the week but hadn't seen each other since last Saturday night. Brigitte was more than ready.

"Nine. If you're looking for bargains, you'll want to be there then. If you just want to have a good time, ten thirty or eleven is fine. But mornings are definitely the best. This Saturday afternoon will be especially crowded because a lot of people will probably still be celebrating Bastille Day. Unless they drink entirely too much Friday, they'll be up and ready to go again after noon."

"That's right." Brigitte felt unaccountably lonely. "I plan to walk over and see a little of that huge military parade on the Champs Élyssés tomorrow. And I want to watch some of the fireworks all over the city to see how they compare to our American Fourth of July ones."

Eva sighed. "Wish we could watch them together, but I'll be corralling a group of students." Her voice took on its tour-guide tone of instructiveness. "Remember not to bring your passport to the flea market Saturday, and carry what cash you think you'll need in a money belt."

"I know about the pickpockets. You warned us enough during the tour."

"I'm sorry. Repeating myself seems to be an occupational hazard."

Brigitte laughed. "Forget it. I understand. As to our meeting time, you should know by now I'd rather sleep late than hunt a bargain. What if we rendezvous somewhere near the place about eleven?"

"Sounds good." Eva seemed excited as she gave Brigitte travel directions and designated a specific meeting place. "I'll be wearing a green blouse."

"Okay. Be on the lookout. I'll be in red, and I'll try to be on time."

Eva laughed. "I'll believe that when I see it. See you later."

Brigitte slowly replaced the receiver on its cradle and stretched back onto her fluffy pillows. She and Eva had come a long way since that first day in the library just a month ago.

Tomorrow should be perfect. Brigitte could wake up and dress as slowly as she wanted, and Eva could get up early and be there as soon as the vendors at Les Puces, as the locals called the flea market, set up their wares. She'd said she was looking for a special birthday gift for Jeanne and wanted to find it at the best price possible. If she and Eva could arrange all their meetings like this one, they might manage to form a relationship that suited both of them.

❖

"Good morning," Eva said as she flipped through the canvases that leaned against each other in one of the large boxes sitting in an old woman's stall.

The woman was still arranging the boxes she'd just unloaded but paused long enough to respond. "Hello. If you find a masterpiece, just let me know."

"I'm looking for an original Picasso at a cut-rate price." Eva winked.

"But of course. I'm sure you'll find a great variety to choose from." The woman stopped and took a sip of coffee from a huge white cup.

After several minutes, Eva selected a small canvas and pulled it out to inspect more carefully. "It's for my aunt, and it has to be just right."

"Why a Picasso?"

"Just because I heard he used to wander through this place looking for things to inspire him."

"That's true. I remember my mother pointing him out when I was a girl. She said he stopped by her stall once and asked if he could sketch her for a painting he planned to do of two women running on the beach." The woman smiled faintly at the memory. "He said he admired her large arms and legs, but she got mad and told him to leave her alone." The vendor raised an eyebrow. "He's a terrible womanizer—well, he was, back then. Evidently he found some models for his two running women, as you can see in this copy."

Eva laughed but slid the painting back where she'd found it. "Thanks for reminding me about that. I think I'll try to find my aunt something by a woman."

"As you wish. That might be more appropriate."

"See you later," Eva said as she left the stall. "Thanks for your time. I may be back." She'd bring Brigitte with her and see what she thought of the small painting.

"Over here," Eva called as Brigitte strolled toward the overpass, looking as stunning as always.

"I thought I'd never get here. I didn't realize this place was so far away from the city center."

"Yes. It's at one of the old gates. Feel like hearing a bit of historical trivia?"

Brigitte twisted her face into a wry expression, then smiled as she nodded. Her hair was as shiny as her white blouse. "Do I have a choice?"

"No. That's one of the risks of dating a tour guide."

"Is that what this is? A date?"

"Naturally. We're finding out if we're compatible. That's how I define a date."

"Okay. I suppose we're off to a good start, don't you? I'm only five minutes late."

"Yes, but you brought a purse instead of doing what I suggested."

Brigitte looked down at the black purse that hung by a slender strap around her neck. "But it's so cute, and it sets off my outfit, don't you think?"

"Surely you left your passport at the hotel?"

"Of course. It's locked up in the safe there. At least I half listened."

They began to walk toward the crowd. "And I expect you to listen to my trivia now." Eva was thrilled to see Brigitte in such a playful mood. She seemed to have lightened up after the tour ended. "More than a hundred years ago," she said, "people known as pickers or moon fishermen would scavenge through trash bins at night and sell their treasures at several places throughout Paris. The city fathers finally got tired of the mess and had all the trash cans within the city limits sealed, so the pickers had to gather their goods outside the city."

"In turn, they brought their wares to the gate to sell, eh? Pretty smart." Brigitte looked around as they walked. "This place is huge."

"Yes, supposedly it's the largest antiques market in the world, but you'll find plenty of other things here. And two other markets are taking place in Paris right now, both located at old gates too."

"What are we waiting for? I want to see what kind of unusual jewelry I can find."

Brigitte's eyes shone like sapphires as she picked up her pace, which helped make the flea market seem like a magical place to Eva.

❖

"Since you're my own private guide today, tell me why this is called a flea market," Brigitte asked as they strolled past the stalls stacked high with antique furniture.

Eva glanced at her, delighted to show off her knowledge. "Gladly. Some people say the name originated in the Middle Ages, when the aristocrats sold their cast-off flea-infested clothes to the peasants."

"Ugh. That makes me itch."

Eva chuckled. "Others say it was named for the flea-infested furniture similar to all these pieces around here."

"Double ugh. Remind me not to sit down or try anything on." Brigitte glanced around with mock horror.

"I'm sure everything's a lot more sanitary than it used to be."

"Maybe, but I'm not taking any chances. I'll stick to jewelry. That should be relatively safe, don't you think?"

"Hmm. I suppose. You do know what the name Les Puces means, don't you?"

"Of course. The fleas."

Eva nodded.

"So nothing's sacred, I assume. Well, I'll just have to grin and bear it, as my grandmother used to say."

Just then they heard music and soon passed an elderly blind man pounding on an ancient piano. Brigitte did a little dance step, then suddenly wrapped her arms around Eva. "Let's dance." She whirled Eva around a few turns. A few people stopped to watch them, and Eva loved the way Brigitte took charge and seemed as free and unashamed as a child. When they stopped, Brigitte panted for a few seconds, then said, "When I was very young, my little friend back in Louisiana and I used to dance like this. I haven't thought about her in years."

"Where is she now?" This was the first time Brigitte had mentioned any of her old friends, except the mysterious Rosa who'd taught her to tango. Eva was surprised she'd mentioned this one.

Brigitte's joyous expression faded, and she looked sad and a bit angry as she released Eva and began walking again. "I have no idea. My grandmother made me stop associating with her, and her family moved away from our small town several years later."

"Stop associating with her? Whatever for?"

Brigitte's face flamed almost as red as her pants. "Oh, just a silly game she caught us playing. It still embarrasses me to talk about it. Isn't that ridiculous? After all these years."

"Nothing's ridiculous, especially things that happen to us when we're children. I'd like to hear about it, if you feel like sharing. Here, let me buy us a crepe, and we'll sit over there on the grass."

Brigitte couldn't believe she was actually confiding in Eva about her early experiences of sexual discovery. As she described the game she and her friend had played, and how she'd felt when her grandmother had discovered them and then scolded them, she thought she'd die of embarrassment. She concentrated on her fruit crepe and watched the passing crowd when she finished, nervous about meeting Eva's eyes.

"Thank you for telling me about that," Eva said, as she took Brigitte's now-empty hand. "I'm sure it wasn't easy for you to be treated like that. To me it sounds like a small splinter, but it's probably festered in you so long it's as painful as a cancer."

Brigitte finally got up enough courage to meet Eva's level gaze. "You don't think I'm just being silly?"

"Of course not. Your grandmother was totally wrong to react like that. What a stupid woman, to make you feel ashamed of something so natural. Did you ever have another friend like that little girl?"

A wave of sadness washed over Brigitte. "No. I was a loner all through school. Rosa was my only friend, and she had to leave town when I was about eight, so I didn't have anyone to trust. Luckily, Rosa wrote me from time to time, and even though Grandmother didn't like it when I got those letters, she did let me keep them. I guess she thought since Rosa was so far away in New Orleans it couldn't hurt for me to hear from her once in a while."

"Well, it evidently turned out for the best," Eva said. "And now, if you're ready, let's go hunt you some flea-less jewelry, and you can help me find a present for Jeanne."

And just like that, Brigitte felt…lighter, as overwhelming burdens from her past burned away like early morning fog on a sunny day. She hoped they were gone for good.

❖

They were rummaging through a jumble of necklaces when suddenly Eva heard Brigitte catch her breath. Eva glanced at the necklace she was holding up like a spoil of war, and a shock of recognition almost knocked Eva off her feet.

"It's not a priceless treasure, but somehow I'm sure this is exactly what I came here to find," Brigitte said, apparently entranced with the piece of costume jewelry. Eva could understand why. Its cranberry-red centerpiece would nestle perfectly in the hollow at the base of Brigitte's white throat, and the five teardrop stones hanging from the silver setting of the central stone would point toward her glorious breasts. Eva almost licked her lips. The chain that Brigitte was now holding around her neck, three large beads and three small ones linked by intricately fashioned silver strips, would support the pendant.

"Here, let me fasten it for you." Standing behind her, Eva lifted the collar of Brigitte's blouse and slid the clasp into place. Then an intuition so powerful it felt almost like a blow hit Eva out of nowhere.

She'd done this before, she knew, with such a strong certainty she couldn't imagine where it came from. *I bought this piece for her and gave it to her as an anniversary present.* Eva had never had such a strange experience.

She shook her head and turned Brigitte slowly to face her. "Let me see how it looks," she said. To her horror Brigitte wore the same vacant expression she had several times during the tour, the times she'd seemed almost to leave her body. What was happening? Eva couldn't do anything but stare at this unusual, beautiful woman she was almost afraid to get to know any more fully.

A dark-haired man with blue-green eyes fastened the clasp of the beautiful red necklace he'd just surprised her with. "Happy fifth anniversary," he said. "I'm so sorry to have to tell you this, but I have to go out for an hour before our feast tonight. You know I'll be counting each second I'm away, though. I'll return soon, my one and only love."

"I understand, dearest one. I'll be ready when you come back to me. Godspeed." Brigitte fingered the necklace, its red pendant warm to her touch. "You couldn't have chosen a more beautiful gift, beloved. *I'll keep it forever. Hurry home.*"

Standing in the tent at the flea market, surrounded by antique jewelry, Brigitte shook her head. "What the…"

"My words exactly," Eva said. "Where did you go?"

"I don't know. One minute I was here, and the next I was… somewhere else. Some *time* else—very long ago. And I think you were there too."

"Me? I've been right here in Paris, in 1972. You're the one who keeps disappearing on me."

"You were fastening this very necklace around my neck. I'd know your touch anywhere. And this piece is one of a kind. It feels exactly the same as it did wherever, whenever I was." Brigitte clutched its central stone as if it could solve the mystery of what had been happening here in Paris.

But Eva would think she was completely bonkers. She needed to snap out of it. Brigitte couldn't keep from wondering, though, why she was so certain Eva had been the man who'd given her the necklace she was now holding.

"How much?" she asked the seller, whose smug expression indicated he'd overheard her conversation with Eva and knew she'd pay whatever he asked.

He named a price and she agreed.

After Brigitte paid the shopkeeper, Eva whispered, "You should have bargained. He'd have come down at least ten or fifteen percent."

"It doesn't matter. I'd have paid twice that much. I have to have this."

❖

It was half past one, and Eva was beginning to drag. She'd been up since five thirty and hadn't slept well because she'd been excited about seeing Brigitte again. "I've looked everywhere for something for Jeanne's birthday, but that painting I saw early this morning is still the best choice I've come across. If you're ready to leave, I'd like to stop and buy it."

"I'm ready, but first I'd like something cold to drink. What about you?"

Eva nodded her agreement.

Brigitte returned a few minutes later with two drinks. She handed one to Eva and stuffed her change carelessly into her small purse, which she wore slung over one shoulder and across her chest.

Eva shrugged in frustration at Brigitte's careless invitation of pickpockets. Evidently Brigitte had so much money she didn't have to worry about losing some of it. They'd almost reached the stall where she'd spotted the painting for Jeanne earlier when Brigitte shouted, "Son of a bitch. That kid grabbed my purse right off me," her face red and her blond hair flying.

"Do you see him?" Eva yelled, then spotted a blue blur racing away from Brigitte. She darted behind the next stall and intercepted him, grabbing him by the arm and pulling him back toward Brigitte.

When they all stood face to face, she said, "This pretty lady is a guest in Paris. What will she think about us if you act like that? Give her back her purse this minute."

The kid scowled and slowly held out the black bag.

"Tell her you're sorry and you won't do it again."

He spit on the ground, but Brigitte grabbed his other arm. "Why did you take my purse?"

"*Maman* is sick and needs some medicine. I have to have money for that."

"And just how much would be enough?" She opened her purse and raised an eyebrow. "Tell me the truth."

"A hundred francs."

"That's all?"

"Yeah."

"Okay." She held out a hundred-franc note to him, and he snatched it from her and stuffed it into his pocket. "And take good care of her. Do you understand?"

"Yes, pretty lady. Thanks. I won't forget you." He pulled off his cap in tribute, then ran away.

"You'll make him think crime does pay," Eva said, though she was touched by Brigitte's generosity, howsoever misguided.

"Sometimes we all need a little help, and I believe this is that boy's time. Besides, I can afford it, and, lucky for him, I'm feeling generous."

Eva took Brigitte's arm and squeezed it. "The people of Paris thank you, and for their sake, I hope you judged the boy correctly. I don't want to see him in a court of law in the future." She threaded her arm through Brigitte's and guided her across the market to the art vendor's stall.

"Ah, I thought you might be back," the same woman from early morning said. "You've come for the painting for your aunt, eh?"

"Yes. I hope you haven't sold it." Eva glanced at the pile where she'd found the painting earlier.

"I put it in the back so no one else would discover it. It's meant for you, I believe." The woman pulled it from behind a jumble of old photo albums.

"What do you think, Brigitte? Do you think Jeanne will like it?"

"I've only met her twice and don't know her taste. What do you say?"

"Blue's her favorite color, and I think she'd like the carefree way the women are running along the beach. She also likes Picasso, though I can't stand him. It's a fairly good copy of the original."

"Why don't you like Picasso's work?"

"He obviously painted this one during his neoclassical period of the 1920s, when Leigh and Emily were here in Paris. They might have seen the original hanging in an art shop somewhere. I do like the bright blues and oranges in it."

"Yes, the colors are striking."

"But I don't like the way he shows the women's legs, feet, and hands as huge in proportion to their bodies, and I don't like how he paints the flopping bare breast on the woman in the front. I enjoy beautiful nudes, but his seem crude and vulgar." Eva scowled. "He's such a womanizer, yet he doesn't seem to actually like women very much."

"Why don't you tell me what you really think?" Brigitte laughed. "I thought all Frenchmen were womanizers."

Eva bristled. "First, Picasso isn't French, as I'm sure you're aware. He's Spanish. Second, we French aren't as puritanical about sexuality as you Americans, but many of us aren't as dissipated as you imagine. In fact, we're very capable of being faithful to our partner, if we've chosen wisely."

Brigitte's smile vanished. "Hmm. Obviously I've hit a nerve, and apparently you don't know me very well if you consider me puritanical. I'd say it's time to call it a day. We've been on our feet a long time and we're both tired." She put her hand on her purse in front of her. "I plan to remain in Paris at least through the month, and you know where to find me. Oh, and wish Jeanne a happy birthday for me. I hope she likes her Picasso."

She turned and walked away, and Eva felt like kicking herself for ruining such a lovely day.

CHAPTER TWENTY-FOUR

Eva paced on the cobblestones of the medieval Court of Honor. Strange how she could barely hear the noise from the traffic in this busy area near Boulevard Saint-Michel. Here, behind the high wall that separated her from the street, and surrounded on the other three sides by the wings of the two-story Hôtel de Cluny, she felt confined yet safe, hearing only the murmurs of tourists and the coos of the pigeons that scurried beside her back and forth near an old well.

It hadn't been easy to call Brigitte and apologize for losing her temper at the flea market this past weekend. Brigitte's casual remark about all Frenchmen being womanizers had hit a sore spot and caught her off guard. Perhaps she was being unrealistic, expecting her parents to live up to her ideal of a perfect couple when they obviously weren't a good match. But she could expect anyone with whom *she* became involved to live up to her standards. Brigitte was evidently capable of a loyal and lasting friendship, judging by what she said about her friend Rosa, and she'd clearly admired Emily and Leigh's relationship. But what did Brigitte want for herself?

She'd swallowed her pride and her doubts and invited Brigitte to visit the Cluny Museum with her today. She loved the Cluny and wanted to share it with Brigitte—but she had an ulterior motive as well. She wanted Brigitte to see the red necklace worn by the woman in each of the six medieval tapestries displayed in this museum.

As she paced—waiting for Brigitte, as usual—the walls surrounding her turned from a dank gray into an almost golden tan when the sun appeared. She studied the carvings that adorned the various windows and pointed archways, especially the grapes and scallop shells carved into the stones of the Gothic building. During the Middle Ages, an abbot had built a mansion over the ruins of some old Roman baths, and it had eventually become this museum. Eva loved places like this for their sense of history, their stability. They made her feel rooted, grounded, secure.

Just then Brigitte rushed through the deep-red entryway, her customary white blouse making her new red necklace stand out. "What a creepy place," she said in greeting as she neared Eva. "That steep slate roof and those ancient towers make me feel like we're on a filmmaker's location for a vampire movie."

Eva shrugged. Brigitte had a way of jerking her out of the past, tugging up her roots, and making her feel vulnerable. It wouldn't do much good to explain that this building was one of the only two remaining medieval homes in Paris. Americans had little concept of the past and how vital it was in shaping the culture of a country.

Placing her hands on Brigitte's shoulders, Eva touched each of her cheeks swiftly with her own. She'd never greeted Brigitte in the French way before, but she wanted to take their friendship to another level, and the traditional *bisou* was a good way to begin. "Hello. It's nice to see you. I want to apologize again for losing my temper the other day. It wasn't really directed at you. I just have some strong feelings about honor and fidelity, and I overreacted. Forgive me?"

Brigitte looked pleased and touched Eva's cheek with three fingers. "It's okay. We all have our hot buttons, though I certainly didn't mean to push yours." Her eyes were as soft and blue as a periwinkle petal. "So, what exactly is this place you want me to see?"

Eva smiled, then transitioned into her tour-guide persona. "Officially, this is the National Museum of the Middle Ages. It houses everything from golden Visigoth crowns to stained glass and sculptures from Notre-Dame. We can give it all a look, but I especially want you to see the collection of tapestries known as *The Lady and the Unicorn*."

Brigitte beamed. "Of course. I've been meaning to look for them but wasn't sure where to find them. When we visited Nohant, didn't you mention George Sand and a fellow author discovered them somewhere?"

"That's right. I'm surprised you remember that detail. I crammed a lot of information into that excursion and only mentioned this in passing."

"For some reason that detail grabbed me—maybe because I'd never heard it before?—and made me like George Sand even more than I already did. Tell me more."

Eva sighed in mock impatience. "Okay. The tapestries were in the upstairs rooms of an old château in northern France, and the mice and the damp were ruining them." They entered the ground floor of the museum, and Eva squeezed Brigitte's hand. "Sand and her friend had some experts from Paris clean the tapestries, and years later— less than a hundred years ago—the town fathers sold them to this museum for the relatively small amount it cost to repave their local cattle market. It was the town's loss and the world's gain."

Brigitte squeezed her hand in return, then continued to hold it. "Thanks for sharing this place with me."

As they walked together side by side, viewing and discussing the assortment of alabaster plaques, choir stalls, and other tapestries, their linked hands and the occasional contact of their shoulders made the collection of artworks from the Middle Ages seem even more special to Eva.

"Why do you want me to see the unicorn tapestries?" Brigitte asked as they wandered through the ground-floor exhibits.

"You'll understand when we get there," Eva said, and smiled like a seductress. "At least I think you will. Something at the flea market reminded me of them, and I want to see if you agree with my theory."

Finally they climbed the steps to the first floor and entered a cool, dimly lit room. On the curved wall in front of them hung six huge tapestries.

"Amazing," Brigitte said. "Each of these has to be at least ten feet by ten feet. What's that in meters? About three and a half? When did you say they were made?"

Eva nodded. "You're right about their size. And they were made about 1500, in Flanders, which was the center of textile making at that time. What strikes you most about them?"

Brigitte tried to take them in, but their age, their size, and their complexity overloaded her senses. "Uh, the red background in all of them?"

Eva nodded. "Yes. Definitely. What else?"

Focusing on each one in turn, Brigitte felt like a slow student unable to answer her teacher's simple questions. "Okay. Here's exactly what I see. Green trees and bushes, plus a unicorn, a lion, and a lady on a circle of green vegetation. Also some flags and a few other animals."

"That's right," Eva said, and Brigitte felt a flush of pride and something a bit more intimate. "Why don't we look at each tapestry closely now, and you'll probably spot what made me think you'd appreciate this exhibit."

Brigitte walked over to the first tapestry and studied it. "I see a well-dressed woman taking something to eat from her maid with one hand while she holds a wild bird with the other." Then she pointed. "Just look at the woman's clothes. What rich-looking fabric, and it's embroidered practically all over. And that necklace—Wow! That's it, isn't it? That's what you wanted me to notice." She couldn't believe it. "It looks like the one I bought at the flea market."

"Yes." Eva gently spread back the tips of Brigitte's collar and lifted the necklace that lay in the hollow at the base of her throat.

Eva's fingers brushed Brigitte's skin as she slowly released the piece of jewelry and straightened her collar, and Brigitte resonated to Eva's touch like the tight-stretched tabla she'd once heard in a recording of some Hindu ragas. As the sensual vibrations spread through Brigitte, Eva swallowed with visible effort, then said, "The necklace you bought made me think of the ones in these tapestries, though I'm not sure why. So I hoped maybe you could help me solve that little mystery."

Eva winked at Brigitte as if they were fellow detectives. "As we examine these tapestries, remember that the first five of the six represent the five senses. The one we're looking at now is supposed to correspond to taste."

Concentrating on the first tapestry, Brigitte fingered the necklace that hung around her neck. A vision of Rosa in the tub, blood covering her arms and throat, flashed through her mind. Brigitte's mouth instantly became dry yet tasted like she'd just sipped sangria someone had dropped several copper pennies into. But then the more pleasant tastes of merlot and chocolate cake, mousse, and brie rushed in and coalesced in her memory to overpower the taste of blood.

She forced herself to focus on Eva's hand that grasped the back of her arm just above her elbow, grateful for the support it gave her. "Mmm. Taste. Okay. Let's go look at tapestry number two."

After they moved the short distance to the next one, Eva released her hold on Brigitte's arm and murmured, her lips so close to Brigitte's ear she could feel the warmth of her breath, "This one's supposed to represent hearing."

"Yes." Brigitte nodded and studied the work of art that had obviously taken more patience to create than she could even begin to comprehend. "That makes sense. Notice how calm the lady looks standing there playing that little pipe organ." In fact, the lady's expression reminded her of Eva, who could have a very soothing effect on her if she wasn't setting off alarm bells in her oversensitized body or infuriating her. "Seeing her maid and the animals around her listen to her play makes me wonder what the tune she's performing sounds like." And standing near Eva made Brigitte want to get to know her much more intimately.

Surrounded by the mumble of lowered voices from the crowd around them, Brigitte once again heard the *clatter* and *clink* that had pulled her from her deep sleep the night she found Rosa in the tub. The sounds had become familiar to her since then, waking her up every few nights. They still made her shudder.

But now, as Eva continued to comment softly on the tapestry, with its millions of tiny stitches, Brigitte could almost hear the mournful, breathy melody the lady's large hands were producing as her maid pumped the organ's bellows. It had a soothing tone, Asian, in a minor key and gradually drowned out the metallic sounds that had so often kept her from sleeping.

Brigitte fingered her necklace, the organ's foreign sound continuing to pull her away from the horrors in the past she thought she'd finally escaped. And when Eva hummed a strange, lonely sounding tune, put her hand in the small of Brigitte's back, and gently guided her to the next tapestry, Brigitte put the sounds of Rosa's suicide to rest.

"There's so much red in this one," Brigitte said, almost trembling now. "All of the maid's gown and part of the lady's, plus that overwhelming background. At least the lady's face and the entire unicorn are white. Why is she holding up a mirror and letting the unicorn look at itself in it?" She immediately saw the blood in the white tub and on Rosa's alabaster body.

"You tell me," Eva said. "These tapestries are wide open to interpretation. The only thing most people agree on is that this one represents the sense of sight."

That was easy, but Brigitte couldn't share what first came to mind. How she wished the tub were still gleaming white, filled only with Rosa and the bubbles she'd always loved to soak in. Even now Brigitte felt as stained by Rosa's blood as Lady Macbeth must have in her famous "Out, damned spot!" speech.

But as she strung together some interpretation about the purity of the unicorn and how it was more attractive than the lady, she realized that, in a way, Eva was playing the role of the unicorn for her. Brigitte needed, craved to forget the past and begin a new life here in this marvelous city, and somehow Eva was helping her do just that.

As she stood and gazed at the third tapestry, her arm brushed Eva's, and a peaceful sense of companionship, of sharing the same space with someone she actually cared for, filled her. She moved her arm slightly against Eva's, and the gaze Eva poured on her made the red of the tapestry recede somewhat, and the unicorn's white, gentle face became her focus. She sighed with a contentment she hadn't felt since before she'd discovered Rosa dead.

They wandered over to the fourth tapestry, and suddenly the odor of menstrual blood overwhelmed Brigitte. She was almost tempted to check the back of her khaki skirt, although she knew she would find no stain. But then, things became clear. Each of these tapestries was triggering one of her senses and somehow making her relive, sensation by sensation, what she'd experienced the night she'd discovered Rosa dead. And by reexperiencing the taste, sound, sight, and odor in this way, she was on her way to assimilating her horrific experience and then, perhaps, accepting it and letting it rest.

"Don't tell me what this one represents." She grasped Eva's arm. "The maid is holding out a basket of flowers for the lady, and the monkey has obviously stolen one and is sniffing it."

"You're right. This one's supposed to represent smell. How did you know?"

Brigitte grinned. "Oh, I have my ways." She didn't want to tell Eva she hadn't been able to shake the odor of Rosa's blood. It assaulted her at the oddest times, though this time, its presence made sense. "What's the deal with the monkey?" she asked, to direct Eva's attention away from her.

Eva looked thoughtful. "I'm not sure. The first thing that came to mind when I looked at the tapestry is the phrase *monkey mind*."

"Monkey mind? What's that?"

"When I was in India, I learned to meditate. According to the Buddhists, we all have drunken monkeys jumping around in our heads, and the best way to tame them is to meditate every day. That helps calm the monkeys, so they don't keep us anxious and afraid all the time."

"So the sweet smell of the flowers is taming the lady's mental monkeys, eh? Psychologically speaking."

"Yes. That's how I see it today. I may change my mind tomorrow, though."

"That's interesting and makes sense in a strange way. Thanks for the interpretation." She kept her hold on Eva's arm, clasping it the same way Eva had held hers earlier, and again a kind of peace that had eluded her since she'd witnessed Rosa's death swept through her. She could become really fond of Eva.

"Obviously this one represents touch," Eva said, as they reached the next-to-last wall hanging, and rubbed two fingers down Brigitte's cheek to demonstrate this fifth sense. The peace that had filled Brigitte just seconds ago vanished, and her cheek felt hot where Eva tracked. She was surprised Eva didn't jerk her fingers back and shove them into her mouth to cool them.

"The lady in this panel reminds me of you in several ways," Eva said, still stroking Brigitte's face.

Brigitte pressed against Eva's fingers, unable to get enough of them, wishing Eva would touch her all over with them. But she forced herself to formulate rational sentences. "Really? How, besides that green velvet gown with its gold trim and chain belt? I'd kill for an outfit like that."

"The long blond hair, for starters. And, of course, the necklace. It looks more like yours than any of the ones in the other tapestries. But standing there with her hand on the unicorn's horn and the lion sitting docilely on the other side of her, she looks so composed, so regal."

Brigitte's arousal grew, and she wasn't sure if Eva's recent touch or her kind words had caused this response. She certainly felt far from composed and regal. "Thanks. But what about that little monkey the lady seems to be staring at? Why does it have a chain attached to its collar?"

"Ah, the monkey again." Eva spoke of it almost fondly. "Its chain is fastened to some type of weight, so showing the animal tamed like this could symbolize that the lady has achieved control over her anxieties and found her inner strength and composure."

"Wow. You've put a lot of thought into this." *Inner strength and composure.* Eva's words struck a chord deep inside Brigitte, and she caressed her necklace, drew a deep breath, and stood up very straight. If only she could be totally honest with Eva about her weird experiences, but that was impossible, so she said the first thing that came to mind. "Very interesting. And probably as reasonable as any of the other thousands of theories people who've visited this exhibit have dreamed up."

After they moved on to the sixth and final wall hanging, they stood silently in front of it for several minutes. "What about this one?" Brigitte finally asked. "How does it relate to the representations of the five senses we've just seen?" She fit her hand into the curve of Eva's waist and guided her to their right, the thrum of foreign music pulsing through her like the tango music had the night they'd danced.

Eva seemed totally absorbed in the scene they stood in front of now, but Brigitte detected a slight quiver when she removed her hand from Eva's waist. It was almost as if their unconventional tango here in this dark room was ending.

"This last tapestry is the hardest one for me to make sense of," Eva said. "It's the only one where the lady's standing in front of a tent, and what interests me most is that she's taken off her necklace and is placing it in a small chest."

Missing the softness of Eva's small waist, Brigitte forced herself to focus on the final tapestry. "Yes, and look. Both the lady and her maid are wearing red in this one. The unicorn and lion are both on their knees to her. And the monkey's tiny now and crouching at her feet."

"Yes." Eva seemed excited, as if they'd found an essential clue. "The lady's completely conquered her inner monkey. Good for her. But I'm not sure why she's putting away her necklace. And what do you think their red clothes symbolize?"

Brigitte felt a rush of excitement too, as if she and Eva were about to finish putting together an intricate jigsaw puzzle, like she and Rosa used to do to pass the time. "What about the words embroidered across the top of the blue tent behind her: *À Mon Seul Désire?*"

Eva shook her head slowly. "Those words supposedly supply the key, but they've been translated into English in so many ways they've just ended up confusing scholars."

"What do others think they mean?"

Eva scratched her head. "Obviously, they've been interpreted as *My only desire*. But scholars have also argued for *By my will alone*, *To calm passion*, and *Love desires only beauty of the soul*. Which one would you agree with? Take your pick."

"None of the above." Brigitte wasn't sure why she'd rejected all the options, but none of them felt right to her. She paused, then said, "I know this was supposedly a wedding present from a French lord to his future bride, so what would he have been trying to tell her in this elaborate, very expensive way?"

Eva merely shrugged, as if she'd considered all the options and rejected them too.

They stood silently for a while. "Now I understand why you wanted me to see this exhibit. The necklace is the key, don't you think? What does it represent? And why was I so drawn to it at the flea market?"

"My thoughts exactly."

"Do you believe in past lives?" Brigitte said the words before she could stop herself.

"Past lives? What do you mean?"

"My friend Rosa and I read *A World Beyond*—a book written last year by a woman named Ruth Montgomery. In it the author revealed that in a past life she'd been alive during the time of Christ as Lazarus's third sister, Ruth, who isn't named in the Bible, and had watched Jesus be circumcised."

Eva laughed. "So she says. And you believe her? How could she ever prove some ridiculous claim like that?"

Brigitte felt like Eva had just slapped her. "I'm not sure what to think about such things, but obviously you're not open enough to discuss them."

Eva clutched Brigitte's shoulder. "I'm sorry. I shouldn't have been so judgmental. It's just that I feel a lot more comfortable talking about ideas and theories than about voodoo and superstitions."

Brigitte winced and turned toward the exit.

This time Eva grabbed Brigitte's hand. "I really do want to apologize. I'm just uneasy talking about something like these past lives you brought up. The other day at the flea market when you bought your necklace, I had that lightning-flash certainty I'd bought it for you at one time. It was just an instant intuition, but then you went into one of those trance states that I saw you have several times during the tour. You have to admit that's not normal behavior."

"Yes, I know—"

"But it also intrigued me. I couldn't get it out of my mind, and coming here to see the tapestries with you has made me realize that neither of us is crazy." Eva blew out a deep breath. "If you can put up with my skepticism, I'd like to try to understand things like this better. I can't put my finger on whatever's happening to you and between us, but I feel something, and I'm willing to explore it if you are."

Brigitte stared at Eva, her chest aching as the words reverberated through her. Eva was offering her an opportunity for a relationship. Could this thing with Eva, whatever it was, develop into something more?

"Okay," she said. She'd enjoy this fantasy and where it went from here. Eva knew about and seemed okay with her past profession. And now she was willing to explore Brigitte's psychic experiences. Brigitte didn't have any other secrets that could possibly come between them.

CHAPTER TWENTY-FIVE

I can't believe you haven't taken a river cruise. It's on every tourist's itinerary." Eva couldn't keep her eyes off Brigitte, whose tight white sweater made her breasts even more delectable than usual. Eva had begun to have visions similar to the one about the necklace, but now her visions involved holding those breasts, of putting her mouth on them and—

Brigitte gazed at her with a sincere expression. "I suppose that's why I've chosen not to take this cruise. I've wanted to experience Paris as it actually is, not like it's simply a city I'm passing through." She seemed so wistful Eva tried to get her mind off sex and focus on Brigitte's words. "I want to get to know it, the good and bad, so I can decide if it would be a good place to live permanently."

"Really? You'd move here? That would be wonderful." The summer fling Eva had considered might be longer than she'd thought, and the prospect made her legs shaky and weak.

"You really think so?"

Brigitte looked so uncertain and hopeful, Eva wanted to hug her. But she wouldn't stop with just a hug. "Of course. Just think of all the fun we could have. I could show you the city as it is now, and you could show me how it used to be."

Brigitte scowled, and Eva rubbed her shoulder to make sure she realized she was halfway teasing.

"I'm sorry. I meant what I said. I've been thinking about what you said about past lives and have decided it'd be great to be able to see Paris as it once was. Especially if we both used to live here at the same time."

Just then the long, slender boat they stood on pulled away from the jetty, and they began their trip up the Seine. "The night cruise is my favorite," Eva said. "The lights make the city even more beautiful than it is by day. All lit up like this, it's almost like a fairyland."

They leaned against the metal railing as the craft began to move a bit faster. "A cool fairyland, isn't it?" Brigitte pulled down the sleeves of her sweater. "I'm glad I wore this."

"Me too." Eva couldn't help but let her eyes linger on Brigitte's breasts, but fortunately Brigitte was gazing at the Obelisk and didn't see how desperately Eva wanted to feel them pressed against her.

"How different things are today in Paris than they were during the Revolution," Brigitte said, shivering slightly as the boat picked up speed. "Less than two hundred years ago, Marie Antoinette had her head cut off and the entire country was in an uproar. Now the peace talks to end that stupid war in Vietnam are the most important political event of the summer."

How ironic. Brigitte's mind seemed to be on anything but sex, yet that was all Eva could think about. She eked out a suitable reply. "Yes, Paris deserves a rest. Don't forget that just thirty years ago we were an occupied city. Of course, I don't remember it. But since I was a child I've seen Paris struggle to recover from the devastation the Germans caused."

Just then, the Louvre came into view, and Brigitte pointed toward it. "You're right. It's hard to imagine they were ever in control here. Thank God they didn't confiscate all your national art treasures and ship them back to the Fatherland."

Brigitte's concern for the culture of France warmed Eva. "You know a lot more about history than most of the Americans I've met. I'm so glad we're getting to know each other." As the dark river slid by quietly and the architectural treasures of Paris appeared before them like frames in a slide show, Eva felt more drawn to Brigitte than ever. She put her arm around her waist and hugged her close. She longed to pull her into the shadows, run her hands under that tight white sweater and—

"Thanks. Me too. Oh!" The dark bulk of the Conciergerie floated into view. Even the lights couldn't illuminate it entirely. It hunched there like a huge rhinoceros half-covered with muddy water.

"Something wrong?" Brigitte trembled. "Are you cold?" Eva asked.

"No, not in the way you might think. If I tell you something, will you promise not to laugh at me?"

"Of course I won't laugh at you. Is it something about past lives?"

Brigitte pulled her gaze away from the Conciergerie and focused on Eva. "How did you know?"

"Just a lucky guess. It seems to be a subject we're both interested in exploring." *Second only to exploring your body.*

"You're right. I was afraid to go into detail about my strange experiences during the tour, but I suppose I can trust you enough now to tell you."

Eva squeezed Brigitte to her, trying to convey that she'd try to understand whatever Brigitte wanted to share with her.

Taking a deep breath of the river air, which always somehow reminded Eva of burnt paper, Brigitte described her experience in Marie Antoinette's cell. "It was like I became the queen for a few minutes. I could feel exactly the same sensations she did, and I can tell you, it wasn't a pleasant experience."

Eva let go of Brigitte's waist, and Brigitte thrust her hands in the pockets of her sweater. How much wine had Brigitte drunk before they met at the jetty? But Eva steeled herself to discuss this strange revelation. "So you think you were Marie Antoinette in a past life?" There, that didn't sound judgmental, did it? Didn't some people fantasize they'd been important historical figures to make themselves seem more important?

But Brigitte surprised her. "No. I felt like I was simply paying her a visit, empathizing with her for a while. I was separate from her, yet I was her, but only during that brief period of time."

"And did you lose touch with your present self when you were being Marie Antoinette?" Brigitte's strange confession began to intrigue Eva.

"Completely. When I woke up from my vision, if that's the proper term, it took me a moment to remember who and where I was."

"Oh." Eva recalled how irritated she'd been when Brigitte stopped paying attention to her lectures. "Did the same thing happen to you at Versailles and at Nohant?"

"Yes, and once when I was alone at Père-Lachaise. How did you know?"

"I wondered where you'd gone. You seemed to suddenly disappear, and I missed you. In fact, it made me angry the first few times it happened, but I gradually decided not to take it personally."

"Angry. Why on earth?" Brigitte seemed concerned as well as puzzled.

"I'm just touchy. It's not easy for me to speak in front of a group, and when you didn't seem to be listening, of course I thought you were bored." Great. Now Brigitte would think she was a total incompetent.

Just then Notre-Dame slipped into view, and the great Gothic cathedral seemed to breathe a benediction over them. "I love those flying buttresses," Eva said, frantically changing the subject. "During the Middle Ages, cathedral cities in France competed to see who could build a cathedral with the highest arch. They were as competitive as sporting events are to us today. The flying buttresses were the main support that enabled the architects to design taller and taller structures…until they began falling down."

Brigitte put her warm hand over Eva's, which had grown chill since she'd removed it from Brigitte's waist to grasp the metal rail. "Nice try, but I'm good at detecting attempts to avoid a sensitive subject. What's really on your mind?"

Eva looked at the lights that enhanced Notre-Dame's beautiful structure, and a sense of calm settled over her. "I'm practicing to speak before a judge and jury. When you didn't listen to me, I felt like I'd failed and I'd never be able to hold the court's attention. Sorry. That was selfish of me, I know, but I do want to be a good lawyer—"

Brigitte pulled her hand back as if Eva's touch stung her. "Wait a minute. A lawyer? I thought you were a professional tour guide."

Eva was glad Brigitte couldn't see her blush as she explained her situation. "I didn't think I'd inspire much confidence in my group members if I told you what an amateur I am."

"So you're not really what you seem?"

"Are you? Are any of us?"

Brigitte was silent for a long while as the riverboat slid under the ornate bridges and between the concrete walls that bordered the Seine.

The reflections of the city sparkled in the water and compounded the light that surrounded them.

As the Eiffel Tower came into view, Brigitte turned to Eva and put her arm around Eva's shoulders. "You know, I really admire this symbol of Paris. It's so tall, straightforward, and unadorned. It seems as if it's proud of its framework and not afraid to show its true self. Everywhere I go in the city, I look up and see it, and it reminds me of what I aspire to be." She gazed at Eva with love shining in her eyes. "Thank you for telling me who you really are. Maybe someday I'll know myself well enough to be able to do the same."

Eva wanted to kiss Brigitte, here on the open deck with the Seine under their feet, the stars over their heads, and the lights of Paris surrounding them. And so she did. As they stood there entangled, the cold breeze lost its bite, and the warmth of Brigitte's hands ignited a bonfire within her. She felt at one with the wind and the stars and the river as she and Brigitte bridged the distance between them that not that long ago had felt impossibly wide.

They kissed for an eternity, and as they stood together as intimately as two lovers carved from the same block of granite, they sighed simultaneously.

"The Rodin Museum, day after tomorrow, one o'clock sharp?" Eva murmured after the cruise ended and she put Brigitte into her taxi. She ran her hand gently over Brigitte's cheek.

Brigitte seemed starstruck but managed to whisper, "One o'clock, very sharp. If I can wait that long. Sometimes I hate your job. Why can't you just come back to my hotel with me tonight?"

"I can't think of anything I'd rather do, but I have clients, and I can't let Jeanne down. If I go with you I'll never want to leave." After another lingering kiss, Eva stepped back and the taxi rolled away, taking Brigitte with it.

Chapter Twenty-six

Eva walked through the door of her parents' house, and her father immediately jumped up from where he was sitting, reading the daily newspaper, and questioned her. "Who was that tall, gorgeous blonde I saw you with at lunch several weeks ago?" No *hello*. No *How are you?*

She played dumb. "Where did you see us?"

"Eating lunch with her and several other people."

His curious, expectant expression made her feel as if her father had been wanting to question her about Brigitte for days. Well, he could just drool all over himself. Brigitte was hers.

"Oh, you must mean Brigitte. She was a member of one of our tours."

Yves frowned. "Where did she say she was from?" Several drops of perspiration shone on his forehead. He was sweating? He never broke a sweat.

"New Orleans. At first I didn't think I'd like her, but we've ended up becoming friends." Why would he be asking such strange questions, and why was she answering them?

"Brigitte," he whispered, almost to himself. "What do you know about her?"

"Not that much. Her best friend died, and Brigitte came to Paris to recover and is staying at the George V. She's fluent in standard French, loves jazz, and seems very well read and eager to learn about the French culture. I got the impression she's thinking of living here permanently." He raised a brow. "We've been seeing each other some too. She's very attractive."

Eva enjoyed her father's attempt to hide his—what was it? Envy? But she refused to tell him exactly where they'd been and that they planned to visit the Rodin Museum together tomorrow. And she would certainly never admit to him that they were falling in love. After all, he'd never confided in her about his amours. Not that she wanted him to.

"Is Mother here? I thought she might want to go shopping."

Yves looked around as if he didn't know who she was referring to. "Your mother? No, I don't think she's been in town for weeks. I've been out of the country for the past few days and just assumed she's still at the coast, as usual."

He seemed so unconcerned Eva felt like shaking him.

"Well, I'll let you get back to your newspaper, Father. Sorry to have disturbed you."

He wiped his sweaty forehead with a crisp handkerchief and tucked it back into a pocket. His grin looked strained. "Don't let any beautiful American women get you into trouble," he said. "I wouldn't trust any of them." He chuckled to himself and turned away, dismissing her like he always did.

"I can take care of myself," she murmured to his retreating back. "And I will." Disliking her father so intensely made her uncomfortable.

Brigitte glanced around to make sure the museum guard wasn't looking, then lightly smoothed her hand just inches above the arched back of a marble woman lost in the embrace of her lover and touched the woman's hip for an instant. In her mind she was caressing Eva. "Too bad Rodin didn't sculpt two women," she said. "I'd never be able to keep my hands off a statue like that."

Eva jerked Brigitte's hand away. "Well, you better, or the guard will appear out of nowhere and throw us out of here." She frowned. "Or, worse yet, Father will track us down and have us arrested for God knows what. I told him about you yesterday, and I'm sure he's madly jealous."

Eva's voice had lost its tour-guide authoritativeness, but Eva still frowned with disapproval at Brigitte's flouting of the museum's rules.

However, judging by the way she played with Brigitte's hand that she still held, Brigitte ventured Eva would be willing to let Brigitte run her hands over *her* as thoroughly as she was burning to do.

"How can they expect anyone with any feelings to not touch these statues? They're made to be caressed, just as women are." Brigitte moved closer and stared at Eva with so much desire she was afraid the guard might arrest her for public lewdness. She whispered, "Being stroked will help polish them, make them shine."

"And wear them out."

Brigitte didn't back away, and Eva was almost panting, her heartbeat visible in the hollow of her throat.

"You should be ashamed. You brash Americans think you can waltz over here and do whatever you want with our national treasures."

Eva smiled, but Brigitte detected a trace of acid in her words. She'd gone a whisper too far. She'd learned how very protective Eva was of her country's art. She stepped back from both Eva and the sculpture and raised her arms. "Look. No hands. But you can't keep my eyes away from it." She locked her gaze on Eva's breasts for a long moment before she transferred it to the sculpture that half-reclined in front of them.

Brigitte circled the work of art, admiring it from every angle. The man's palm rested lightly yet possessively on the woman's smooth hip, as if absorbing the heat that radiated from it. The woman had placed her arm, almost as muscled as the man's, around his head in a tight grip, and both seemed lost in their kiss, as if nothing mattered except the fusion of their lips.

Brigitte recalled kissing Eva on the cruise and couldn't remember anything that had ever given her so much pleasure. She squirmed as she envisioned exploring Eva's entire body with her lips, as she was bursting to do.

The sun lit the underarm of the marble woman wrapped in her lover's embrace. Her breasts, their legs and feet, their entire bodies glowed with a warmth Brigitte had never experienced in a work of art. "What a masterpiece," she murmured.

"Yes. It's divine. *The Kiss* is the perfect name for it." Eva sighed. "He really captured their passion, didn't he?"

Brigitte ran two fingers along Eva's bare forearm. "If I can't touch any of the art in Paris, may I touch its most beautiful admirer?"

Eva flinched, then stepped closer to Brigitte, grinning. "If I can keep you out of trouble that way, I suppose it's a small sacrifice to make." The golden rings in Eva's blue-green eyes flared, and Brigitte slid her arm slowly around Eva's waist, brushing her breast suggestively.

Eva gasped, and her eyes threatened to melt Brigitte, who felt as if she were made of wax.

As they wandered arm in arm among the sculptures in the small museum dedicated solely to Rodin's masterworks, they gradually moved almost as one as they admired the way Rodin had made stone and metal come to life.

All too soon, Eva looked at her watch. "Ready to go? I don't have much time."

"No. I'd like to stay here forever, but I suppose we have to."

"We can sit in the garden for a little while, if you want, before I have to leave."

Brigitte nodded, and Eva led her to a secluded spot, perfumed by masses of flowering shrubs surrounding them. "Hmm. What a nice afternoon. Very stimulating." Brigitte rubbed her hand up and down Eva's thigh, lost in her nearness. Then, almost in one of her trances, she gazed into Eva's eyes and let Eva draw her face to her lips.

Brigitte's lips tingled, ached, as if her entire body had been asleep and was coming awake. Sensations jetted through her she'd never considered possible. Eva's strong hands grasped her cheeks, her neck, her breasts, modeled her like clay, made visions shatter her. She was Sleeping Beauty, Pinocchio, Pygmalion's Galatea, waking into life because he so fiercely desired his creation to be human. But her Pygmalion was a woman.

Brigitte's blood sang through her veins, her cheeks and nose vibrated, her shoulders felt weak as their lips joined for an eternal moment.

"Wow," she said, when she finally gained enough strength to pull away. "Are you sure your name isn't Rodin? You certainly know how to transform stone into flesh." She sighed, her body tingling.

Eva appeared dazed too. "I was just about to ask you the same question." She glanced at her watch. "Damn. I have to meet my tour group at the Louvre. I'll be tied up with them the rest of the day." She pulled away a fraction, and Brigitte groaned at their separation. Eva swiped absently at her mussed hair. "I'm putting them on a late train to Pisa tonight. Can I see you tomorrow morning? Say ten? Is that late enough for you?"

"I'll be counting the minutes. I hope I can sleep." Brigitte pulled Eva close once more. "Can you hear my heart? It reminds me of a drummer riffing like crazy."

Eva chuckled, placed her hand over Brigitte's left breast, and squeezed gently. "Don't let it slow down. We'll tango tomorrow morning." Then, with a promise shining in her eyes, she was gone.

Brigitte sat in the garden outside the museum until the caretaker came out to close the gates. "Good night," he said.

"Good night." She was certain this would be the longest night of her life, and the best morning.

❖

As Brigitte lay in bed trying to sleep, reliving her afternoon with Eva like listening to a favorite song over and over, she thought of Rosa. But instead of contemplating her death, she recalled happier days. Just as she began to doze, a scene from her childhood unwound in her mind and lulled her to sleep.

Brigitte slipped out of her grandmother's house, then skipped down the trail of crushed oyster shells to Rosa's cottage, tucked under the cypress trees and so far away it was almost invisible.

"Come on in, little one. What beautiful swamp irises you've brought me. Would you put them in a vase?" Rosa, her red hair rolled up with bobby pins all over her head, sat in her bathtub full of bubbles.

Brigitte loved the colorful bubbles, but they always popped when she poked them.

Rosa stood up, naked, and kissed her on the cheek, like she always did. Grandmother never kissed Brigitte, though she did give her a stiff hug once in a while. But it was all right that Grandmother didn't hug her more, because she smelled like onions and garlic, not sweet like flowers.

After Rosa dried off on a white towel and pulled on her pretty underwear and what she called her negligee—it was really a thin red housecoat—she sat in front of a big round mirror in her bedroom and carefully put on her makeup. She was so pretty.

Brigitte sneezed, but she stared as Rosa patted her face powder on with a pink powder puff, then rubbed a little pad around in a red container of rouge and dabbed some high on each cheek. After she blended it with the powder, her eyes seemed brighter and her cheekbones higher.

Using a pair of silver tweezers, she plucked her dark eyebrows. They were already thin, but Rosa wouldn't let a single hair mess up their arch. "I have to look perfect for Mr. Dupuis this afternoon," she said. Rosa crimped her eyelash curler on the top lashes of one eye and squeezed the curler shut for a long time, then did the same thing to the other eye. It worked like magic. Her lashes looked longer and curlier than ever.

"We need to hurry. It'll be dark soon, and he doesn't like for me to keep him waiting. We're driving to New Orleans tonight. Will you take my bobby pins out?"

Rosa's hair was as soft as a kitten as it fell into long curls. Brigitte wanted to rub one of them against her cheek, but Rosa picked up her brush and quickly smoothed her hair into beautiful waves that fell to the top of her shoulders. It was as red and shiny as the feathers on Grandmother's favorite laying hen, and she ached to touch it but knew better than to try now that it was ready for Mr. Dupuis.

"Would you get my stockings out of the chifforobe?" Rosa said, taking off her negligee. Her kind voice made Brigitte's stomach feel funny.

She handled the stockings carefully. Once, Brigitte had hit the corner of Rosa's dressing table with one and torn it, and Rosa almost cried. She said they were made of a new material called nylon and were really scarce because of the war overseas. But Mr. Dupuis always managed to locate some to bring Rosa.

By the time Brigitte handed her the hose, Rosa was slipping her black garter belt over her lacy panties. They were a lot fancier than the big white ones Grandmother wore. Today, Rosa even let her help her put the five little hooks into the metal eyes that held the contraption together over her stomach.

Then she pulled the narrow elastic strap down the front of one leg and fastened it to the top of her hose. "Will you make sure the seam on the back of my leg is straight?"

After Brigitte inspected the thin line and told Rosa it wasn't crooked, Rosa pulled the back strap down and let her fasten the little rubber and metal gripper to the hose. Then they fixed the other leg, and Brigitte ran her hand up Rosa's leg to make sure neither hose had any wrinkles in it. She loved the feel of Rosa's firm skin encased in the smooth nylon.

Rosa looked at her nice wristwatch Mr. Dupuis had given her for Christmas. "Heavens. Mr. Dupuis will be here before you know it. I better hurry."

She pulled a snow-white satin blouse out of her chifforobe and put it on, then a long blue straight skirt that clung to her hips just right, tucked her blouse in, and cinched a patent-leather belt tight around her waist. Brigitte helped Rosa slip on her blue high-heel shoes that made her look like a movie star, and Rosa covered her own lips with bright-red lipstick, blotted on a Kleenex, and put a dab on Brigitte's lips.

"You better run along now, little one," Rosa said, patting some of her special perfume behind each earlobe and on the underside of each wrist. As she clipped on the little gold earrings Mr. Dupuis had given her and slipped gold bracelets on her right wrist—they were a present from him too—Rosa started to disappear, *like she was turning into a ghost.*

Chapter Twenty-seven

I'm coming. Just a minute."
The knock on Brigitte's hotel door was louder than she'd expected from Eva, but if Eva was as keyed up as she was, that was understandable. Brigitte had been dressed and waiting for what seemed like hours.

She'd stayed up until the wee hours reading the recently released *The Joy of Sex*, which had made it impossible for her to sleep the remainder of the night. In her experience, joy and sex had never been closely related. Sex had always been part of business, and joy had rarely been part of her life. But if she had to put a name to the feeling that had bubbled up from somewhere deep inside her yesterday when she'd kissed Eva, joy would be the best word she could think of to describe it.

The knock came again when she'd almost reached the door. "Hey, I said I'm coming. You sound as impatient as I feel." But as she slung the door open, she didn't see Eva. A man stood there, an angry-looking man who looked vaguely familiar.

"You don't recognize me, do you?" he said, his gray eyes like pewter. "New Orleans, 1955. I'm hurt but not surprised. I remember you, but all our faces must run together for a whore like you. Or do you even look at us except when you take our money?"

"Who are you, and what the hell are you doing here? I'm busy. Go away." She tried to shut the door, but he pushed his way in.

"I'm busy too, and I won't keep you long. I won't even sit down. Just stay away from my daughter. If you ever touch her, I'll kill you."

"Your daughter. Who—"

"Eva. At least that's what she calls herself now. I know I didn't tell you my real name all those years ago, and I can't imagine why you told me yours. Aren't women like you supposed to hide everything about yourself? How dare you come to my country and try to seduce my daughter."

Now Brigitte remembered this man. He'd been charming when Rosa had first introduced him to her. Rosa said he'd come highly recommended by one of her oldest clients from France and was willing to pay more than the going rate. He preferred blue-eyed blondes, she said, but he didn't like for them to be too smart.

She glared at the man. "So you're Eva's father. She's mentioned you. From what she's said, it's rather ironic you should demand I don't see her again. I should say the same thing to you."

He drew back his hand and she stood up taller. "Go ahead. Show me what you're capable of. If you think I'm going to lie about how smart I am or give you the satisfaction of being the downtrodden little woman you want me to be, you're wrong. You may not realize it, but you did me a big favor all those years ago. I've never again let a man treat me like you did back then."

His expression turned cunning. "Have you told Eva what you were, what you still are, at heart? Once a whore, always a whore, I always say."

Her palm itched with wanting to slap him. "Yes. I've told her about my life in New Orleans. But she's clearly not your natural child. She accepts my past as just that. In fact, she seems to think we might have a future together." Though she and Eva hadn't discussed anything past their mutual desire to ravish each other, Brigitte couldn't resist this opportunity to wound Eva's father.

His eyes ignited, then chilled her as he stared at her. He was still a handsome man, but the years had chiseled lines in his hard face and grayed his hair until it resembled the color of a moonstone. His eyes seemed to diminish in size until they became pinpoints emitting pure hate.

"I suppose you told her how you let me fuck you, you bitch. How you let me use you and even smiled after I did. You stood there and held out your hand and let me buy your body. And you were a cheap lay, an inexperienced swamp rat who didn't have a clue how to handle a real man from Europe."

His words pummeled her much more effectively than his fists could have. But she straightened her spine and pulled her white robe tight around her body. She was almost rigid with fury. "Get out of here, you bastard. I'll leave your daughter alone, but not because you want me to. I can't stand the thought of being close to anyone related to you."

She shoved him out the door and slammed it after him. She had to get out of Paris, perhaps take a train to Germany or Eastern Europe. She couldn't bear to stay in the same city with Eva and not be with her.

If she didn't go, Yves would tell Eva what had happened between them all those years ago, and she couldn't bear to think of him hurting Eva like that. If she stayed, Eva would be constantly reminded of Yves and his women every time they touched.

Brigitte felt like throwing up, but instead she pulled her suitcase from the closet and began to pack.

❖

Eva climbed the stairs to reach Brigitte's suite to try to work off the nervous excitement that had built steadily since yesterday. She'd kept waking up every hour last night, touching her lips and wondering if she'd imagined how wonderful Brigitte's kisses felt.

Who would have thought the strange, aloof woman she'd fought with in the library would turn out to be so alluring in every way? What would happen now? If their kisses were any indication, having sex with her would be a life-altering experience. She couldn't keep herself away, yet she wasn't sure she wanted her life changed.

Hot sex between the sheets was one thing, but in her experience it didn't last forever. She didn't want to modify her career plans, or even put them on hold, if this turned out to be merely the summer fling she'd envisioned earlier. Then, she'd had no idea that Brigitte would consume her as fully as she had. Eva couldn't imagine the flames that had burst out between them in the past few days dying down any time soon.

No, her rational side warned her that she and Brigitte needed to have a long, serious discussion about what they were about to get into, but her brain was so scrambled she couldn't think about anything but running her hands over Brigitte's luscious nude body. She'd aim for a sensible conversation but wouldn't be surprised if her ability to think deserted her as soon as she saw Brigitte.

She knocked on Brigitte's door. No answer. Surely Brigitte hadn't overslept. She'd seemed so reluctant to let her go yesterday at the museum. Maybe she hadn't slept well last night and then hadn't been able to wake up this morning. She knocked again, louder this time. Finally she called out. "Brigitte. I know you're in there. Please let me in."

Now she heard footsteps and the door slowly opened. Brigitte appeared ashen, nothing like she'd looked yesterday sitting in the garden outside the Rodin Museum. Then, she'd glowed from the inside out, but now she looked as pale and cold as a block of unshaped marble.

"Come in, Eva. I'm packing."

"Packing? Whatever for? Have you had bad news from home?"

"You might say that." Brigitte appeared to have trouble moving and simply dropped into the nearest chair. "No, that's not true. I stayed awake all last night thinking about you, about us. And when I cooled off and really considered what was happening, about to happen, I decided that this—whatever it is between us—will never work." She glanced up. "Sit down for a minute, and then I've got to catch a train. I've already called a taxi."

Eva dropped into the chair across from her and stared. Brigitte's vitality, her very blood seemed to have been drained from her. Now Eva understood what people meant when they described someone as being a shell of themselves. Compassion welled up from deep inside her.

"Why do you think that? At least tell me that." Eva felt as if she were at the bottom of a deep well and could barely see the light far overhead.

Brigitte took a long, labored breath and let her shoulders drop as if she were shrugging off a heavy weight. "I'm an American and you're French," she said.

Eva almost laughed. "Is that all? At first, yes, that was a huge problem. But you've opened my eyes. Why, I—"

"No. That's the least of my worries. It's my past that bothers me most. You're a tour guide right now, so it's easy for us to be seen together in public, to be accepted by your friends and family."

Eva adjusted herself in her seat. "So. I'll keep on being a tour guide if that'll make you feel better."

"I don't think so." Brigitte shook her head. "You'd hate me soon enough if you had to give up your dream of becoming a lawyer, of helping people who need you."

"No, I swear I wouldn't mind." Now Eva shook her head, but through the clamor inside herself, she realized Brigitte was right.

Brigitte smiled faintly, as if she realized she'd made a valid point. "Think about that little pickpocket at the flea market. He needs someone like you to defend him."

"He can find someone else." Eva refused to give up so easily.

"No. You're one of a kind. Your country truly does need you."

Eva sighed. Brigitte was making too much sense.

"Besides, what if someone uncovered my past? I can just hear the whispers among the people we'd associate with. A lawyer and a whore?"

"No one would ever find out."

"Someone always finds out."

"But you've changed. People change every day."

"People don't care. They love the gossip, the thrill of feeling superior. They don't want to let others change."

"I don't care. We can run away together, we can—" Eva put her head in her hands and burst into tears. "I want to be with you."

"It's all right, my darling." Eva felt Brigitte stroking her hair and leaned into her touch. "You'll feel better tomorrow. You'll get through the summer, and in the fall you'll become so caught up in your final steps of being licensed, you won't have time to think about me."

Eva looked up, then threw her arms around Brigitte. "Don't go. Please, don't go."

Brigitte slowly loosened herself from Eva's embrace and backed away. "I have to. You know it's for the best. You have a wonderful future ahead of you. I want you to make the most of it."

Eva wiped the tears from her cheeks.

"Now, go. My taxi will be here soon, and I don't want to keep it waiting."

Eva got up and just stood there. "No last hug? No final kiss?"

As if something had broken loose inside Brigitte, she wrapped her arms about Eva, then tilted her face up and seared her lips with a kiss. Brigitte appeared as strong and sure of herself as Joan of Arc must have on her way to be burned at the stake. Then she turned her back and walked into her bedroom.

Eva looked around the room and let herself out. In the hallway, she met the bellboy who was obviously coming for Brigitte's bags.

Chapter Twenty-eight

Damn. I can't find my registration list for the tour that starts tomorrow. Did you put it somewhere? I wish you wouldn't straighten the stuff on my desk. You know how I hate that." Eva riffled through the pile of papers that littered the space in front of her.

Jeanne walked over and picked up a stapled document lying in the outbox on Eva's desk. "It's right here, where you tossed it yesterday. What's wrong? You've been as irritable as a heat rash all day. And I've never seen your desk this disorganized. No wonder you can't find anything."

Eva jerked the papers away from her. "Thanks. I have a lot on my mind."

"I'll say. And you better get whatever it is off your mind by tomorrow. Having twenty American teenagers and their chaperones to escort all over Paris will give you more than enough to think about without worrying about whatever's bothering you right now. What's wrong?"

Eva sighed and walked over to the coffeepot. "Want a cup?" she asked as she poured herself one.

"Yes, please." Jeanne gestured to a small, secluded alcove furnished with several armchairs. "Let's talk."

Settling into a chair with her coffee hot in her hands, Eva sighed again. "I don't know where to begin."

Jeanne patted her arm. "Just tell me how you feel. Maybe that'll help."

After a long silence, Eva said, "Hurt. Confused. That's how."

Jeanne sipped her coffee. "Why?"

Eva stared through the front window of the office. Some people rushed by, intent on pursuing whatever goal motivated them on a bright Sunday morning, whereas others strolled, some arm in arm, perhaps headed to the park to escape the July heat. She and Brigitte could have planned to meet in the Tuileries later this afternoon, take a picnic—damn it. Her throat ached, and she slammed her cup onto the small table beside her and put her hands over her eyes, doubling over. She couldn't hold back the tears that had been building in her again since yesterday, when she last saw Brigitte.

Jeanne knelt beside her in an instant and wrapped her arms around her. "Go ahead. A good cry never hurt anyone. We'll talk about everything afterward and sort it out."

Eva relaxed into Jeanne's embrace and let herself go. Gradually the tears slowed and stopped. She hiccupped and sniffled.

"Here." Jeanne handed Eva her handkerchief. "It's a good thing I'm old-fashioned. You young people run around unprepared for emotional emergencies like this." She chuckled gently and gave Eva a final squeeze. "That's it. You already look better. You're beautiful even with a red nose and eyes."

Eva's throat spasmed again, this time with gratitude for Jeanne's presence in her life. What would she have done without her all these years?

Jeanne sat back down and picked up her cup of coffee. "Do you feel like talking now, or do you need some more time? I'll be here whenever you're ready."

Eva straightened in her chair, blew her nose twice, and picked up her cup too. "Sorry our coffee's not still hot."

"That's the least of our worries," Jeanne said with a smile. "It was too hot to handle for a while anyway." She sat silently, seeming as patient as the Sphinx.

"Brigitte left town."

"So? The tour was over. She enjoyed it and then moved on to the next city on her agenda. Why are you so upset about that?" Jeanne set her cup back down.

"Brigitte left—"

"I heard what you said." She slowly retrieved her cup. "But you need to give me some idea about why that upsets you so much."

"We were involved. Then she basically decided she wasn't good enough for me and left. I didn't want her to." Eva took a sip. There. Those were the facts as she saw them.

"Why would she think she's not good enough for you? She's an intelligent, gorgeous, wealthy woman." Jeanne smiled mischievously. "She's good enough for me."

Eva frowned. "Don't joke about it. You don't understand. She used to be a prostitute. She's not proud of her past and was afraid she'd ruin my reputation and my career."

"So that's why I liked her from the very beginning," Jeanne said. "She's not only intelligent, gorgeous, and wealthy, but she's also noble."

"Oh, Jeanne." Eva lowered her cup to her saucer with a clatter. "This is serious. I'm hurting here and you're making light of everything."

Jeanne looked properly contrite. "Did she tell you about her past?"

"Yes. When we were in Nohant." She shook her head slowly. "She seemed embarrassed about it, but I let her know I considered it over and done with, so she seemed to let it drop. It must have bothered her a lot more than I realized."

Jeanne frowned. "I would imagine so. Is that the only reason she dropped you? Did she get tired of sleeping with you and just tell you that to let you down easy?"

"What do you mean?" Eva blew out a breath.

"You mean you hadn't even had sex with her? I can't imagine. Why, she's—"

"Okay. That's enough. After the tour was over, and I mean over, we dated. We went to hear jazz, danced the tango at Chez Moune, shopped at the flea market, saw the unicorn tapestries together, took a night cruise on the Seine."

"And all that time you never even—"

"Okay, okay." Eva's ears burned. "We kissed during the cruise, and we went to the Rodin Museum—"

"Ah, then at the Rodin Museum you—"

"Yes, yes. We couldn't keep our hands off each other. But I had to leave and go put that group on the train, and we planned to see each other yesterday morning…"

"And that's when she told you she was leaving. If you didn't sleep together, what did you do all that time?" Jeanne seemed genuinely puzzled.

"We talked. We got to know each other. We learned to trust each other. I like her. She liked me."

"And that's why you're hurt." Jeanne put her hand on Eva's shoulder.

Eva jerked her shoulder back. "Hurt. Who said I was hurt?"

"You did, not five minutes ago. You said you were hurting and confused, and I was making light of everything." Jeanne held on, stroked her like she was calming a wild horse.

"I did?" Eva gazed out the window again, trying to regain her composure. "Well, I don't remember saying that, but I damn sure am."

"Which one?"

She slowly met Jeanne's probing eyes. "Both. Hurt and confused." Damn. Jeanne would make a hell of a prosecutor.

"A few weeks ago, you didn't even like Brigitte, though she is gorgeous. She irritated you, infuriated you even. What happened between you two?"

Eva felt like a common criminal on the stand, forced to answer the same question again. "I told you. We did things together. We liked each other. We trusted each other. I thought we had something special."

"And that's why you're so upset?"

"Of course. If we'd just slept together we'd probably have gotten it out of our systems, and maybe I could have accepted her reasons for leaving without too much of a problem."

"Or maybe she wouldn't have left."

"Now I'll never know."

"And you'll always wonder."

"And I'll always miss her."

"Do you feel better now?" Jeanne gazed at her with sympathetic eyes.

"I feel more objective about it…I guess."

"Then why do you still look so sad?"

Eva shrugged.

"I wonder what happened to change her mind so suddenly." Jeanne looked thoughtful.

Eva sighed heavily. "I guess I'll never know. But I do know that I need to get back to work. Thanks. Maybe I can manage to keep my mind on it a little better now."

CHAPTER TWENTY-NINE

Brigitte sat in the first-class dining car of the Orient Express and fingered the petals of the rose that adorned her table. The crimson sun blinded her momentarily as it penetrated the window across the aisle. If only Eva were sitting opposite her—challenging her, arousing her, claiming her. But perhaps even Eva had been only a fantasy, like her dream in which Simone had made her believe she could be her true self and still have the woman she wanted.

Brigitte couldn't escape her past. Who could have ever guessed Eva's father would turn out to be one of her clients from long ago? So much for living happily ever after in Paris. She'd had to lie to Eva not only about why they couldn't be together but also about when she actually planned to leave. It had taken her an entire day to pack and to store most of her belongings at the hotel.

She shook her head. One of the three men in black business suits who sat at the table across the aisle lowered the shade. Their voices were low, almost whispers, only an occasional word of their Oxbridge English drifting her way. Did Yves know these men, do business with them? Their heads almost touched, and Brigitte basked in the excitement shimmering from them. A beautiful young woman about Eva's age, perhaps their secretary, sat with them, looking rather old-fashioned in her long-sleeved, high-necked lace blouse and midcalf straight skirt.

The men reminded her of the Englishmen in Bram Stoker's *Dracula*, which she'd read ages ago, who were chasing Dracula across Europe to the Black Sea hoping to destroy him. The book had introduced her to the Orient Express, and since then she'd associated it with adventure and intrigue.

She stared into the globed glass of wine she cradled in her hand, wishing it were a crystal ball in which she could discover an exciting yet satisfying future with Eva. At least this dinner had met her expectations so far.

Her Tokay perfectly accompanied the nutty-tasting pâté de fois gras served as the first course. As she swirled the wine the waiter had handed her, its bouquet of fresh strawberries and vanilla almost overpowered her. It smelled like Eva. Usually she preferred French wines, but this Hungarian vintage seduced her as she rolled it over her tongue and softly chewed. She spread the delicate pâté, sprinkled with mustard seeds, onto brioche and alternated bites of it with sips of wine.

She was beginning her second glass when a young woman, her hair as dark as Eva's, glided toward her. Had Eva followed her? She took a closer look. No, this woman's eyes were dark, not blue-green. Her white satin blouse set off her scarlet pantsuit, just as her pale skin and teeth seemed even lighter compared to the bright lipstick covering her full, pouting lips. But just the thought of Eva had made Brigitte's breath come more rapidly, and the open neck of the woman's shiny blouse made Brigitte yearn to touch Eva's breasts. The stranger held the arm of a large older man who seemed to want nothing more than to pamper her. As the train abruptly rounded a bend, she grasped the man's forearm to steady herself, revealing blood-red nails. No, this definitely wasn't Eva.

Brigitte lapsed into her imagination to help her forget Eva. Was this woman Countess Elena Andrenyi and her husband the count, reincarnated to accompany her? When she'd first read Agatha Christie's *Murder on the Orient Express*, in her midteens, she'd imagined herself as this very woman, a beautiful young American married to a Hungarian aristocrat. Part of the group who avenged the murder of her sister and her two children, the countess never bloodied her hands. She appeared fragile, yet was stronger than anyone realized. She and her twelve co-conspirators literally got away with murder.

The stranger paused at the table in front of her and let the man pull out her chair. As he rounded the table to sit with his back to Brigitte, the woman stared at her with an expression that made her sweat. It suggested lusty sex between satin sheets, with the woman's nails raking Brigitte's back to produce beads of blood as red as the color of her nail polish. Brigitte stared back, and the woman transformed into a demure, harmless creature more likely to be Count Dracula's victim than his consort.

Brigitte took a large swallow of wine and shook her head. The wine was potent. Usually she held her alcohol better than this. Despite her sudden dizziness, she forced herself to refocus on *Murder on the Orient Express*. She'd read the novel so many times she finally promised herself that someday she'd travel on the famous train, but not as the wife of a man as stodgy as the count. She'd escort someone as beautiful as the countess.

The large man sat down and blocked her view of the temptress, so her mind jumped tracks as she spied another familiar-looking woman sitting alone three tables away on the opposite aisle.

Mabel Warren, the first lesbian Brigitte had encountered in print, had popped up in another novel set on the Orient Express—Graham Greene's *Stamboul Train*. The woman she had just spotted sat sipping from a tumbler filled with a brownish drink she immediately imagined as whiskey, for Mabel Warren was an aging alcoholic in her fifties. This woman emptied her drink and imperiously signaled the waiter for another one.

The present-day Mabel lit a cigarette and glanced at her wristwatch, and then she half turned to look over her shoulder. Finally, an attractive blonde in her late twenties sauntered in. The woman with the drink, her cropped hair mussed, jumped up and signaled the blonde, obviously trying to show her off to the rest of the passengers. The young woman, who looked nothing like Eva, glared at her companion as if she was acting ridiculous and sat down like she would rather be anywhere else, stroking her own long hair.

How was Eva doing? If she and Eva had slept together the night they tangoed, would Brigitte have been able to relax, to share herself completely? By then she'd already confessed her past profession, but she hadn't revealed her strange visions. After she'd told Eva about them, she'd felt unencumbered, but if they'd had sex after their steamy session in the Rodin Museum, would the shadow of Eva's father have spoiled it? She was almost glad he'd intervened before they'd made love. To find out about him after the fact would have certainly devastated her.

Yes, perhaps Yves had done them both a favor by interrupting their plans. But why was she dwelling on this when she was not only traveling first class on the Orient Express, but in a private compartment for the overnight trip? She needed to forget Eva and what they could have had. Thank God her life in New Orleans and the generous terms of Rosa's will had made her able to afford to travel in style, with a comfortable bed, mosaic-floored private bath, constant hot water, and fluffy white towels in her own living space.

But she couldn't forget Eva that easily. If only she were here. They could have an intimate conversation over their wine, then stroll back to their compartment. There they would slowly undress each other and spend the entire night having fabulous sex, in their own secluded universe.

But Yves had made sure that wouldn't happen. Brigitte sighed. She couldn't tell Eva what kind of man Yves was. And someone as idealistic as Eva, who wanted to devote her life to upholding the law, truly wouldn't mesh with someone like her, who'd flouted the law for decades. No, Eva and she would never know what it was like to make love to one another.

She sighed and looked back at the other passengers in the dining car and finished her second glass of wine.

The three men were British diplomats, she fancied, on their way to Budapest. They would travel across Austria into Hungary, where they'd spend the night near the train station in a famous old hotel. At dinner, the men would comment on the buildings that still lay in ruins in some sections of the city and remark that it looked like the Hungarian Revolution had ended last month, instead of fifteen years ago. The Soviets clearly hadn't managed to help their satellite countries rebuild as successfully as the countries of Western Europe had.

Engaged by her fictitious scenario, Brigitte decided that one of the men would be a spy, though she didn't know which one. And their secretary would be having an affair with one of them, the one with wavy hair.

Brigitte cut a spear of asparagus into small bites and tried it. Delicious. Firm with just enough crunch.

Just then the large man seated with his back to her dropped his napkin and bent toward the aisle to retrieve it. The eyes of the dark-haired young woman who had initially made her think of Eva blazed at her like a forest fire. The man wasn't actually her husband. Brigitte quickly revised her story. He was her mother's new husband, escorting her back to Vienna. The young woman had run away from home when her mother married him. He was obviously a philanderer who'd wed the rich older woman only for her money, but he'd blinded her so completely she even trusted him to track down her rebellious daughter and return her to the family mansion.

The man had located the daughter in Paris and soon made a pass at her. But the fiery young woman had slapped him and declared she was a lesbian and would inform her mother and everyone she knew in Vienna of that fact if he insisted on taking her back. He did insist, believing he could win her over during the lengthy train ride, but obviously he wasn't having much luck. The woman would slip out of her private berth tonight and knock on Brigitte's door, having watched for her after dinner and located her compartment.

She wouldn't say much, but their eyes would catch fire and their bodies would follow. Like Eva's and hers should have. If only Yves hadn't showed up, if only she'd never met him, if only she'd never been a...

Brigitte sighed and tried a potato. Ah, so fresh, and with more taste than its American counterpart, though perhaps she was simply hungry. And the sauce was a masterpiece of cream and butter and some unknown ingredient. Perfect. Her steak was rare, exactly as she'd requested, and required almost no chewing. She stared at the blood that oozed from it and ribboned the white cream sauce. Would she ever be able to see blood, or a sunset, or a red necklace without thinking of Rosa? Would she ever be able to see a brunette, especially one with blue-green eyes, without thinking of Eva?

Eva had helped her quit having nightmares about poor Rosa dead in her tub, but now they'd returned.

The train rocked, but then Brigitte realized it had been her head. She could see the notes of the soft music that filled the car, flowing like a waterfall. Had someone laced her pâté with LSD? She drank more wine.

On her new plane of awareness she fantasized that the older woman she'd noticed earlier was actually a famous German novelist who enjoyed the leisure of train travel to devise the plot of her next book. Definitely a lesbian, a Gertrude Stein type, she hired attractive secretaries more to inspire her than to do her typing and filing. She herself enjoyed those menial tasks because they gave her the time and the opportunity to polish her work. She wasn't a wildly popular novelist but a serious literary type who intended for her books to eventually be classics. However, her secretaries kept her in touch with the more superficial world she tended to overlook yet craved occasionally.

Which of these women would notice Brigitte tonight and later knock on her door? Perhaps all of them? God, if only Eva would show up, tap on her door…

Dessert was a raspberry tart—a flaky delicacy full of vanilla pastry cream and topped with fresh raspberries coated with an apricot glaze. She savored the tang of the fruit blended with the sweetness of the cream and the glaze. It tasted like Eva. But she couldn't go there. She needed to sleep, to escape her longing for Eva in dreams that took her far away from this world where she'd been forced to walk away from the woman she wanted so much, that she was dying inside without her.

Hopefully a good night's sleep aboard the Orient Express would help her forget Eva, but she decided to have one more glass of wine in case it didn't. She emptied the bottle while the other diners drifted away.

Finally deciding to stand, she wavered and nearly tripped over her chair as she lurched into the corridor, reeling from table to table to steady herself. She was disappointed. She'd expected the Orient Express to move more smoothly.

❖

Brigitte careened down the narrow corridor of the first-class coach to her private compartment after prowling through several cars and exploring the fabulous train. During her tour of the first-class sleeper, she noticed two of the three men in business suits sitting in a two-berth compartment at the opposite end of the car. She giggled, amused at how serious they looked. The third one was entering an adjacent room with his arm around the large man who had sat with the woman with blazing eyes. Hmm. What was going on here?

Through her veiled awareness she glimpsed the gorgeous young countess in another compartment with the prim-and-proper woman who'd eaten with the three men. Her face grew even warmer when she realized the brunette temptress would be sleeping only a wall away. The older lesbian and her blond companion were staying on the other side of her and seemed very cozy. Now she was totally confused.

She sank into the damask armchair in her spacious room and tipped her spinning head back. The rhythmic noise of the iron wheels, combined with the wine, lulled her almost to sleep, but then she heard a thud and a loud whisper.

"You crazy fool. You better be careful."

Shaking her head, she tried to determine where the sounds came from but couldn't say for sure. By the time she jumped up and opened her door, the corridor was empty and quiet.

She must have been dreaming, so she stripped off her clothes, managed to pull on a filmy gown she'd bought in Paris, and slid into bed. She was gliding across northern France, she mused dreamily as the slight vibration of the train lulled her to sleep.

A hand on her shoulder shook her awake.

"What the—"

The small, surprisingly strong hand clamped her mouth shut. "Shhh. You'll wake the others. I thought you wanted me here."

As her eyes adjusted in the dusky light streaming under the door to her compartment, she discerned the sable-brown eyes of the young woman she'd admired earlier. Her eyes glowed almost red as she bent closer, her heavy perfume intoxicating.

"What are you talking about?" Brigitte whispered.

"I saw the way you stared at me during dinner. Do you think I can't tell when a woman desires me?" She threw off her dark robe and stood there as white as a marble statue, finally slipping under the sheet next to her. "I'm Scarlet, and I'm all yours."

Brigitte was sure she was dreaming this time, but the flesh under her hesitant fingers was warm and smooth. She slid her hand down Scarlet's side to her small waist and up the swell of her hip. Scarlet snuggled closer and rubbed her full breasts against her arm, and then she caught the hem of Brigitte's gown and eased it over her head.

Relaxing into her dream, Brigitte settled back into the comfortable bed as Scarlet stretched out on top of her and smoothed soft hands over her face.

"You're very beautiful, you know," Scarlet murmured, then bit her lower lip as gently as if she were tasting a raspberry. Brigitte countered Scarlet's teeth with her tongue, rolled her over, and nipped her cheek.

"Ah, you're as feisty as you are lovely," Scarlet murmured as she sank her teeth into Brigitte's neck.

She bucked, but Scarlet held on, and soon Brigitte was wandering in a huge field of wildflowers, their colors and smells surrounding her until Scarlet slowly released her and she dropped onto her pillow.

Brigitte slept for a while, until the train slowed and she became aware of someone sitting on the bed next to her. The person had evidently opened the shades, and the full moon glittered on long blond hair. "Who are you and—"

Again, someone hushed her, this time by merely placing a finger over Brigitte's lips. "I'm Ruby."

Gradually she could make out the green eyes of the blonde who had sat with the older woman at dinner last night, though a thin red ring circled each iris. "What's going on? Are you two playing a trick on me? How did you get in here? I thought I locked my door."

"Ha. You couldn't have kept us out, even if we'd had to bribe the conductor, which we didn't. You were easy. And Scarlet said you're delicious."

Why was this happening to her? She'd close her eyes and go back to sleep, and when she woke up it'd be morning and she'd be in Germany with her feet planted firmly on the ground.

As she squeezed her eyes shut, a hot hand caressed her leg, then slid up toward her stomach. Fingertips brushed her mound and circled her navel, massaging her belly. "Ah, you smell so fresh," Ruby muttered. "How I'd love to eat you and then lap your warm sauce. You'd melt in my mouth like tender beef."

She was growing tired of this rubbish, so she reached down to grab the imaginary woman, only to encounter a handful of silklike hair.

"Let me love you," Ruby whispered as she followed Brigitte's hand upward and bit the other side of her neck.

Energy rushed through her with the power of a locomotive or a flash flood. She was caught in the whirlpool torrent, a hurricane, a tornado, a tidal wave surging through her, breaking every internal barrier she'd ever built. Finally exhausted, she collapsed against her pillow again, the smell of incense coiling through her like a snake.

The third time she awoke, she sat up in bed and stared at the figure in the damask chair across from her bed. The window shade was closed again, but she could make out faintly glowing eyes.

"I didn't want to wake you," a soft voice said. "I would have sat here and watched you sleep."

"Who are you?" she asked, though this had to be the young woman who'd sat with the three men last night.

"I'm Coral." She rose hesitantly and approached.

"I suppose you want to seduce me, then bite my neck." Brigitte was past disgusted with this nonsense, but something kept her from dismissing this phantom she'd somehow conjured to her room. She needed to find out why she was having these visions and why her breasts and clitoris were pulsating like the throat of a warbler in full song.

"I want to love you, but you have to let me."

Coral sounded so apologetic that Brigitte lay back and patted the bed beside her. "Come here. You can't do any more damage than your two friends have." How could this beautiful dream woman possibly hurt her? In her long, high-collared gown, Coral looked like a girl playing boarding-school games.

But Coral's stroking hand felt like it belonged to a grown woman. The pulsations in Brigitte's clitoris grew from birdsong to kettledrum, spreading outward as Coral's gentle, rhythmic touch ignited an explosion from the depths of her body. It inched upward, seeming to seek the light, lava moving uphill, Etna and Vesuvius and Krakatoa combined as the glowing red substance rushed through her and finally seemed to blaze through the top of her head.

When Brigitte exploded, Coral cupped her face and kissed her eyes, her cheeks, her mouth. Her shoulders dropped, and as Coral kissed her way down her body and thrust deliciously long fingers into her with a scream of triumph, Brigitte melted into the mattress in surrender.

This could have been Eva with her, she realized. Eva would have made her burst into flame like this. But Eva was in Paris, and Brigitte was hurtling away from the City of Light.

A shriek startled Brigitte awake to the sun shining around the edges of the room-darkening shade. Then a loud boom sounded and the train shook, threatening to jump the tracks. It gradually stopped.

She ripped off her gown and threw on navy slacks and a pullover. She'd had some weird dreams last night, probably from all that wine, but that explosion was definitely real. Strangely, she wasn't hungover, even after drinking an entire bottle of Tokay. She felt energized, as powerful as the engine of the Orient Express.

She yanked her door open and rushed out into the corridor just as everyone else did. Two of the men still wore pajamas, as did the older woman whom she'd envisioned as a writer. The three women who'd visited her dreams were dressed and stood in a small circle, and when she glanced at them she could have sworn their eyes momentarily flashed red. What an imagination. To her embarrassment, her body began to throb like it had last night.

"Did you hear that sound? What happened?" the writer asked. "Why have we stopped in the middle of nowhere?"

"How do you know we're in the middle of nowhere?" one of the men asked.

"Because I looked out the window, silly."

The writer evidently knew the man, who seemed as if he'd like to choke her.

"Where's the conductor? He should be able to tell us what's going on," said the woman who'd called herself Scarlet last night, sounding exactly the way she had in the dream. Brigitte must have overheard her at dinner.

The conductor rushed into their coach. "Ladies and gentlemen. We've had an explosion in the first-class dining car. We're not sure what occurred, but it's nothing to worry about." He settled his features into something resembling serenity. "We're in Germany now, and as soon as the local authorities straighten things out and we replace the dining car, we'll be underway." Then he became magnanimous. "In the meanwhile, you'll have your breakfast in the other dining facility. The staff will do everything possible to ensure that it meets the same standards as the one you paid for."

Grumbling, everyone glanced at each other and began to return to their rooms. Brigitte studied Scarlet, Ruby, and Coral, tempted to chuckle as she recalled last night's marathon. How ridiculous.

The coach hummed with anxious, excited voices in several languages, just as her body still hummed from last night.

"Someone planted a bomb, intended for the first-class passengers at breakfast, but it exploded early."

Brigitte trembled. She could have been killed.

Later, as she ate a mushroom-and-cheese omelet in the new dining car, the older woman, the one she'd assumed was a novelist, paused at her table and said, with a British accent, "May I join you?"

"Of course." Perhaps she could discover who these people really were and why they were on this train.

"Horrid way to wake up this morning. That was a close call." The woman caught a busy waiter's attention and immediately ordered black coffee and toast. "Have you traveled on the Express before?"

"No. And I'll never forget this experience."

The woman grimaced. "Yes. Almost being killed will do that to you. But on the upside, riding this train is like being in a time warp. That's why I insist on taking it every chance I get." She looked around the dining car fondly. "So much romance and intrigue embedded in the very fabric of the accommodations."

Brigitte warmed to the woman. "That's exactly how I feel."

"I try to convince everyone I direct to travel this way. Of course, the big-name stars insist on flying. Time is money for them." She shrugged. "I prefer making B movies because the actors are usually impressionable nobodies who'll do exactly what I ask. We're all riding together on this occasion, except for the extras we'll pick up in Budapest."

"You're shooting a movie in Budapest?"

The woman buttered a piece of toast. "Yes, a horror flick called *Dracula's Daughters*. Audiences never seem to tire of vampires."

Brigitte almost choked on a piece of omelet. "I suppose you're right. Why do you think that is?"

The woman frowned and drank some coffee. "Hmm. It's almost impossible to untangle the interwoven fabric of violence, sex, love, and healing. The vampire speaks to that complex aspect of life."

Brigitte shivered, didn't know how to respond.

The woman finished her coffee and gave her a smoldering look. "Thanks for the company. If you're traveling as far as Budapest, look me up. We're staying in the big old hotel near the train station, and I have a private room."

Brigitte smiled weakly and murmured her thanks. The woman would most likely show her a side of Budapest she wouldn't see on a tour, but she'd had enough adventures. She wanted Eva, not some poor substitute. And her alcohol-induced visions last night, combined with the explosion this morning, had upset her more than she cared to admit.

If Eva had been with her—as she had been so much of this summer—maybe she could have coped better. But alone, she felt adrift, like a kite with its string cut. The bomb in the dining car, which was rumored to be a terrorist attack, could easily have ended her life, and she would have lost her chance of ever seeing Eva again.

Life was so short and could end at any moment. She'd been so obsessed with her memories—dwelling on her past with her grandmother, her mother, and Rosa—that she'd let them suck the life out of her. Is that what her three mysterious visitors last night had been trying to show her? Or was it something more positive?

She gazed out the window at the landscape rushing by. She'd travel around a bit, spend the rest of the summer alone, visiting the parts of Europe she'd always dreamed of seeing. She'd leave Eva alone too, let things between them settle. In the fall, though, she'd return to Paris. She needed to stop running away from her past, she needed to run toward her future, and telling Eva everything would help her do just that. And instead of trying to protect Eva, she'd let Eva decide if she wanted to try for a future together. She would trust Eva with her heart.

Chapter Thirty

Eva's father entered the café like he owned it. He always gave people that impression, no matter where he was. He believed he owned people too, she thought as she watched him head toward her.

"Yvette. I'm glad you agreed to meet me for lunch."

"It's Eva, Father. Will you ever remember that? I was surprised when you called. It's not like we make a habit of this." In fact, it was a once-in-a-lifetime occurrence. "What a nice café. Not one of your usual haunts."

"No. I thought you'd like to try something different, more upscale than you can probably afford right now, on a tour guide's salary. I tipped the maître d' so we'd have this nice private table too."

"What do you want to tell me? Is it something about Mother?"

"Don't be upset. Your mother's fine, though I wish you'd had some time this summer to go spend a few days with her at the coast like you used to. She misses you."

"Is it about Louis then?"

He shook his head. "No. I wish I could say he was okay. You know I worry about your brother. He needs to learn to be a man. I simply wanted to visit with you, to remind you what your life will be like when you establish yourself as a lawyer and can leave your menial job escorting foreigners around Paris."

"It's not all that bad. In fact, I've met some interesting people."

Yves tasted the wine the waiter had handed him and signaled for him to pour, then gazed into his wine as he swirled it. "Indeed." He took a large swallow. "What have you been doing except working?

Having a bit of fun, I suppose? Still seeing that tall blonde? What was her name? Brigitte, wasn't it?"

His smug expression angered Eva. "I was, but I'm not anymore." She couldn't believe they were having this conversation. He'd never asked her about her personal life.

"Why, what happened?" He raised a brow.

"None of your business."

He smiled urbanely. "Doesn't a father have a right to be concerned about his daughter?"

What was he up to? "All right. She broke it off a couple of weeks ago because of our differences."

"Your differences?" He swirled his wine again.

"Yes." Was she experiencing one of those altered states like Brigitte had? "She reminded me that she was an American and I'm French."

"Oh. Is that all?"

"Isn't that enough? Even you know how much I dislike Americans and their so-called culture."

"Right. I'd forgotten." He pinched off a bit of bread and buttered it sparingly.

"Also…she's ashamed of her past and said she was afraid someone might find out about it." She couldn't believe she'd just told him that.

"So?" His quirked eyebrow accented his expression of curiosity.

"She said if we were in a relationship it might damage my career."

"Oh. I see." He let out a long sigh, as if relieved about something, and swallowed the rest of his wine, then poured himself another glass.

Eva sat very still. What was going on with him? He usually drank in moderation.

"I have something to tell you about your American…friend. This Brigitte."

Suddenly it all made sense. Father staring at Brigitte in that café, asking about her later and sweating as he did so, and now this mysterious luncheon rendezvous. "You know her, don't you, Father?"

He stopped his glass halfway to his lips, then lowered it with a guilty expression. "Ah. Yes. I have to say that I do." Just then the waiter set a large Caesar salad down in front of him and a smaller one for her.

"What? How? She said this was her first time in Paris."

He set his glass to one side and unwrapped his silverware with a showy flourish. "I met her a long time ago, in New Orleans, while I was there on a business trip."

Something hardened inside Eva. "Tell me."

He hesitated, then shrugged. "I heard of her from several of the men I still do business with in New Orleans occasionally." He puffed out his chest. "They described her as eminently desirable and especially selective of her clientele, even back then, near the beginning of her career. Naturally I assumed she would gladly admit me to her select group of admirers."

"Naturally. How could she resist such an opportunity?"

He chewed his lettuce. Then, toying with a crouton, he said, "I took her to dinner at one of the oldest, most expensive restaurants in New Orleans. I spared no expense, treated her like she was a lady instead of a—"

"Now, now, Father. Remember, she's still a friend of mine." Eva was beginning to understand why he'd invited her here. He must have been afraid Brigitte had recognized him and revealed his identity. As if that had ever mattered to him before when he paraded his women in public.

He rearranged the lettuce on his plate. "When we returned to her apartment, naturally I expected a return on my investment. And I got it."

"Of course," she murmured. Sex as a business transaction. The thought revolted her.

He carefully smoothed back his hair. "I treated her like I always treat the women I entertain." He smiled in seeming satisfaction. "But all too soon, after a spirited exchange, she showed me the door and told me to never contact her again."

His obvious self-pity almost nauseated Eva, and suddenly she lost her appetite, even though she'd taken only one bite of her salad.

"Of course I complained to her manager, but she informed me that Brigitte made no promises and, in essence, chose her companions herself."

He ate another bit of lettuce and gazed at her as if he expected her to understand, even sympathize. "I resented the outcome of my investment, which left a very bitter taste in my mouth." He winced as if he'd found fault with his salad.

"And that's it? You never saw her again?"

Yves appeared almost wistful now. "I caught glimpses of her from afar, but we never spoke. I had no inkling of what she expected from a man and refused to let her humiliate me again." He put his fork down as if a sudden thought required all his energy. "If I'd known she liked women, I might have felt differently, but I assumed any woman in her position was interested only in the opposite sex."

Eva leaned across the table toward him, suppressing a desire to throttle him. "Why did she decide to leave Paris so suddenly, Father? Did you visit her and convince her to leave me alone?"

His flush revealed that she was correct. He glanced around and said in a lowered voice, "For Christ's sake, Yvette. I just told you what kind of woman she is." He stared at her, then impaled his Romaine like it had offended him. "I thought the most prudent course of action was to simply make her disappear and save you the embarrassment of becoming intimate with someone like her."

"Because you've always saved us that type of embarrassment, Father?" Eva couldn't keep the sarcasm from her tone.

"I'm a man, a Frenchman. I can do exactly as I please, with whomever I want. It's my right. People even expect it of me." He shoved his salad plate away.

"Why would my being with Brigitte embarrass the family, then?"

He stared at her in seeming disbelief that she could be so obtuse. "You're a woman, for God's sake. Granted, you're a queer one, which is another story altogether." He laughed with what sounded like derision. "But you're still a woman, and I'll be damned if you'll give my friends and acquaintances cause to laugh at me." He touched the corner of his wine-stained mouth with his linen napkin.

"Well, I'm a Frenchwoman, Father. And I'm also your daughter." She settled her own napkin in her lap, pushing her salad plate away also. "You have no right to tell me with whom I can associate. And you have no business threatening any friend of mine." She aligned her knife and fork symmetrically. "If you pull something like that again,

I'll tell Mother exactly what you've been doing behind her back all these years."

Just then the waiter arrived with the main course, and her father smoldered in silence.

When the food lay before them, he glared at her. "You think your mother would listen to you? Or if she did, that she'd give a damn?" He actually sneered. "She's so cowed she'll accept anything I do or say. She believes she's lucky to have me, and she is. What other man would have endured her silliness all these years?"

Eva cut a small bite of meat. "Her silliness and her fortune? That's why you married her, isn't it?" She raised the morsel to her mouth, then stopped, staring at the man she called her parent. "You have about as much feeling for her as you do for me."

"Bah. You don't know anything, and I don't plan to waste my breath talking to you about things that don't concern you." He snapped his fingers as if he could dismiss his entire marriage in a second. "We're here to discuss your little tryst with a certain whore from New Orleans, aren't we? Well, talk away. What do you want to know about her? Did you bed her? Perhaps we can compare notes." His eyes gleamed with what appeared to be curiosity and envy.

Eva took another bite of her meat and then slowly dipped a fried potato in mayonnaise as her father looked at her expectantly.

"I'm waiting for your account of your acquaintance with Brigitte," he said.

She had no idea why she sat there and endured his filthy questions. She felt as paralyzed as if she were gazing at a cobra, like she wanted to behead him but didn't have the strength to wield her knife. "We toured Paris together, we learned to appreciate each other and where we came from, and we began to believe we might somehow be special to one another. But you'd never understand that, would you, Father? The only special person in your life is yourself."

He brushed her comments away with a wave of his hand. "How can you find anything to appreciate about a common whore who, as far as I'm concerned, will always be one."

"To be truthful, in my eyes right this minute, you're more of a whore than Brigitte ever was."

He spit his bite of meat into his hand, then glanced around to see if anyone had overheard her.

"What in the hell does that mean?"

"You married for money, didn't you? And then you proceeded to break the terms of your business arrangement by cheating on Mother at every turn." His glare should have incinerated her, but it only fueled her. "At least Brigitte wants to change, to forget her past. If she likes women, and I'm a woman, why shouldn't we have a chance to decide if we enjoy each other's company?"

He stood and flung his napkin onto the table. "Bah. Do as you wish. I washed my hands of that woman years ago, and I wish I could do the same with you. But I can't."

Then he sat back down, motioned the waiter over, and paid the check. An expression almost of defeat flitted across his face as he rose again, more slowly this time. "If you can tame her, you have my blessing. But that's a very big *if*."

Eva slowly finished her meal after her father left. Brigitte must have been trying to protect her from learning about her past liaison with Yves. But Eva didn't want or need to be sheltered. She could make up her own mind—if she ever saw Brigitte again.

CHAPTER THIRTY-ONE

Tuesday, September 5

"I'm sorry to see you under these conditions, Father." Eva stood talking to him after the small private ceremony for Louis. He'd been her younger brother, and she loved him though they had little in common.

Yves gazed at her with eyes that reminded her of melted lead instead of ball bearings. He seemed to be closer to her own height now, instead of towering over her, and his shoulders were more rounded than squared.

He swiped at his eyes and she almost grasped his arm, but he backed away a fraction, and she restrained herself.

"Why did Louis throw everything away like that?" he murmured, as if talking to himself.

Eva shook her head, her grief like a dark wool cloak. "I don't know. Drugs can promise a lot, but I've never bought into their allure."

He looked at her as if seeing her with brand-new eyes. "I realize that. And I'm glad."

This time she did take his arm. "Thank you."

He stood up a bit straighter. "By the way, have you heard from Brigitte?"

She shrugged. "No. I have no idea where she is."

He raised an eyebrow in seeming surprise. "Too bad. I hope she's not in Munich at the Olympics. That's a bad situation. But maybe she hasn't given up on you yet." A muscle quirked in his cheek as he eyed a nearby guest. "I need to mingle now. And your mother probably would appreciate having me by her side. She's going to need my support now more than ever."

His glance at his wife told Eva all she needed to know about the future of her parents' marriage. She'd lost a brother but perhaps she'd one day salvage her relationship with her father.

Her heart shifted into a faster rhythm. Had Brigitte gone home, or was she still in Europe? That possibility helped Eva's woolen depression ease a bit.

She accepted a glass of wine that a nearby waiter offered her and stood back, alone, watching her parents stand side by side across the room and converse with one of their few guests.

If only Brigitte were beside her. Why hadn't Brigitte simply told her about her father's visit that morning in the hotel? Why had she made up excuses and left? Didn't she want to fight for what they had?

Eva sighed and walked over to join Jeanne, unable to answer the questions that haunted her.

❖

Saturday, September 9

"Taste of Paris. Eva speaking. How may I help you?" Eva sorted through the applications for her upcoming tour as she offhandedly answered the telephone. Jeanne was out of the office for the day, but luckily business was slow since most of the tourists had deserted Paris in late August.

"Eva…"

She dropped the papers she was holding and focused every ounce of her attention on the sultry voice she'd know anywhere. "Brigitte?"

"Yes. It's good to hear your voice." Brigitte sounded simultaneously eager and anxious.

"My God. Where are you? I've missed you so much. When can I see you?" Eva had dreamed of, expected this call for so long she'd almost worn it out, like an LP record she'd played constantly for months. And the one time she hadn't been thinking of Brigitte, she'd called.

"Do you really want to see me?"

The voice affected every part of her body—her heart pounded, her brain buzzed, and her mouth felt dry. "I can't think of anything I'd rather do," she managed to say.

"Good. I'm at the George V again, in my old suite. Can you come over tonight about seven?" Brigitte's voice was more confident now.

Eva looked at the CLOSED FOR THE DAY sign lying on the desk by the front door of the office. "I can come right now if you want." Jeanne wouldn't be happy, but she'd understand if Eva left early just this once.

"No." Reluctant, yet decisive. "I have some shopping to do. Don't eat before you come. All right?"

"I'll be counting the minutes. Can I bring anything?"

"Yes. Now that you mention it, wear a dress you enjoy dancing in, and be sure to bring your tango shoes."

"We're going out later?"

"You'll see. Until then?"

"Until then." Eva slowly lowered the handset into its cradle. Brigitte was back in Paris! Eva could finally take her life off hold.

Eva drew in a long breath and raised her hand to knock. She took a step back, her heart stampeding. It would be so much easier to just get back on the elevator here in the George V, to run away and lose herself in her studies, her profession. But she straightened her spine and returned, then rapped softly on the door of Brigitte's suite.

No one answered for so long, Eva had already turned around to leave when she heard Brigitte's voice. "Just a minute. I'm coming." She sounded strong and sure.

Eva still had time to dash around the corner. Brigitte would think she'd decided not to come, that someone had knocked by mistake. But Eva pivoted and stood there, finally certain this was where she wanted to be.

The door opened a crack, and blue eyes that still reminded her of the sea on Turkey's southern coast sized her up. Slowly, Brigitte revealed herself. Barefoot, wearing a short black dress, she'd evidently let her hair return to its natural blond softened by darker roots. She looked years younger, like she'd lost some of her hard edges, her makeup accentuating her features rather than masking them.

Eva couldn't move her mouth. She didn't know what to say. They stared at each other, Eva resisting her desire to run, pulled into those blue eyes.

Brigitte finally broke their silence. "Come in," she said, and Eva welcomed the words of reprieve.

When they sat face-to-face in Brigitte's living room, Brigitte on the sofa, Eva finally said the only thing she could think of. "Father told me about your affair with him."

"Affair? Is that what he called it?" Brigitte's stare could have melted steel.

This silence lasted even longer than their previous one. Eva felt as if she were waiting for a verdict. What was Brigitte thinking? "He said that you had sex once, but then you refused to see him again. He seemed upset, said you'd humiliated him."

Brigitte cleared her throat and took a long drink of the water from the glass that sat on the table beside her. "Humiliated him?" She scoffed. "Did he tell you I'd just gotten into the life, so I played along with the dumb-blond act Rosa said he liked?"

"He said you were just beginning your career and that you were eminently desirable, with a select clientele."

Brigitte's smile had a bitter tinge. "At least he got that part right. Did he describe how he lorded it over me the entire evening, displaying me like a crown jewel at Antoine's, while with every remark, he showed me how thoroughly beneath him he considered me in every way?"

Eva flinched, remembering her father's account of the evening. "No. He said he treated you like a lady instead of a..."

"Whore. That's the word he used, isn't it?"

"Yes." The word felt like solidified bile as Eva forced it out.

"At least he used one honest word."

"What really happened that night, Brigitte?" Eva didn't want to hear, but she had to if she and Brigitte were going to have any future.

"Basically, he used me sexually like a piece of toilet paper, and afterward I felt filthy. That's why I refused to ever see him again. But in a way, he did me a favor."

Eva felt as if Brigitte had stabbed her in the heart, but she had to keep going. "A favor?"

Brigitte straightened her back. "Yes. I started taking college classes after that, and reading even more about current events." She smiled, finally. "I made it a point to clarify with every one of my clients that I was his equal, intellectually as well as socially."

"Good for you," Eva said.

"Yes. It was good for me. I started calling myself a companion, instead of using the common derogatory words for someone in my profession, and the more I demanded that my clients treat me as an equal, the more I thought of myself that way."

As Brigitte spoke, Eva saw more fully why she admired and desired her.

"I provided a valuable service, just as a jeweler or a movie star did, and I expected to be appreciated, not demeaned for it."

Eva gripped the arm of her chair. "I wish you'd told me all this instead of making up some excuses and leaving."

Brigitte met her gaze but didn't speak. She rose from the sofa. "How about a glass of wine?"

"Yes. Thanks. That's exactly what I need." Eva was glad for a reprieve. Having to face what her father had done had been like slamming into a brick wall. She felt bruised, battered, possibly like Brigitte had that night so long ago in New Orleans. But they needed to share this so they could leave it behind them.

As Brigitte handed her a full glass and sat down with her own, Eva asked, "Why didn't you tell me the truth six weeks ago? Why now?"

Brigitte drew a long breath. "I didn't want to hurt you by letting you know how much I loathed your father. He showed up not long before you did and told me to leave you alone. I couldn't bear to think about my involvement with him every time I saw you. And I couldn't stand to tell you how I felt about him, what sort of a man your father was. I feared you'd think about his loathsome behavior every time you looked at me." She frowned. "I was afraid you and I truly couldn't have any type of future together. My one night with him would always taint it, come between us, because I couldn't let you know about it or risk him telling you."

Eva sipped her wine and didn't speak for a long while. "You and I hadn't known each other very long and were still consumed by lust. I can see how you might say what you did and leave. And in a way, I'm glad you did."

Brigitte stared at her with clearer eyes. "You can? You are?"

"Yes. I needed time to come to terms with Father on my own. And I have. Plus, some things have changed in his life, and he may be the better for them."

"I'm glad, for both of you." Brigitte smiled for the first time that evening.

"But you haven't answered my other question." Eva felt like a trainload of spoiled American teenagers had just rolled away from the station, leaving her relieved and free. "Why did you come back?"

Brigitte's smile grew. "Oh, I wanted to see if you were in the mood to have a picnic and to dance with me."

"A picnic and dancing?" Eva held up the bag she'd dropped beside the sofa. "I just happen to have a hearty appetite and some tango shoes. So the answer is yes."

Brigitte's eyes narrowed. "Are you sure? I didn't think you liked Americans very much."

"Who told you such a thing?" Eva widened her eyes innocently. "I love Americans."

Jumping up, Brigitte started toward her coffee bar. "Wonderful. Because this American just happens to be famished."

CHAPTER THIRTY-TWO

Eva relaxed into her metal chair as she sat on the small balcony across the table from Brigitte and examined the food spread out in front of them on large platters. "You must be starving. Just look at all this. Cheese, ham, olives, fresh bread, crepes, strawberries, pears, and chocolate. Oh, it all smells so good. So this is what you were shopping for this afternoon."

"Yes." Brigitte appeared proud of her purchases. "And I had the hotel staff make these lovely trays for us."

The sun was beginning to set, and Eva stared out across Paris. "It's a beautiful city, isn't it? I'm so glad you came back. Where have you been?"

Brigitte spread a generous portion of brie onto a piece of soft bread she'd broken from a large, crusty loaf. "Oh, the typical tourist sites. The Alps, the Parthenon, the Sistine Chapel, the Prado. It's all glorious, but I couldn't think about anything but Paris, and you. The Eiffel Tower is still my favorite."

Eva glanced out the window. "I'm so glad. Look. You can almost see it in the distance."

"But that's the wrong direction. What kind of tour guide are you, anyway?" A smile quivered on Brigitte's lips.

"One that will be retiring in a year or so, I hope. As soon as I pass my bar exam." She watched Brigitte devour a crepe. "Hey, what kind was that?"

Brigitte licked the side of her mouth provocatively, then ran her tongue along her upper lip. "Umm. Smoked salmon, cream cheese, and capers." She picked up an olive and sucked it into her mouth.

"No fair. That's my favorite kind. Was that the only one?"

"Let me see." She sorted through the assortment of crepes. "I think this might be one. Want it?"

As Eva reached for it, Brigitte pretended to take a bite. Eva grabbed it from her. "Hands off. That's mine."

Brigitte shrugged and then stood up. "If you feel that way about it, okay. More wine?" she asked. "We have a nice merlot and a pleasant pinot noir."

"Pinot noir." Eva accepted a glass and swirled it, savoring its mixed aroma of cherry, rose petals, and leather. "Thank you. This smells delicious."

Brigitte sipped her merlot, then picked up a small strawberry and held up it to Eva's nose. "Smell this. It's from the mountains."

Eva inhaled deeply. "Ah. Nothing's better than a wild French strawberry. It's better than any perfume." She took it from Brigitte's fingers and crushed it until the juice began to run. "Here. See how delicious it is."

Brigitte gently held Eva's hand up to her mouth and touched the strawberry with the tip of her tongue. "You're right." She sucked it into her mouth. "It's wonderful." Brigitte licked Eva's fingers clean. "Don't want you to stain your dress," she said, letting her gaze slide down the tight-fitting white dress Eva wore.

"No, we can't have that, can we?" Eva murmured.

They decimated their feast and sat in silence as the lights of Paris began to blink on and replace the vanished sun's rays. "Would you like to hear some music on my new record player?" Brigitte asked out of the darkness.

Eva roused herself. "New record player? Another recent purchase?"

"Yes. I was on a roll this afternoon. Want to listen to a recording by Erroll Garner? We could enjoy him together this time."

As they walked back inside, Brigitte snaked her arm around Eva's waist and led her to the plush love seat. The sounds of Garner's genius at the piano washed over Eva, and she sighed, contented. Then a question occurred to her. "Are you planning to live here permanently? I mean, here at the George V?"

Brigitte brushed Eva's bangs to one side of her forehead and placed a kiss there. "In Paris, yes. At the hotel, no. I've decided to look for an apartment. I stored most of my luggage here at the hotel while I was gone, but I think they're getting tired of me and all my property." She gestured to her new record player. "As you can see, it's mushrooming daily."

"Hmm," Eva said. "Jeanne has started dating someone she says is special, so she just might be getting tired of me too."

Brigitte's hand drifted down to Eva's cheek, followed by a kiss there. "I could use a roommate. Someone to show me the city, help me improve my French."

Eva turned toward Brigitte and rested a hand on her shoulder. "Your French is perfect, though I might know someone who'd like to show you all of Paris's secrets."

"Does this someone know how to tango? That's one thing I require in a roommate." She ran her hand up Eva's calf. "Hmm. Somehow I bet she does." She gestured toward Eva's purple bag sitting on a nearby end table. "And it appears she brought her tango shoes with her." Brigitte assumed a stern expression. "I do, of course, require proof of her dancing ability."

Eva rose and pulled her shoes from her bag. "That's fine. But you have to supply the music."

"Agreed. I have just the thing."

Eva hadn't worn her special shoes in so long she was nervous putting them on. What if Brigitte was actually serious? She was anxious about her bar exam but sensed her whole life depended on the result of this particular test.

But when the music poured over her, she stood and assumed a serious expression to match Brigitte's. Brigitte sat on the love seat fastening the strap of one of her medium-heeled shoes around her ankle as Eva grabbed a long red silk scarf that lay on the back of a chair and flung it over her shoulders. Whirling around the room with the scarf wrapped around her shoulders, she then tossed it over Brigitte's shoulders and pulled her to her feet with it. A strumming guitar filled the room, accompanying a female voice singing in Spanish. *Ah yi, yi, yi.* The raspy voice called her to the dance.

Brigitte glided toward her, and Eva slung the scarf to the other side of the living room. The tango beat filled Eva with its passion as she led Brigitte a few steps, Brigitte's right hand resting on Eva's left shoulder, Eva grasping that hand possessively. She'd wrestle the devil himself for this woman.

In the center of the living room, Eva stepped behind Brigitte, and they both flung their arms upward in time with the beat. Eva bent her knees and slowly ran her hand down and then back up Brigitte's silk-covered legs, the left one stretched backward, straight and inviting. Eva gasped with pleasure as she stroked the firm flesh encased in such a strong yet yielding substance.

As the vocalist sang of the sweetness of the tango, Eva wrapped her arms around Brigitte from behind her, then slowly pulled her arms up and back, strength rushing through. She held both their arms extended and out like wings, as if they could fly away together into space and time.

She twirled Brigitte to the music's rhythm, and then Brigitte knelt in front of her, momentarily submissive. Eva passed one leg over Brigitte's head, rested it briefly on Brigitte's shoulder, then rose, exhilarated by Brigitte's beauty and her intense focus on only her. Eva grabbed Brigitte's hands and drew her up toward her, but then they whirled away from each other and Eva experienced a profound sense of loss.

Eva half turned away from Brigitte, half pulled her back, and Brigitte spun into her arms. Eva felt as if she'd captured an exotic jungle cat and exulted in her prize. Eva lowered Brigitte halfway to the floor, then pulled her back up. She couldn't live without her. They swirled together, and then, with Brigitte's left leg straight, Eva's pressed tight against it, Eva held her in a tight embrace against her breasts, panting with desire.

With Brigitte's right hand on Eva's shoulder, Eva ran her left hand slowly up Brigitte's side, beginning at her upper thigh and continuing upward. She could almost feel the air sparking beneath her fingers.

But suddenly, Brigitte seized control. She held Eva as she threw her head back and rested completely in Brigitte's left arm. One slight move and Eva would have landed helpless on the floor. But she relaxed into Brigitte's power as Brigitte feathered her hand from Eva's throat down the center of her body, brushing her crotch.

Eva ignited, like natural gas lit by a match. She could practically smell sulfur and almost blacked out from the sensual rush that Brigitte's hand evoked, but she managed to stay conscious. She didn't intend to miss a second of their tango.

They straightened, then kicked through a complex set of moves together and ended up in a tight embrace, Brigitte's hand in Eva's hair caressing her scalp with strong fingers. Brushing noses, they stared at each other with a searing, serious gaze, their hair hanging free and in their eyes, their lips inches apart, as if they were straining to touch, to merge. The guitar and the woman's voice died away, yet Eva didn't move as Brigitte's caress moved to her neck. The odor of spring rain suddenly washed over her, though it was a dry September day.

"You've cut your hair, haven't you?" Brigitte said after the music died away. She stared at Eva's neck, seeming transfixed.

"Yes. It needed some attention. It's too much trouble when it gets too long."

Brigitte shook her head as if clearing something from her mind, then led Eva over to the record player. Brigitte kept her arm around her as they both removed their shoes and stood there with bare feet. Then she took the record from the player and laid it nearby. "How did you like this one? I just bought it."

"It's wonderful to dance to. And you're wonderful to dance with."

Brigitte appeared bedazzled as she turned to Eva. "It's meant to be, I think. I don't want to ever let you go."

"Then don't." Eva put her arm about Brigitte's waist. "I want you, my beauty. More than I've ever wanted anyone." The words bubbled from her mouth like expensive champagne.

Brigitte slowly turned Eva in her arms, then lowered her head and brushed her lips over Eva's forehead. Eva closed her eyes and sighed with pleasure as twin kisses blessed her eyes and her ears. When she finally opened her eyes, she looked down at the top of Brigitte's head. Brigitte was halfway kneeling, kissing Eva's nipples that were straining to escape from her sheer dress. Brigitte pushed one narrow strap aside, then the other, and slowly pulled the clingy fabric down below Eva's breasts.

"Let's take this to the bedroom while I can still walk," Brigitte whispered, and Eva had no choice but to say yes.

❖

Eva's eyes gleamed like aquamarines as Brigitte led her to her spacious bed and laid her on it. Brigitte felt as if she were offering a beautiful sacrifice to the goddess of love. No, not a sacrifice but a tribute, an offering of thanks, a way to show her reverence for the women who had lived during the centuries before them, to the one who lay stretched out in front of her, and to the mysterious powers of the universe that had led them to one another.

Eva was the woman Rosa had sent her to Paris to find. Their tango tonight had proved it. When Brigitte had seen the taut skin of Eva's neck earlier, she'd relived her vision of the mysterious woman who'd momentarily interrupted her final dance with Rosa. The face of the woman was no longer fuzzy. She was Eva.

Now Eva lay motionless before her, gasping as she eased Eva's white dress past her waist, over her hips, and down her slender legs. When Eva lay there totally nude, Brigitte stood still for a moment, awash in Eva's vulnerability, her beauty. Quickly stepping out of her own flimsy black dress, she lay down beside Eva and stretched Eva's arms over her head, as Eva had done to her during their dance.

Brigitte smoothed her hand along the inside of one of Eva's arms, then the other. The bluish veins lying just beneath the surface of the white skin near the inner side of Eva's wrists reminded Brigitte of river deltas—rich, fertile areas where the world's great civilizations had been born and thrived. Rosa had shed her blood, but Eva's pulsed through her.

She traced across to Eva's small breasts, their nipples sharp enough to cut flesh, yet as smooth as mousse. Delicious. She sucked. She licked. She reveled as Eva yielded them to her, these precious, priceless gifts.

Momentarily sated, Brigitte continued her journey, traveling downward, as if on a voyage into the humid jungles of the Congo, the Amazon. Heat rose from Eva, and the room seemed steamy as Brigitte neared the fecund tropics of her desire. It had been an endless trip, but oh so worth it. Eva panted, then jerked as Brigitte, dying of thirst, drank from the source of the heat that was making them both sweat.

She scalded her tongue in it, painted Eva's inner thighs with it, lost herself in it. She rode down a river of blood, pulled by the swift currents, tossed about by the river's fury, rushing toward an unknown destination, then plummeted over a breath-shaking waterfall.

At the bottom, she floated, relaxed, trusting the cooling fluid that surrounded her to keep her from drowning, finally quenching her thirst.

"God, Brigitte. What did you just do to me?" Eva's words penetrated her consciousness, pulled her upward to Eva's lips, her breasts, her silken skin.

"I'm not sure," Brigitte whispered.

Go to Paris reverberated through her.

She kissed Eva's soft lips, so full yet firm. "But I do know one thing."

Eva sighed, her breath sweet. "What's that?"

"I want to do it over and over, for the rest of my life, my darling." Brigitte kissed her again. "Here in Paris. With you."

About the Author

Shelley Thrasher, world traveler and native East Texan, has edited for BSB since 2004. A PhD in English, she taught in college for many years before she retired early and still teaches a fine arts course online. She has published poetry, short stories, and essays, as well as one scholarly book. Shelley and her partner Connie, with their two dogs, cat, and parrot, live near Dallas, Texas. Her first novel, *The Storm* (2012), was a GCLS historical romance finalist and a Rainbow Awards runner-up for best debut novel. Her second novel, *First Tango in Paris* (2014), is based on her travels abroad.

Books Available From Bold Strokes Books

Kiss The Girl by Melissa Brayden. Sleeping with the enemy has never been so complicated. Brooklyn Campbell and Jessica Lennox face off in love and advertising in fast-paced New York City. (978-1-62639-071-3)

Taking Fire: A First Responders Novel by Radclyffe. Hunted by extremists and under siege by nature's most virulent weapons, Navy medic Max de Milles and Red Cross worker Rachel Winslow join forces to survive and discover something far more lasting. (978-1-62639-072-0)

First Tango in Paris by Shelley Thrasher. When French law student Eva Laroche meets American call girl Brigitte Green in 1970s Paris, they have no idea how their pasts and futures will intersect. (978-1-62639-073-7)

The War Within by Yolanda Wallace. Army nurse Meredith Moser went to Vietnam in 1967 looking to help those in need; she didn't expect to meet the love of her life along the way. (978-1-62639-074-4)

Escapades by MJ Williamz. Two women, afraid to love again, must overcome their fears to find the happiness that awaits them. (978-1-62639-182-6)

Desire at Dawn by Fiona Zedde. For Kylie, love had always come armed with sharp teeth and claws. But with the human, Olivia, she bares her vampire heart for the very first time, sharing passion, lust, and a tenderness she'd never dared dream of before. (978-1-62639-064-5)

Visions by Larkin Rose. Sometimes the mysteries of love reveal themselves when you least expect it. Other times they hide behind a black satin mask. Can Paige unveil her masked stranger this time? (978-1-62639-065-2)

All In by Nell Stark. Internet poker champion Annie Navarro loses everything when the Feds shut down online gambling, and she turns to experienced casino host Vesper Blake for advice—but can Nova convince Vesper to take a gamble on romance? (978-1-62639-066-9)

Vermilion Justice by Sheri Lewis Wohl. What's a vampire to do when Dracula is no longer just a character in a novel? (978-1-62639-067-6)

Switchblade by Carsen Taite. Lines were meant to be crossed. Third in the Luca Bennett Bounty Hunter Series. (978-1-62639-058-4)

Nightingale by Andrea Bramhall. Culture, faith, and duty conspire to tear two young lovers apart, yet fate seems to have different plans for them both. (978-1-62639-059-1)

No Boundaries by Donna K. Ford. A chance meeting and a nightmare from the past threaten more than Andi Massey's solitude as she and Gwen Palmer struggle to understand the complexity of love without boundaries. (978-1-62639-060-7)

Timeless by Rachel Spangler. When Stevie Geller returns to her hometown, will she do things differently the second time around or will she be in such a hurry to leave her past that she misses out on a better future? (978-1-62639-050-8)

Second to None by L.T. Marie. Can a physical therapist and a custom motorcycle designer conquer their pasts and build a future with one another? (978-1-62639-051-5)

Seneca Falls by Jesse Thoma. Together, two women discover love truly can conquer all evil. (978-1-62639-052-2)

A Kingdom Lost by Barbara Ann Wright. Without knowing each other's fates, Princess Katya and her consort Starbride seek to reclaim their kingdom from the magic-wielding madman who seized the throne and is murdering their people. (978-1-62639-053-9)

Season of the Wolf by Robin Summers. Two women running from their pasts are thrust together by an unimaginable evil. Can they overcome the horrors that haunt them in time to save each other? (978-1-62639-043-0)

The Heat of Angels by Lisa Girolami. Fires burn in more than one place in Los Angeles. (978-1-62639-042-3)

Desperate Measures by P. J. Trebelhorn. Homicide detective Kay Griffith and contractor Brenda Jansen meet amidst turmoil neither of them is aware of until murder suspect Tommy Rayne makes his move to exact revenge on Kay. (978-1-62639-044-7)

The Magic Hunt by L.L. Raand. With her Pack being hunted by human extremists and beset by enemies masquerading as friends, can Sylvan protect them and her mate, or will she succumb to the feral rage that threatens to turn her rogue, destroying them all? A Midnight Hunters novel. (978-1-62639-045-4)

Wingspan by Karis Walsh. Wildlife biologist Bailey Chase is content to live at the wild bird sanctuary she has created on Washington's Olympic Peninsula until she is lured beyond the safety of isolation by architect Kendall Pearson. (978-1-60282-983-1)

Night Bound by Winter Pennington. Kass struggles to keep her head, her heart, and her relationships in order. She's still having a difficult time accepting being an Alpha female—but her wolf is certain of what she wants and she's intent on securing her power. (978-1-60282-984-8)

Windigo Thrall by Cate Culpepper. Six women trapped in a mountain cabin by a blizzard, stalked by an ancient cannibal demon bent on stealing their sanity—and their lives. (978-1-60282-950-3)

The Blush Factor by Gun Brooke. Ice-cold business tycoon Eleanor Ashcroft only cares about the three Ps—Power, Profit, and Prosperity—until young Addison Garr makes her doubt both that and the state of her frostbitten heart. (978-1-60282-985-5)

Slash and Burn by Valerie Bronwen. The murder of a roundly despised author at an LGBT writers' conference in New Orleans turns Winter Lovelace's relaxing weekend hobnobbing with her peers into a nightmare of suspense—especially when her ex turns up. (978-1-60282-986-2)

The Quickening: A Sisters of Spirits novel by Yvonne Heidt. Ghosts, visions, and demons are all in a day's work for Tiffany. But when Kat asks for help on a serial killer case, life takes on another dimension altogether. (978-1-60282-975-6)

Smoke and Fire by Julie Cannon. Oil and water, passion and desire, a combustible combination. Can two women fight the fire that draws them together and threatens to keep them apart? (978-1-60282-977-0)

Love and Devotion by Jove Belle. KC Hall trips her way through life, stumbling into an affair with a married bombshell twice her age. Thankfully, her best friend, Emma Reynolds, is there to show her the true meaning of Love and Devotion. (978-1-60282-965-7)

The Shoal of Time by J.M. Redmann. It sounded too easy. Micky Knight is reluctant to take the case because the easy ones often turn into the hard ones, and the hard ones turn into the dangerous ones. In this one, easy turns hard without warning. (978-1-60282-967-1)

In Between by Jane Hoppen. At the age of fourteen, Sophie Schmidt discovers that she was born an intersexual baby and sets off on a journey to find her place in a world that denies her true existence. (978-1-60282-968-8)

Under Her Spell by Maggie Morton. The magic of love brought Terra and Athene together, but now a magical quest stands between them—a quest for Athene's hand in marriage. Will their passion keep them together, or will stronger magic tear them apart? (978-1-60282-973-2)

Rush by Carsen Taite. Murder, secrets, and romance combine to create the ultimate rush. (978-1-60282-966-4)

Secret Lies by Amy Dunne. While fleeing from her abuser, Nicola Jackson bumps into Jenny O'Connor, and their unlikely friendship quickly develops into a blossoming romance—but when it comes down to a matter of life or death, are they both willing to face their fears? (978-1-60282-970-1)

Homestead by Radclyffe. R. Clayton Sutter figures getting NorthAm Fuel's newest refinery operational on a rolling tract of land in upstate New York should take a month or two, but then, she hadn't counted on local resistance in the form of vandalism, petitions, and one furious farmer named Tess Rogers. (978-1-60282-956-5)

Battle of Forces: Sera Toujours by Ali Vali. Kendal and Piper return to New Orleans to start the rest of eternity together, but the return of an old enemy makes their peaceful reunion short-lived, especially when they join forces with the new queen of the vampires. (978-1-60282-957-2)

How Sweet It Is by Melissa Brayden. Some things are better than chocolate. Molly O'Brien enjoys her quiet life running the bakeshop in a small town. When the beautiful Jordan Tuscana returns home, Molly can't deny the attraction—or the stirrings of something more. (978-1-60282-958-9)